LADIES WHO LYNCH

JASON WRIDE

The characters and events portrayed in this book are fictitious. Any similarity to real persons, living or dead, is coincidental and not intended by the author.

No part of this book may be reproduced, or stored in a retrieval system, or transmitted in any form or by any means, electronic, mechanical, photocopying, recording, or otherwise, without express written permission of the publisher.

Jason Wride ©2022

ASIN: B0BC6ZTZ9H

Cover design by: Doug Crookston ©2022

To Angela Stevens for always being there to read my *very* rough first drafts and give advice, guidance and plenty of tough love. And Laura Zollner for helping me come up with the initial idea.

To all my test readers: Ainhoa, Kasia, Daphne, Olivia and Lilian. Without your valuable input I could have never brought these *Ladies* to life.

To Maggie Truelove, who proofread an earlier draft of the novel, and who sadly passed away this year. And Charlotte Stace for proofreading the final draft.

To all the cafes, and the amazing staff working at them, who provided plenty of coffee, cake and conversation whilst I sat for hours and procrastinated endlessly:

- Chapter 72 on Bermondsey Street, London
- Fuckoffee on Bermondsey Street, London
- Scooter Caffè on Lower Marsh Street, London
- Common Ground on Little Clarendon Street, Oxford

To Doug Crookston for creating another awesome cover.

And finally, to my boy, Scabby. Rest in peace, little buddy.

'You fit into me
like a hook into an eye
a fish hook
an open eye'

— **Margaret Atwood**

PROLOGUE

Siobhan emerged from the bowels of Charing Cross station and burst onto the dazzling streets of London's West End. Her brain still buzzed from the two beers she'd downed earlier, and she barely noticed the cold wind whipping off the high walls, her leather jacket hanging open to reveal her favourite *Iron-Maiden* T-shirt.

'You okay back there, Angie?' she glanced back at the new client, an older woman with tightly-permed brown hair and bright-red lipstick.

'I'd prefer Angela, if you don't mind,' the woman replied breathlessly, struggling to keep up in a long overcoat and high heels.

'No worries. My bad. It's just down this way.'

Siobhan turned a corner and caught a glimpse of herself in a shop window, her cropped red hair ablaze in the reflection of the glowing streetlights and flashing neon signs. That's right, people. Make way. Don't make me go all Scarlet Witch on your arses. She smirked at the approaching pedestrians who scattered in the thudding echo of her Doc Martens.

A trio of drunken businessmen stumbled out of a nearby pub and blocked the way, their shouts and laughter bringing her back to reality.

'Jesus! Get out the way, you fucking eejits!' She barged past them and crossed the street to a dimly-lit Thai restaurant. 'Can you believe those bozos? They think they own the world with their *Peaky Blinders* haircuts and fancy suits.' She swung open the door, ignoring the 'Closed' sign, and led Angela through an empty dining room.

The owner, Queen Bea, stood behind the bar, talking loudly on the phone. Her green-and-gold sequined dress clung to her svelte curves, shimmering in the gloom, her immaculate beehive hairstyle reaching up to the ceiling. They exchanged a knowing look, and then Siobhan ushered Angela through a bamboo curtain into a private, VIP-only room. The room had just one table, surrounded by a collection Asian-inspired artwork and ornaments, and she stopped in front of a golden lucky cat adorned with colourful Swarovski crystals.

'Are you ready?'

'Yes.' Angela nodded.

'Good. Because after this, there's no turning back.'

She lowered the cat's paw and an oak-panelled wall slid open, revealing a secret lift.

They stepped inside and it took them down to a cylindrical corridor that was once part of an old passageway connecting Charing Cross and Embankment station, but instead of harsh white tiles and fluorescent lighting, the walls were lined with discreet spotlights and painted a tasteful light grey.

'Welcome to the London and Districts International Emergency Support-Centre for Women, or Ladies HQ, as we like to call it.' Siobhan spread her arms theatrically. Then she took Angela into her office, which was located about halfway down.

'Do you want a drink before we start? Tea, coffee, water – some brandy maybe?'

'I'm fine. Thank you.'

'No worries.' Siobhan slipped behind a black desk, which was empty apart from a large flatscreen monitor and a plain white folder labelled 'Confidential'. 'Right. Let's get started.' She opened the folder and took out a contract. 'So, as agreed, you, Mrs Angela Stevens, will be donating the total sum of five-hundred-thousand-pounds to the London and Districts' International Emergency Support-Centre for Women. Is this correct?'

'Yes, it is.' Angela took a deep breath and straightened her back.

'Perfect. Before we continue, I just need to remind you that we'll be filming everything that happens tonight. Don't worry though. It's just for our records. None of this footage will ever see the light of day. Unless something goes majorly tits up, that is. Now. The quicker we get this done, the quicker we can get to the fun stuff, am I right?' She handed Angela a pen and smiled.

'What's this?' Angela pointed to the bottom of the page.

'It's your signed confession.'

'I think I'm going to need that brandy.' Angela put down the pen and rested her hands on the table.

A few minutes later, after a large brandy and some gentle coaxing, she finally signed her name. Then she followed Siobhan through the rest of the labyrinth-like underground complex, until they reached a plain black door.

'Right. This is it. Once you go inside, it'll start automatically. Just remember, if it gets too much there's an intercom on the wall, right next to the door. Press it, and I'll come get you straight away.'

Angela opened the door and Siobhan raced back to the office, turning on the monitor just in time to see her slip off her coat and reveal a fifties-style floral dress and matching apron.

'Woo! You go, girl! Betty Draper in the house, y'all!' she called out.

A children's nightlight illuminated everything in a colourful cascade of twirling stars, and Angela approached an oversized crib in the middle of the room. A middle-aged man, dressed in a baby-blue onesie, lay strapped down inside amongst a pile of stuffed toys and pillows. His balding head and pudgy face were barely visible in the gloom, but Siobhan could see his close-set eyes darting about anxiously as the lights swept over them.

A moment later Angela appeared above him, and he let out a frightened cry. Then, to Siobhan's surprise, she leant over the white bars and began to sing:

'*Hush, little baby, don't say a word, mamma's gonna buy you a mockingbird. And if that mockingbird won't sing, mamma's gonna buy you a diamond ring—*'

'Fuck you, lady!' The man yanked on the straps, his face contorting into an angry grimace. But they didn't budge.

'Well, that's not very nice now, is it?' Angela took a dummy out of her apron and put it in his mouth.

Continuing to sing, she walked over to a small table and picked up a hunting knife. The serrated blade glowed ominously and the man spat out the dummy, shaking his head.

'No. Wait. Please! I'm sorry. I'm sorry. I won't swear again, I promise.'

'What about all those young girls. Are you sorry about them too?'

The stars continued to rotate and she edged closer.

3

'I don't know what you're talking about.' He looked away, avoiding her fierce gaze.

'I think you do.' She raised the knife above her shoulder.

'No. Stop! You've got the wrong guy.' He burrowed deeper into the pillows. 'You have to believe me. I've got a wife and kids of my own. I'd never do anything to hurt a child. Let's just talk about this. Please. I'm begging you.' The words came out in a torrent, his voice getting higher and higher, tears staining his ruddy cheeks.

'There, there,' she cooed. *'Hush, little baby, don't you cry, nobody loves you, and it's time to die.'*

She thrust the knife into his open mouth and Siobhan watched, transfixed, as his eyes bulged and a torrent of blood sprayed all over the stuffed toys and pillows…

PART I

TWO YEARS EARLIER

1

The shrill alarm rang out in the gloom, growing louder and louder, and Anaïs reached around blindly, regretting her decision to stay out until three am.

Finally she hit the snooze button and turned over, burying her throbbing head into the pillow to avoid the nightlight that rotated on the ceiling.

'Hey! Wake up, sleepy head!' Jenny, her flatmate, yanked back the duvet, unveiling Anaïs' matching unicorn-themed shorts and vest. 'Nice PJ's.' She smirked, walking over to the window and throwing open the curtains.

Anaïs squinted into the bright morning light and let out a long groan. 'No! Close them. Please! I've got a migraine coming on.'

'Sounds more like a *Migraini* to me. It stinks of alcohol in here.'

'That's not funny.' Anaïs got up and stomped into the bathroom, slamming the door behind her.

After a quick shower, she hastily applied some makeup, then swept through the ground-floor apartment like the Tasmanian Devil: packing her rucksack, throwing on a striped crop top and black dungarees, and guzzling down a mug of black coffee in a twirling tornado of green and blonde hair.

She gave herself a quick once-over in the hallway mirror, frowning at her reflection. Then she wheeled her bike outside.

Soon she was cycling through the narrow, graffiti-laden pathways of Brick Lane, passing the entrance to the Nomadic Gardens and ducking through a low underpass as a train thundered by overhead. But when she reached the main street, her head started to pound again.

She pulled into the curb, taking a moment to recover, and caught a glimpse of a little pharmacy tucked away down a quiet side-street. The neon-green sign flickered gently in the sunlight, and she decided to run inside.

A bell tinkled when she entered, and a tall, dark-haired man in black trousers and a white coat appeared, stopping her in her tracks.

'Good morning, my dear, I'm sorry I startled you. I just unlocked the door. Although you know what they say, the early bird catches the worm.'

He spoke in an old-fashioned, slightly high-pitched way, enunciating each word and lingering on the last syllable of each sentence, which Anaïs thought strange as he didn't look much older than thirty.

'Uh… yeah, sorry, I was just popping in to get my prescription.' She gave him a slip of paper.

'Of course, let me see.' He took the slip. His long slender fingers brushing against hers. 'Anaïs Dubois – what a beautiful name. Are you French, perchance?'

'My dad was, but I've lived in London my whole life.'

The thought of her late father sent a pang of sadness through her chest. He'd died in a car accident in Switzerland almost ten years ago, and she wished more than anything that she could spend one more day with him, feeling his big warm hugs, listening to his funny stories, and going for drives down to Brighton and the South-East coast in his vintage convertible Mercedes.

'Are you okay, my dear?' the man asked, a look of concern on his face.

'Yes, sorry, I just zoned out for a second.' She gave an embarrassed smile.

'That's perfectly okay. So, what am I getting for you today? Ah, Sumatriptan. Wait! Don't tell me – migraines?'

'Uh, yes, that's right.'

'Terrible things. I suffer from them myself. For future reference, you should get some lavender oil. It works wonders. Not that I want to deter you from taking tablets, of course. It's my livelihood after all.' He let out a little giggle. 'And, if all else fails, you can't beat a good head massage.'

He leered at her with deep-set blue eyes and thick black eyebrows. And with his slicked-back hair and clean-shaven face, she thought he resembled a maître d' at a fancy restaurant, or the creepy wolf from the old Betty Boop cartoons she watched as a kid.

'Lavender oil and head massages – got it.' She nodded, wishing she'd just waited and gone to *Boots* or *Superdrug* like she usually did. 'Great. I'll be right back.' His mouth opened wider and he flashed a pair of sharp incisors, compounding the wolf comparison. Then he disappeared behind the counter.

She checked her phone and read a text from her mother, Diane, who owned a high-end modelling agency in Chelsea and lived in a sprawling country-house in Strawberry Hill:

Good morning, ma puce. Don't forget, I'm having a little soiree this evening for my birthday. Nothing too fancy, just some drinks and nibbles, but a dress wouldn't go amiss. Anything but those ghastly dungarees you're so fond of. See you at 7. Bisous, Maman.

'Shit!' she muttered. Taking a bus, and then two trains to the other side of London was the last thing she wanted to do, but she knew her mother would be upset if she cancelled. And what was so bad about the dungarees?

'Here you go, Mademoiselle.' The man returned with a small bag, interrupting her thoughts.

'Thank you.' She opened her rucksack and a pile of flyers came tumbling out. 'Shit!' She crouched down but another jolt of pain made her wince.

'Let me help you.' He knelt beside her and gathered up the stray sheets. 'What's this?' He glanced at one of the flyers: ' "*The London College of Fashion's Equality Council is Proud to Present, Fashionistas for Feminism – With Special Guest Speaker, Margot Conti: Professor of Feminist, Gender & Sexuality Studies at Cambridge University.*" Sounds very impressive, and I see its being held at WunderBar. Isn't that near here?'

'Yeah, I work there a few nights a week. The manager's letting us have the function room upstairs for free.'

'That's very kind of them. Do you mind if I keep one? I can put it up in the window.'

'Uh, yeah. That would be great.' Anaïs took out her purse. 'How much do I owe you?'

'It's on the house. Put the money towards your cause.'

'Are you sure?'

'Yes, I insist. Just promise me you'll come back again.'

'Thank you. I'll donate it to one of the charities we support. I should really get going.' She edged towards the door.

9

'Of course, it was a pleasure to meet you, my dear. My name's Victor, by the way.

'Nice to meet you, Victor. Have a good day.' She smiled and left.

She arrived at the college campus about twenty minutes later and rushed through the reception area with her head down. She approached the stairwell, but Professor Humphreys, a notoriously letchy professor in his late-forties, suddenly appeared, blocking the way.

'Whoa, there, young lady!' He reached out and grabbed her by the shoulders. 'You should watch where you're going. You don't know who you'll bump into.'

'Oh! Sorry, Professor Humphreys, I was in a world of my own.' She shrugged him off and stepped back. The smell of tobacco, mixed with the cheap cloying aftershave he wore, made her want to gag, but she clenched her jaw and smiled through gritted teeth.

'Uh, uh, uh, what have I told you? It's Bill, remember?' He lifted his finger close to her mouth, and she fought the urge to slap it away.

'Sorry, but I really need to go. I'm already late.' She tried to step past, but he thrust out his arm and leant against the wall.

'That's okay, I'll give you a hall pass.' He threw back his head and let out a haughty laugh.

The sun caught his face, and she could see the long black hairs protruding from his nostrils. Like spider legs reaching towards her. She fantasised about grabbing hold of them and kicking him in his corduroy-clad balls but managed to restrain herself.

'Oh, before I forget,' he continued, 'there's a networking event tomorrow evening at the Ace Hotel in Shoreditch. There'll be lots of reps from the industry there, and it's only a ten-minute walk from where you live. How about we meet somewhere for a quick drink first and then go together. Say seven-thirty? You can invite your flatmate, Jenny, too, if you like – the more the merrier.'

'I'd love to,' she lied, a little disconcerted that he knew where she lived. 'But I'm already going to an event in Brick Lane. Maybe you could pop by. You might find it useful.' She handed him a flyer and gave him a knowing look.

'Uh, yes, very important stuff.' He took it with a sheepish smile.

'Well, I should get going. Have a great day, *Bill*.'

The rest of the day went by without incident, and she cycled home after her last lecture, quickly changed into a green summer dress and oversized white cardigan, before making the arduous journey to Strawberry Hill. She arrived just after seven and pressed the intercom on the high stonewall.

A moment later the wrought iron gates opened automatically and her mother appeared in an off-the-shoulder, figure-hugging purple dress, her blonde hair perfectly styled in an elegant bun, her bare neck dripping in diamonds. She was joined by Andréa, one of her oldest friends and Anaïs' Godmother. But they were both overtaken by Andrea's two-year-old German Shepherd, Chewie, who bolted out of the house and leapt up on Anaïs, almost knocking her over.

'Whoa, boy! I'm happy to see you too, but you're getting way too big to jump on me. You're like a grizzly bear.' She wrestled him down and stroked his head.

'Good evening, ma puce. I'm glad you could make it.' Diane hugged her and they exchanged kisses.

'Happy birthday, maman.' Anaïs smiled. 'You look so glamorous. Like Meryl Streep.'

'Meryl Streep is almost seventy, darling. I'm barely forty-seven.'

'Forty-nine,' Andréa corrected her.

'I meant a younger version, obviously.'

'Well, I suppose that is a compliment,' Diane replied. 'I'm glad to see you made an effort this evening. That's a pretty dress. It's a shame about the hair though.'

'I like it,' Andréa spoke up. 'It's very, umm, punk – is that the right word?'

'Thanks, Andi.' Anaïs gave her a quick hug. 'Did you come straight from the office?' She glanced down at the black trouser-suit and bright-white running trainers, which made the woman look even skinnier than she already was.

'Come on,' Diane interrupted. 'We can talk inside. The champagne and canapés are waiting.'

'I thought you said it was going to be a little soiree.' Anaïs gave her mother a quizzical look.

'It is, darling, but we're not savages.'

When they got inside, Diane led them into the dining room, where they found Anaïs' second Godmother, Jackie.

'Ah, now we can get the party started.' Jackie stood in a multi-coloured dress and matching headscarf, an empty glass of champagne in her hand.

'It looks like you already did.' Anaïs grinned.

'Don't be cheeky, missy. Now, get your cute little behind over here and give your Auntie J a hug.'

Anaïs' grin grew wider and they embraced, Jackie trapping her in a bear hug, despite her diminutive stature, and squeezing tightly.

'So, how you been, honey?' Jackie asked, finally releasing her grip.

'I'm okay. I've just been super busy with work and assignments. Nothing exciting. How about you? Have you arrested any interesting criminals lately?'

'My days of catching criminals are long gone. Since I became Chief-Superintendent all I do is sit on my big behind all day, drinking coffee, eating pastries and attending meeting after boring meeting.' She rolled her eyes.

'What about you, Andi?' Anaïs asked. 'How's Stjerne-Tec doing? You must be top of the Footsie-One-Hundred by now.'

'I'm not sure about that. We did just sign a very lucrative contract with the Federal Intelligence Service in Berlin, though. We'll be providing them with our newest security and surveillance technology, along with full IT and network support for the next five years.'

'Wow! That's amazing! Congratulations. Berlin will be so cool. I'll have to come and visit when you're out there.'

'Thank you.' Andréa smiled. 'It's crazy to think that my father came over from Denmark in 1969 and opened a little electrical shop in Kingston and now we're a multinational corporation with offices in London, Copenhagen and Berlin. If he was still alive, I don't think he'd believe it. I can hardly believe it myself,' she added as two waitresses came in carrying silver trays filled a selection of canapés.

'Ooh... what do we have here?' Jackie took a blini and put the whole thing in her mouth. 'Mmm... what is this?' She chewed loudly, closing her eyes in ecstasy.

'It's smoked salmon mousse, layered over crème fraiche and topped with red caviar,' Diane said, matter-of-factly.

'Well, la-di-da. Who knew pretension tasted so good?'

'Sometimes I wonder how the three of you are such good friends,' Anaïs said, picking up a champagne flute from the table. 'You're all so different. Like chalk and cheese.'

'More like chalk and chocolate.' Jackie laughed. 'Although it is crazy how long we've known each other – almost forty years – we're like sisters from another mister. Did I ever tell you the story of our first week at Lady Gwendolyn's?'

'About a million times.'

'I remember it like it was yesterday.' Jackie ignored Anaïs' sarcastic reply. 'I was terrified, walking into a huge classroom, full of rich little white girls, all whispering and giggling at the afrohaired black girl. Diane and Andi were the only ones who came and introduced themselves at breaktime. I'll never forget Andi saying her name, "It's pronounced Andreia, like Princess Leia!"' She mimicked Andréa's voice. 'And then I said, who's that? You should have seen the look on her face. And you know what?'

'You still haven't seen that *damn* movie,' Anaïs butted in, knowing the story by heart.

'When did your daughter become such a little smart Alec?' Jackie glanced at Diane.

'I'm kidding. Carry on… I like hearing this story, honestly.'

'I've forgotten where I was now.'

'You told me you hadn't seen any movies because your father said television was evil, and the Devil lived inside it,' Andréa joined in.

'Ah, yes, and then Diane said, "That can't be true. Everybody knows the Devil lives under Andréa's bed."' Jackie laughed.

'I did say that, didn't I?' Diane spoke up.

'You did. And I still sleep with a nightlight on.' Andréa shot her a dirty look.

'Don't worry, Andi, so do I,' Anaïs added.

'Anyway, that's when Issy Harrington and her cronies came marching over and started making monkey noises,' Jackie continued. 'You should have seen your mother telling them off with all her fancy words, and then fighting them when they wouldn't listen. She was like a pocket-sized thesaurus with fists.'

'Well, I was captain of the debating team.' Diane shrugged. 'Although sometimes you have to fight fire with fire.'

13

'I wish I'd seen that. My mother, the street fighter.' Anaïs grinned.

'Yes, well, I only condone violence in extreme circumstances.' Diane's face turned serious. 'And in this case, it backfired.'

'Yeah, we all got detention for a month.' Jackie shook her head.

'Apart from me,' Andréa corrected her.

'That's because you snuck off when things got heated, as usual. Although, in hindsight, it was a good thing.'

'Why's that?' Anaïs played along.

'On our last day of detention, your mother and I arranged to meet Andréa in the park and then go into town. But Issy and her older sister, Felicity, ambushed us with a gang of older girls. Then they stripped us down to our underwear and tied us to a tree.'

'I still can't believe they did that.' Anaïs shook her head.

'I can't believe they threw white paint all over us.' Diane frowned. 'My poor mother almost had a heart attack when I got home. I had to have half my hair shorn off, and I was still finding paint lodged in all kinds of orifices for almost a month afterwards.'

'Ew! Maman, too much information.' Anaïs scrunched up her face.

'You just ruined the ending.' Jackie scowled.

'I didn't ruin anything. Everyone knows what happened next, even Chewie,' Diane replied. 'They threw the paint. We turned into statues. And then Andréa found us and ran for help. The end.'

'Fine! I was only telling it as a build up to my toast anyway. And if you think your mother was horrified, imagine how mine reacted when her little African princess came home looking like a porcelain doll. Now, does everyone have a drink?' Jackie looked around. 'Good. Let's raise our glasses to forty years of friendship, and hopefully forty more. Oh, and happy birthday to this one too.' She glanced at Diane out of the corner of her eye and raised an eyebrow.

2

The following evening Anaïs paced up and down the function room of WunderBar, her phone stuck to her ear, as the penultimate talk ended and a polite smattering of applause broke out amongst the audience of mostly female students. 'Where the hell is she?' she muttered, listening to the endless ringing tone. 'Come on, Margot, pick up…' She ducked past the fake black trees that lined the room, their fairy-lit branches casting her shadow on the wall, where gothic-inspired murals of *Snow White*, *Rumpelstiltskin* and *Little Red Riding Hood* watched her with dark sinister eyes, and she finally hung up.

'Here, drink this.' Jenny appeared with a shot glass filled with a clear liquid.

'I can't drink now. I'm meant to be hosting this thing. Although, if Margot Conte doesn't turn up in the next five minutes, there'll be nothing to host.'

'Hey, just relax. She'll be here. And nobody wants a host that looks like they're about to have a nervous breakdown. Come on. Drink. I got the barman to pour me a Grey Goose – I know it's your favourite, Miss Frenchy-Pants.'

'I guess one shot won't hurt.' Anaïs took the glass and downed it.

'Better?' Jenny asked.

Anaïs nodded.

'Good. Now just go and tell everyone we're having a short break, or I can go up and do a little Beyoncé, if you want – *Who runs the world? Girls!*' Jenny raised her fist and sang out of key.

'You can save that for when I actually want people to leave at the end of the night.'

Anaïs stepped up to the microphone, but a booming New York accent stopped her in her tracks.

'Hold up! Coming through… Make way people…' A statuesque woman strode purposefully through the crowd, wearing dark-rimmed glasses and a white blouse, unbuttoned at the top, showing off her olive skin and pronounced clavicles. She stopped in front of Anaïs and put her hand over the microphone: 'You're Anaïs, right?'

'Yes–'

'Great! I'm in the right place. That's always a good start. Love the *locay*, by the way.' She glanced around. 'Good choice. Makes a change from stuffy lecture theatres and soulless conference rooms.'

'Thanks. Do you want some time to prepare?'

'Nah, it's fine, I went through my notes in the cab. Sorry I was late by the way. Traffic's a bitch in this city. I'll just get straight down to it. Let's get this show on the road, right? Can you get me a gin with a dash of tonic and a spritz of lemon? And don't be shy with the gin. It's been a day!'

Anaïs scurried off while the woman introduced herself to the audience.

It wasn't long before the whole room fell silent, hanging on her every word, enraptured by her thoughts on mainstream feminism versus radical and Marxist ideas, and nodding their heads in agreement with her arguments against the patriarchy, objectification, and the male gaze.

Anaïs watched from the back of the room, her mind flitting to her run in with Professor Humphreys the previous day. She glanced around but, as expected, he was nowhere to be seen. She couldn't see the strange guy from the pharmacy either, which was a relief.

She turned her attention back to Professor Conti, who continued to educate and entertain the audience, mixing her forthright views with funny anecdotes about her own experiences working on Wall Street in the late-eighties and nineties, and cutting remarks aimed mostly at the smattering of men in attendance, although it was all in good jest, evidenced by the constant eruptions of laughter and
applause.

After a short question and answer session, things came to an end and Anaïs approached the woman.

'Thank you so much. That was amazing!' she gushed. 'You were like a rock star up there.'

'Thanks, hun. It's funny you should say that. I always wanted to be Janis Joplin when I was younger. I guess this is the closest I'm ever going to get.'

'Can I get you another drink?'

'Thanks, but I should get going. I'm only here for the weekend and there's lots of people to see. Great job tonight, though. You've got a big future ahead of you.'

'Thank you so much, Professor Conti. That means so much coming from you,' Anaïs spluttered, slightly taken aback.

'Please, call me Margot, but never Maggie! You have my information. Keep in touch. And if you're ever in Cambridge, let me know.'

'Yes. I'd love that, Prof–I mean Margot.' She escorted the woman outside and then ran back upstairs.

'Oh. My. God. How epic was that?' Jenny grabbed her by the elbows as soon as she re-entered the room.

'I know. I can't believe how well it went.'

'Professor Conti is such a boss!' Jenny added.

'Do you want a drink?' Anaïs asked.

'I'd love to, but I need to go meet Tom. We're having a late dinner in an Indian place around the corner.'

'Everyone's leaving me.'

'Don't worry, we'll celebrate tomorrow, I promise.' Jenny gave her a hug and then rushed off.

Anaïs mingled with her other friends, and they soon got into the party spirit, dancing, drinking and chatting animatedly until the bar closed at midnight.

When they got outside, one of the girls suggested going for a drink in a nearby late-night bar, but Anaïs was tired after the stress and excitement of hosting the event and decided to go home.

After saying goodbye, she crossed the road and went into a brightly-lit mini-market, picking up a bottle of white wine and some hummus. She gave Jenny a quick call as she strolled down the snack isle, but it went straight to answerphone so she left a voice message:

'Hey, you, thanks again for coming tonight. I really appreciate it. I hope you had a nice dinner. I'm just in the shop. Let me know if you want anything, otherwise I'll get you a little surprise. Oh, and if you and Tom are doing any weird sexual stuff in the kitchen again, please go up to your room. I'll be home soon. Love you.'

She ended the call and picked up a bag of crisps and some Maltesers for Jenny, which were her favourite, then went to pay.

Outside she strode along the quiet street, hugging the bag to her chest and lowering her head against a sudden downpour, when a sharp pain tore through one side of her head.

'Not now,' she grumbled, remembering that she'd left her tablets on the bedside table. And things got even worse when she saw a white van parked in the narrow laneway that led to her flat, its hazard lights blinking on and off.

When she got closer, she noticed the driver's side door was slightly ajar, but the cab was empty. She could hear the rhythmic clicking of the lights and the rain thudding against the roof, and she held the bag closer, sliding past. There was nobody at the rear of the van either, and she approached the shadowy underpass that led to the Nomadic Gardens and her flat beyond.

A train hurtled by overhead, and she glanced up, temporarily transfixed by the luminous carriages, flashing by one-after-another, until a fierce stab of pain brought her back to reality.

Suddenly the whole world turned black, and the bag slipped from her grasp, the wine bottle exploding as it hit the ground.

For a moment she was completely disorientated. Then she felt something dragging her backwards. A vice-like grip digging into her neck and shoulders. She tried to struggle free. Instinctively reaching for her phone. But it slipped from her grasp, and she was bundled into the back of the van.

'What's going on? Let me go!' she cried, before falling silent as a blunt object slammed into her solar plexus, sucking the air out of her lungs.

She lay prone on the floor, struggling to breathe, and the attacker pinned her down, tying her wrists and ankles. Then he lifted the material covering her face and forced something into her mouth. A strange, metallic-tasting liquid slid down her throat, and she coughed and spluttered, her whole-body going into spasm. But the attacker was unrelenting, his hefty bodyweight keeping her in place.

Within seconds the doors slammed shut, and she heard the engine roar to life as the van accelerated away. The jerky motion sent her rolling across the floor, and she crashed into the side-panel.

'Stop! Please! Why are you doing this?' she shouted. Her eyes wide with terror but seeing nothing. 'Somebody answer me! My family has money. We can give you whatever you want. Just let me go. I'm begging you.' She sobbed quietly, praying someone would reply. But her pleas went unanswered. The silence deafening.

Soon the van sped up, and she squeezed her eyes shut, trying to focus.

Then the hallucinations started...

3

The rest of the journey went by in a psychedelic blur of non-stop colours and unrelenting visions, until the van finally came to a stop, bringing Anaïs temporarily back to reality.

For a moment everything went black again and all she could hear was the soft pitter-patter of rain on the roof. Then the backdoors swung open with a skin-crawling screech.

'Please, you don't want to do this,' she cried. 'Let me go. I won't tell anyone, I promise.' She waited for a reply, but her captor remained silent.

Without warning he grabbed her ankles and dragged her outside. She landed on the gravel floor with a heavy thud, the impact taking the wind out of her.

She curled up in the foetal position, desperately trying to catch her breath, but he gripped hold of her armpits and yanked her up to a sitting position.

'Who are you?' she cried. But he didn't answer. Then, to her surprise, he untied her wrists and ankles and ripped the bag off her head.

She looked up in confusion and let out a blood-curdling scream when she saw a snarling, red-horned demon, looming over her, its long, forked tongue flicking in and out of its blackened mouth.

'No! You're not real.' She squeezed her eyes shut and shook her head.

When she opened them again, she was relieved to see that it was just a man in a red-and-black tribal mask.

'Who are you? What did you give me?' Her fear morphed into anger, and she glared up defiantly. 'Answer me, you fucking psycho!' But he still refused to talk, his eyes hidden behind the dark slits in the garish mask.

'Why don't you take off that stupid thing and show me who you are, you fucking coward!'

Before she could say anything else, he reached out with a large, black-gloved hand and grabbed her by the hair. She tried to wriggle free, but he lifted her up and dragged her along a narrow pathway until they reached a muddy clearing. There was a dark forest up ahead, the foreboding treeline about twenty metres away, and she could see dozens of dark figures lurking in the shadows, their shapes indistinguishable, fading in and out of sight.

Suddenly a flash of lightning lit up the sky, followed by a roar of thunder, and she looked up and watched as the dark clouds pulsated above her, expanding and contracting like a living breathing entity.

Soon another roar ripped through the sky and a tropical deluge blocked out the world.

Anaïs threw back her head, welcoming the cold water on her face. Then, to her surprise, it started to slow down, the constant stream separating into long lines of glimmering beads, like luminous jellyfish floating in the deep dark ocean.

She glanced around in wonder, watching the strange phenomena unfold, until suddenly the rain stopped moving altogether, billions of perfectly formed droplets hovering in mid-air, reflecting her image over and over.

She reached out tentatively, but then the droplets turned black, and the stranger's masked face materialized, his impenetrable stare multiplied infinitely, and she let out a gut-wrenching scream. The sound intensified, and the droplets exploded in a cacophony of noise. Then, just like that, she was alone.

For a brief comforting moment, she thought the man had gone. Then she noticed him standing a few feet away, and her stomach lurched. He held a long knife in his hand, his head tilted to one side, and she knew he was smiling behind the mask.

'Why don't you just leave me alone, you fucking pervert!' She turned and ran towards the forest, plunging headfirst into the trees and stumbling blindly through the branches.

It didn't take long for her eyes to adjust, and she found a muddy pathway, quickening her pace as the dark forest writhed and groaned all around her.

She spotted a faint light up ahead and raced towards it. But when she glanced down again a light mist began to rise. It quickly grew thicker, swallowing up the path and covering the forest floor in an eerie white blanket. She tried to ignore it, but slithering white tendrils wrapped around her legs and she fell to the ground, sliding across the muddy surface.

She came to a stop a few feet later and clambered to her feet, her eyes darting around nervously. Thankfully, the mist had disappeared, and she could see that the light was actually a house. Excited, she raced towards it, but then she spotted the masked stranger running parallel to her through the trees. He moved in a jaunty, jagged fashion, like a strange character from an old stop-motion movie. Then, to her horror, he turned and headed straight for her. Terrified, she ran straight into a cluster of bushes that appeared out of nowhere.

She struggled to break free, slowly untangling herself from the sinewy foliage, when a hand grabbed her shoulder and dragged her into a moonlit clearing. She screamed and fought, desperately shouting for help, but the man was too strong, easily pushing her to the ground and pinning her down.

The soft light from above illuminated his masked face, and Anaïs caught a glimpse of his eyes through the dark slits.

'It's you,' she murmured, looking up in surprise. A shared moment of mutual recognition passing between them. Then a fist crashed into her face with an almighty thud and everything went black.

4

A faint ringing emanated from the darkness and Diane stirred for a moment before rolling over and nestling her head deeper into the pillow, clinging onto her peaceful dreams. But the sound persisted, growing louder and louder, until she finally woke up. She snatched the phone off the nightstand and squinted at the bright screen, but she didn't recognise the number.

'Hello,' she answered guardedly, her voice a little hoarse.

'Hi, Mrs Dubois. It's Jenny Frieman. Anaïs' flatmate.'

'Hi, Jenny, you do know it's almost three am, don't you?' Diane sat up.

'I know. I'm really sorry. But I didn't know who else to call. I found your number in Ani's room. I hope you don't mind. I mean it's probably nothing, but I'm a little worried–'

'Slow down, dear, and tell me what's happened.' The urgency in the girl's voice worried her, but Diane tried to remain calm.

'Like I said, it's probably nothing, but Ani was meant to be home over two hours ago, and she's still not back.'

'It was her event tonight, wasn't it? Maybe she's still out celebrating.'

'No, I mean, yes, it was, but she left me a voicemail at twelve-thirty saying she was in the shop and she'd be home soon.'

'Maybe she bumped into someone and decided to stay out a little longer,' Diane suggested, starting to think that the girl was overreacting.

'She would have still called or messaged, or something.' Jenny persisted. 'And her phone keeps going to answerphone too. It's not like her at all.'

'No, you're right. That is strange.' Diane sat on the edge of the bed, rubbing her temples. 'Is there anywhere else she might have gone? To see a boy maybe?'

'She's not seeing anybody at the moment. Not that I know of, anyway.' Jenny sniffed down the line. 'And if she'd gone to see someone, she would have still replied to let me know she was okay.'

'Maybe her battery died?'

'It wouldn't ring if she had no battery. Do you think we should call the police?'

'No. Wait. Let me think…' Diane stood up and put on her dressing gown. Then she stepped over to the window and glanced through the curtains at the rain falling outside.

'Mrs Dubois? Are you still there?' Jenny's voice interrupted her thoughts.

'Yes, yes. Sorry. Just sit tight. I'm going to come to you. I'll call my friend Jackie on the way. She's a Chief Superintendent in the police. She should be able to give us some advice. In the meantime, if you hear anything, call me straight away. Do you understand?'

'Yes,' the girl replied, her voice barely a whisper.

'Good. I'll see you soon. And don't worry, I'm sure it's just a big misunderstanding.'

Diane got dressed and went down to the kitchen, pouring herself a glass of water and then calling Anaïs.

The phone rang for what seemed like an eternity, and she held her breath. What was her daughter up to? She willed her to pick up, but it eventually went to answerphone.

The sound of Anaïs' perky recorded voice left a lump in her throat, and she took a moment to compose herself:

'Hi, darling, sorry to call so late, but I just spoke to Jenny. She's worried about you. Apparently, you were meant to be home a few hours ago. Please call me when you get this and let me know you're okay. Love you.'

She gulped down the rest of the water and then went into the hallway, quickly putting on a rain jacket and a pair of tennis shoes, before grabbing her car keys and going outside.

A few minutes later, she pulled out of the driveway and connected her phone to the car's Bluetooth system. She tried Anaïs' number one more time, tapping her fingers on the steering wheel. Then, to her surprise, someone answered.

A tinny, mumbling voice crackled through the car's speakers and Diane's fingernails dug into the soft leather of the steering wheel.

'Ani? Is that you? You're breaking up.' But there was just a hiss of static in reply. 'Ani, please, let me know that you're okay.' She stared at the digital display on the dashboard, showing Anaïs' name and number. 'Come on! Come on! Work, you wretched thing–'

'Hello? Can you hear me? I don't think there's anyone there...' Suddenly the voice came through more clearly, and Diane could hear a young girl speaking to someone else.

'Oh my God, Ani, I'm so glad you're okay,' Diane blurted, relief flooding over her.

'I'm sorry, but this is Lizzy.'

Diane heard the girl talking to a man in the background, and she lost her patience.

'Lizzy!' she called out. 'Is Anaïs with you? I'm her mother, Diane, I really need to speak to her.'

'I'm sorry, but I don't know anyone called Anaïs. I'm with my boyfriend. We just found this phone on the way home from a party.'

'Where did you find it exactly?' Her mind swirled with dark thoughts, but she tried to remain calm.

'In a little alleyway off Brick Lane, the one that leads down to Allen Park and the Nomadic Gardens.'

The mention of the Nomadic Gardens, which was one of Anaïs' favourite places, made it even worse, and Diane had to focus on the road to stop herself from losing control.

'Was there anything else there?' she asked.

'Um… I don't think so – oh, wait. There was a plastic bag with a broken wine bottle inside and some crisps and Maltesers. There was no purse or ID, if that's what you mean.'

'Where are you now?'

'We just got home. I'm literally standing in my hallway, dripping wet.'

'Would you mind if I came to pick the phone up now? I'm already on my way to Pedley Street. It's just, my daughter's been missing for a few hours, you see, and I'm a little worried.'

'Of course. We're only five-minutes from there. On the other side of the park.'

'Thank you so much, Lizzy. I really appreciate your help.' Diane took the girl's address and typed it into the car's sat nav. Then she pressed down on the accelerator and sped over Chiswick Bridge, towards Hammersmith.

Once she was on the other side of the river, she called Jackie and waited nervously as the phone rang and rang…

'Hello,' Jackie answered groggily. Just as Diane was about to give up.

'Hi, Jackie, it's Diane, I'm sorry to bother you at this hour, but I'm on my way to Ani's, and I needed your advice.'

'Is everything okay?'

Diane paused to compose herself. Then she told Jackie about the conversation with Jenny and the phone call with Lizzy. She struggled to get the last few words out. Her voice on the cusp of breaking.

'Okay, listen to me carefully,' Jackie spoke up. 'I'm going to put a call into the station and get them to file a missing person's report. Then I'll get a car sent out to the scene straight away. In the meantime, I need you to stay calm. Can you do that for me?'

The mention of the word *scene* conjured images of police tape and chalk outlines on the floor and Diane's mind went into a spiral, her eyes glazing over, the streetlights and the road blurring into one through the rain-smeared windscreen. Without thinking, she careered through a red light, almost crashing into a black cab, before yanking the steering wheel to the side and swerving out of the way at the last minute.

'Diane! Is everything okay?' Jackie asked. 'It sounds like the Monaco Grand Prix there.'

'Yes, sorry. I'll see you soon. Thanks, Jackie.' Diane ended the call and put her foot down.

She reached Brick Lane less than fifteen minutes later and went straight to collect Anaïs' phone, thanking the bleary-eyed girl who answered the door, before getting back in the car and driving the short distance to Pedley Street.

She parked outside Anaïs' flat and got out of the car. But before she'd even reached the front door, Jenny appeared, her face puffy and smeared with makeup and Diane's heart sank.

'Have you heard anything?' she asked, although she could already guess the answer.

Jenny shook her head and wrapped her arms around Diane, sobbing into her chest.

'Now, now. Shush… there's no need for that.' Diane patted her back. 'Everything's going to be okay.' But when she told Jenny about the phone and the plastic bag, the girl broke down completely.

'She bought those Maltesers for me! She knows they're my favourite. This is all my fault!' Jenny howled. 'If I'd just stayed with her tonight, instead of going to meet Tom, everything'd be fine.'

Diane ushered her inside and Jenny slumped down on a kitchen stool, while she poured two glasses of water.

'Here, drink this.' She handed Jenny a glass, noticing the empty bottle of wine on the counter.

'I needed it to calm my nerves,' she explained, following Diane's gaze.

'That's perfectly understandable. I could do with a glass myself.' Diane forced a smile. 'Do you know how to unlock this?' She held up Anaïs' phone.

'The passcode's Ani's birthday. Here, let me.' Jenny took the phone.

'Who's the last person she spoke to?' Diane asked.

'It was me.'

'What about messages or emails?'

'I'm looking now…' Jenny kept scrolling. 'There's nothing that looks suspicious, just a few Instagram notifications and WhatsApp messages from girlfriends.'

Diane was about to take a look for herself when the front door buzzed.

'I'll get it.' Jenny leapt up and ran into the hallway.

She returned a moment later with Jackie and a slight-built, blonde-haired man in a rumpled grey suit that looked about two sizes too big for him. He had a narrow boyish face and wispy stubble, although Diane could see from his hard-grey eyes and the feint lines around his tight-set mouth that he was probably in his mid-to-late-thirties.

'Hi, Diane.' Jackie looked at her sombrely. She was dressed in a trouser-suit too, and the formality made Diane feel uneasy. 'This is Detective Parsons. He kindly offered to drive me here tonight.'

'Thank you. It's good you're here. We have Ani's phone. Maybe you can use it to find her.'

'Diane, wait. I need to tell you something,' Jackie interrupted her.

'What is it? What's wrong?' Diane saw the look on her friend's face and began to panic. 'Have you found her? Please tell me she's okay. I couldn't bear it if anything's happened to her. She's all I've got.'

'We just had a call to say that a girl matching Anaïs' description was found in Epping Forest a little while ago—'

'Oh my God!' Diane lifted her hands to her face, the whole room spinning around her. 'Is she alive? Please tell me she's alive?'

'Yes! Yes! She's alive,' Jackie reassured her. 'A man found her while he was walking his dog. Luckily, he was a retired RAF officer, and he managed to perform CPR and get her to a hospital just in time. She's in surgery as we speak. Her situation's critical, but the doctors are doing everything they can.'

'What happened to her?' Diane asked.

'Maybe we should wait until we get to the hospital. We still don't have all the details.' Jackie stepped forward and put a hand on her shoulder.

'I want to know.' Diane looked at her with a determined grimace.

Jackie hesitated, and Detective Parsons spoke for the first time.

'I'm sorry to have to tell you this, Ms Dubois, but your daughter was sexually assaulted.' When he finished the sentence, all the colour drained from Diane's face and she fell silent, while Jenny let out a pained cry.

The detective glanced at Jackie, shuffling a little uncomfortably, then carried on: 'Like Chief Superintendent Njoku said, we don't have all the details yet, but as far as we can tell, it would seem the perpetrator tried to strangle her to death, but they were scared off by the man and his dog.'

'Can you give us a moment, please, detective?' Jackie put her arms around Diane and held her tightly.

'Of course, ma'am. I'll go and start the car.'

5

FIVE DAYS LATER

Jackie opened the door to the private hospital room in a tailored police uniform, her hat tucked under her arm, her usually wild afro hair tied-up in a neat bun, and greeted Diane and Andréa.

'Sorry I haven't been back for a while. I've been tied up with the investigation. How's everyone doing?'

'We're fine. Do you have any news?' Diane asked in a clipped tone, skipping the pleasantries.

'Yes, uh... Detective Parsons and his team have been sifting through the CCTV over the past few days. Unfortunately, there were a lot of power outages on the night because of the weather. We did get footage of a white van reversing into the laneway around the time Anaïs was attacked, though. The angle isn't very good, but we were able to get a partial registration and track the vehicle to an elderly couple in Margate. They reported it stolen a few days ago. The husband is in his seventies though, so I doubt he had anything to do with it. But at least we have something to look for. And if we find the van, I'm confident we'll find whoever's responsible and lock them away for a very long time.'

'Did you get a look at the driver, at least?' Diane asked.

'You can see someone getting in and out of the van, but the view is partially blocked by the wall and the roof of the vehicle. Whoever this person is, they're clever. They knew exactly where the cameras were. And they seem to be wearing some kind of mask too.'

'What kind of monster is this?' Andréa exclaimed.

'It would seem the worst kind,' Jackie said gravely.

*

29

Up until this point, Anaïs lay behind them, staring at the ceiling, eyes unfocused, murky puddles lying stagnant in a barren wasteland, the medication making her lethargic and unresponsive. But she knew the longer she stayed silent, the more chance there was of the man getting away with it.

Focusing all her energy, she tried to say something, but she hadn't spoken since the attack, her throat restricted by the plastic tube the doctors had inserted into her crushed windpipe after the emergency tracheotomy.

Since then she'd been in and out of consciousness, existing in a dream-like state between fantasy and reality. The medication took away the physical pain, but the mental anguish was impossible to cure and a big part of her couldn't help wishing she'd died that night. At least then she wouldn't have to keep reliving the same nightmare over and over again. But now wasn't the time for wallowing in self-pity; she needed to say something before Jackie left.

'Wu...' She tried to lift her hand, her voice barely audible, a mumbled gurgle that made her wince in pain. But nobody noticed.

Swallowing hard, she tried again. 'Wait... Don't go...' This time the words came out in a raspy slur, and everyone turned.

'Ma puce!' Diane rushed over and took her hand.

She tried to continue, but her throat burned, acid reflux clogging her already damaged airways. She coughed and spluttered, wincing with each convulsion.

'Just take your time. There's no rush.' Diane stroked her hand.

Anaïs closed her eyes and took a deep breath. 'Need... to... speak... to... Jackie...' She forced out the words, taking her time to enunciate each one as clearly as possible.

'What is it, honey?' Jackie stepped forward.

'I... know... who... it... was...' She barely had enough breath to finish the sentence, her chest beating heavily.

'Who was it, honey? Tell me.'

She swallowed down the phlegm building up in her throat, her face hardening.

'The pharmacist,' she said, with conviction.

'What pharmacist?' Jackie looked at her in confusion.

'In Brick Lane... he gave me my prescription last week...' She wracked her brain, trying to remember the man's name. Then, to her horror, she was whisked back to the moonlit clearing, the masked figure hunched over her, his piercing blue eyes glowing through the dark eye-slits, his gloved hands wrapped around her neck.

'Sleep, my dear...' His distinctive voice pierced through her head, like nails down a chalkboard, and she sat bolt upright.

'Victor,' she said, barely above a whisper, as if saying the word aloud might make him reappear. Then she fell back onto the pillow and passed out.

6

Jackie drove straight to Brick Lane and parked in front of a police van that blocked the junction leading to the pharmacy, its blue lights flashing silently.

A small group of uniformed officers chatted beside it, but when she got out of the car they quickly stood to attention.

'Morning, gentleman.' She revelled in the way they shuffled uncomfortably in her presence, their eyes facing forward, almost frightened to look at her even though they were all at least a foot taller.

'Morning, ma'am,' they replied in unison.

'Has Detective Parsons arrived yet?' She glanced around.

'He's just over there, ma'am.' One of the officers pointed to a black car across the road.

'Thank you, gentleman. As you were.'

She strode over and Detective Parsons got out to meet her, along with a young Spanish-looking detective.

'Afternoon, Ma'am.' He nodded.

'Afternoon, detective, has there been any movement yet?'

'Nothing much. We only got here a few minutes ago.'

'What have you found out so far?'

'The guy's name is Victor Leopold Farkas. He's thirty-three. Hungarian. Came over to London as a kid after his parents were killed in a car accident in Budapest. And now he runs a little pharmacy here, in Brick Lane.'

'Any record?'

'Nope. He's clean.'

'What about any other family in London, or a partner?'

'He did have aunt and uncle here. He lived with them when he first moved over, but they died in a house fire about fifteen years ago.'

'Doesn't seem like he's had much luck.'

'Nope. He did get a pretty big inheritance though.'

'Hmm, interesting...' Jackie's eyes narrowed. 'Good job, detective.'

'You should thank Detective Pisani. She's the one that got the information so quickly. She's a bit of a tech whizz.'

'Well done, Detective Pisani. 'I'm glad to see the women are showing the men how it's done.'

'Thank you, ma'am. I actually did my Masters dissertation on diversification in the Metropolitan Police and its effects on socio and economically deprived areas. You were one of my inspirations. I wrote a case study on you and your work in Brixton and South-East London. It's a pleasure to finally meet you properly.'

'Really? I'm flattered. When this is over and done with you can show it to me. The only things Detective Parsons ever wrote about me were scribbled on the bathroom stalls when I was his sergeant, and he was a snot-nosed, pain in my behind.'

'I never wrote any of those things, ma'am. But I did say them behind your back from time-to-time.' He smirked.

'Okay, that's enough chitchat. What's our plan of attack?'

'We'll go in through the front with two officers and Detective Pisani will take the others around the back.'

'Perfect. Let's do this.' Jackie strode off and approached the officers.

'Hello again, gents. Are you ready to bring this man in?'

'Yes, ma'am.'

'That's what I like to hear. What's your names?'

'I'm PC Carraway, and this is PC Crookston, ma'am,' one of them answered.

'Huh, Carraway and Crookston. Sounds like an eighties cop show. Right, let's go.'

'Do you want us to go in first, ma'am?' PC Crookston asked.

'What do you think? I haven't been on active duty in over ten years. And look at these nails. They're made for tackling canapés and mimosas, not murderers and rapists!'

'Uh, yes. Sorry, ma'am—'

'It's okay, Officer Crookston, I'm just joking with you. But you two are definitely going first, followed by Detective Parsons, and I'll take up the rear – Lord knows I've got enough of it. Oh, and be as rough as you like with this guy.'

A moment later they entered the shop, and a man, dressed in a white coat, greeted them with a wide smile.

'Good afternoon, officers,' he said, stepping from behind the counter. 'I must say this is a welcome surprise. It's always a joy to see our fine constabulary out and about. To what do I owe this pleasure?'

'Cut the bullshit, Mr Farkas,' Detective Parsons said as the officers rushed forward and slammed him down on the countertop.

'Could someone please tell me the meaning of this intrusion?' He looked up serenely despite the burly officers thrusting his arms behind his back and pushing his head down, ruining his immaculately slicked-back hair and ruffling his pristine coat. 'This all seems rather unnecessary—'

But before he could say anything else, they put a pair of handcuffs on his wrists and yanked him up.

'Victor Leopold Farkas, you're under arrest for the rape and attempted murder of Anaïs Dubois. You don't have to say anything, but it may harm your defence if you do not mention, when questioned, something which you later rely on in court. Anything you do say may be given in evidence…'

As Detective Parsons continued to read the man his rights, the officers dragged him towards the door, knocking over display cases and shelving as they went.

'Stop for a moment, please, officers.' Jackie blocked the entranceway and looked up at the man. He didn't seem like a rapist or a murderer, but when he leered down at her, she saw an emptiness behind his eyes that made her shudder.

'Ah! I see you brought royalty with you.' He looked at the crown and star on Jackie's epaulettes and grinned. 'A Chief Superintendent coming all the way here for little old me. I'm honoured. Although this is a grave mistake. I would never dream of hurting anybody, let alone an innocent young girl.'

'Save it, Mr Farkas. Anaïs is alive and well, and she's told us everything.' Jackie hoped the revelation would cause a reaction, but he didn't even blink. 'Get him out of here.' She stepped aside, and the officers bundled him through the door and into the back of the van as a group of passers-by stopped and watched the drama unfolding.

7

The following evening Anaïs convinced the doctors to discharge her, and she was transported to her mother's house in a private ambulance.

When she got there, a makeshift bedroom had been set up in the dining room with a heartrate monitor, ventilation machine and IV drip. Her mother had also hired a young nurse to look after her. Soon Anaïs fell into a tumultuous sleep, the now familiar nightmares returning, until a tapping sound on the patio window woke her up.

Startled, she looked out at the dark garden, but all she saw was her reflection staring back. Her silhouette illuminated by the soft light of the heart rate monitor and the digital clock on the counter, which showed one-forty-five am.

'Ugh, I look like something out of *The Exorcist*,' she croaked.

She turned away, her head sinking into the pillow with a huff, when suddenly the phone rang. She thought about ignoring it, but the incessant sound bore into her brain like a jackhammer, and she picked up the wireless handset, being careful to avoid the tube in her throat.

'Hello,' she said, a little apprehensively.

For a moment there was silence, an eerie static as empty as a faraway ocean. Then she heard someone breathing. At first it was faint, almost imperceptible, but as she continued to listen, the sound grew louder. More urgent.

'Who is this?' She held the phone closer, but the breathing continued, like the howl of an approaching storm. 'I'm sorry, but I think you've got the wrong number.' Her hand shook, a sense of dread washing over her.

She was about to hang up when someone finally spoke: 'Good evening, Anaïs. I do hope you're well, my dear.'

'No, this isn't real! They arrested you!' she cried out, recognising Victor's distinctive voice straight away.

'Who knows what is real and what is not in this strange world we live in. You look radiant this evening by the way. Even with that unfortunate thing in your throat.'

Anaïs looked at the window and saw the man leering back at her, his eyes glowing menacingly in the soft light. He lifted a gloved hand to the glass, and she let out a gut-wrenching scream.

Within seconds, Diane burst into the room, followed by the young nurse.

'What is it, ma puce? What's wrong?'

'He's here!' Anaïs pointed at the window but when she looked again, he'd disappeared.

'Who's here?' Diane stared at her in confusion.

'The man – Victor! He's in the garden!'

Diane walked over to the window and put her hand to the glass. 'I can't see anybody. You must have had a nightmare or a hallucination. You're on very strong painkillers. The doctors said there might be some side-effects.'

'He's out there. I saw him!' Anaïs' voice rose, her terror turning to anger. 'We need to call the police!'

'I know you're scared, ma puce, but he's already locked away. He can't hurt you now.'

'Can't you just call Jackie to make sure he's still there?' she asked, fresh tears filling her bloodshot eyes.

'It's almost two am, darling. Let's wait until morning. I'm sure it was just your mind playing tricks on you. You've been through so much.'

'If you won't call her, I will.' Anaïs picked up the handset again.

'Okay. Let me do it.' Diane sighed. 'You need to rest your voice.' She took the handset and dialled Jackie's number. Then she wandered into the kitchen.

She came back a few minutes later with a tight smile on her face. 'Jackie's on her way, and she's bringing Detective Parsons and Detective Pisani.'

*

Jackie arrived thirty minutes later, and Diane led her through to the dining room while the detectives went to check the garden.

'What's happening? Is he still locked up? Please tell me you've still got him.' Anaïs sat up, her eyes frantic, as soon as they entered the room.

'Just calm down, honey. The detectives are taking a look around outside now. I wanted to talk to you both alone. Do you mind leaving us for a moment?' Jackie looked at the nurse.

'What's wrong?' Diane asked.

Jackie took a deep breath and straightened her back. 'We had to leave Victor Farkas go a few hours ago–'

'What do you mean *let him go?*' Diane erupted.

'We tried everything we could,' Jackie replied calmly. 'But the man speaks in riddles and he has an answer for everything. We also found the van burnt out in a field near Romford. It had been there a few days and forensics couldn't find anything to link it to the crime or Mr Farkas.'

'Surely you could have kept him a little longer. He's bound to slip up sooner or later,' Diane replied desperately.

'We held him for the full twenty-four-hours, plus a few extra, but we would've needed a warrant to keep him any longer. And there's no way any judge would have granted that with no camera footage, no physical evidence, no DNA, and no witnesses to corroborate Ani's story–'

'Story! This isn't a goddamn story! This is my daughter's life we're talking about. A life that monster almost took. How the hell could you just let him go? And what about the man who found her, the one walking his dog. Surely he's a witness?'

'All he saw was a young girl lying in the woods alone. It's not enough.'

'So when were you planning on telling us?' Diane asked. 'After he'd broken in and finished what he started?'

As soon as she said this, Anaïs broke down in tears and she rushed to her side.

For a moment there was silence. Then Jackie spoke up, 'I was going to tell you first thing in the morning. We've had a patrol car watching the pharmacy since he left. There's no way he could have snuck past them and got all the way out here without being seen. But if there's anything out there that proves he did, we'll drag him straight back in. And this time we'll lock him up for good–'

'Excuse me.' Detective Parsons walked into the room with Detective Pisani.

'Did you find anything?' Jackie asked.

'I'm sorry, ma'am but there's no signs of an intruder. The garden's immaculate. Same goes for the glass – there's not a single smudge.'

'The patrol car outside the pharmacy radioed over too,' Detective Pisani spoke up. 'They rang the buzzer and Farkas was upstairs in his flat.'

'What happens now?' Diane asked. 'Did you check the phone records?'

'I've got my team working on it as we speak,' Detective Parsons answered. 'But if he did call here, chances are he used an unregistered SIM card. The guy's too smart to use anything that could be traced back to him.'

'Does that mean you're not going to arrest him again?' Diane's shoulders slumped.

'Not at the moment. But we'll keep a car parked in front of your house for the next few days. And we'll keep watching Mr Farkas twenty-four-seven. I'll get the Forensics team to come back in the morning too and have a look around when it's light.'

'I can stay here tonight, if you like?' Jackie suggested. 'I don't mind sleeping in one of the spare rooms. I'll even take the couch. If Ani doesn't mind my snoring.'

'That won't be necessary.' Diane ushered them out of the house.

'Diane, can we talk for a minute, please?' Jackie stopped at the front door as the detectives went to the car. 'I know you're mad at me, but I was just trying to do the right thing. I'm sorry. I should have told you straight away.'

'It's too late. You put my daughter's life at risk tonight – your goddaughters – and I'll never forgive you for that. As far as I'm concerned, our friendship's over.'

'You don't mean that. How about we pour a couple of glasses of wine. That always makes things better.' Jackie forced a smile.

'Not this time. From now on, I'll deal with Detective Parsons directly.' She closed the door in Jackie's face and went back to check on Anaïs.

8

TWO WEEKS LATER

Andréa stood in the kitchen of her immaculate penthouse apartment, located on the twenty-fifth floor of a brand-new development in Canary Wharf and measured two identical portions of food for her ragdoll cats, Artoo and Deetoo.

'There you go, my little beauties.' She stroked their soft fur as Chewie watched on silently from the dining room, his big head slumped on his paws. 'Don't look so glum, mister. We're going to visit auntie Diane and Anaïs soon.'

As she said this, his long ears pricked up and she walked over to the floor-to-ceiling glass doors that ran along the length of the sprawling, open-plan living space. She looked out at the ultra-modern high-rise office blocks scattered around her, including the headquarters of her own company, Stjerne-Tec, and thought about Diane – she'd called again the previous night and told her that the man who attacked Anaïs was still hounding them. Andréa had tried to convince her to call Jackie, but Diane stubbornly refused.

Why was she getting dragged into this? They knew she hated conflict. She was more than happy being the quiet one in the background.

She was pulled out of her thoughts by Chewie scratching on the glass as the automated sprinklers came on outside, spraying the plethora of plants and flowers placed with military precision along the sweeping balcony.

'Not today, mister.' She shook her head. 'I know you love the sprinklers, but I don't have time to mop up your mucky paw prints. And we both know you only want to do it so you can shake yourself all over poor Artoo and Deetoo.'

She walked to the front door, picking up her bag and jacket on the way, and Chewie followed.

'Right. Change of plan. We're going to take a little detour to Brixton first,' she said, putting on his lead. 'Don't look at me like that. I don't like going there either, but I need to sort this mess out once and for all. Even if it means banging their stubborn old heads together.'

A little while later, she arrived in Brixton and almost dragged Chewie through the bustling, energetic main street, eager to escape the barrage of sights, sounds and smells that battered her senses, almost overwhelming her.

Finally she reached Jackie's house, which was located on a quiet street lined with grand, old Victorian terraced houses, their once pristine facades weather-beaten and faded, and she breathed a sigh of relief.

'Here we are, mister. We made it. You're such a brave boy, aren't you? Yes you are. What would I do without you?' She rubbed his head and scratched behind his ears, lingering at the rusted gate.

'Well, well, well, look who it is!' Jackie appeared in the doorway, wearing a bright-red dressing gown and holding what Andréa guessed was some kind of rum cocktail.

'How did you know we were here?' she asked.

'I'm the Sheriff in these parts, I know everything.' Jackie tipped the brim of an imaginary hat and took a sip of her drink.

'Are you drunk?'

'Don't give me those eyes, it's the weekend. And, no, I'm not drunk. I'm just having a little early-afternoon tipple. What are you doing here anyway? You hate Brixton.'

'I don't hate Brixton.'

'Mm-hm.' Jackie narrowed her eyes. 'When was the last time you came here?'

'I, um, I don't remember—'

'Liar! You remember everything. You're like the *Rain Man*.'

'Fine.' Andréa sighed. 'It was five-years ago when you got promoted, and you had a house party to celebrate.'

'See! I told you.' Jackie let out a loud belly laugh.

'It's only because we usually meet at Diane's,' Andréa lied. 'Speaking of Diane, I need to talk to you.'

'Is everything okay? She hasn't spoken to me in weeks. That woman can hold a grudge like nobody's business.'

'Let's talk inside…'

'Fine. I take it the furball's coming too.' Jackie glanced down at Chewie.

'Of course.' Andréa looked aghast. 'I'm not going to leave him out here. Anything could happen to him.'

'Come on then.' Jackie stepped aside. 'But he better not make a mess.'

'He'll probably clean up if anything.' Andréa stepped past her and glanced around the cluttered hallway.

'What's that supposed to mean?' Jackie slammed the door behind them.

'Nothing…' Andréa went through to the living room and perched on the edge of the couch.

'Hmm, good. Would your highness like a drink? Herbal tea, orange juice, a Mai Tai maybe?'

'I'll just have some water. Can you get Chewie some too, please?'

'Why, of course. Would he like a pitcher with ice? Maybe a straw too?'

'Not unless it's biodegradable.'

'Huh! *Biodegradable*… is this woman for real?' Jackie disappeared into the kitchen, muttering under her breath.

She came back a moment later with a glass of water and a small bowl for Chewie.

'So, what's happened? It must be pretty serious to bring you all the way out to the ghetto.'

'Well…' Andréa took a sip of water and looked around at the staid brown furniture, covered with a mishmash of colourful throws and pillows, and the African woodcarvings and trinkets that fought for space alongside old picture frames, containing faded family portraits and verses from the Bible. She was about to tell Jackie about Diane when she spotted a picture of the three of them, all dressed in traditional Nigerian outfits at Jackie's wedding to her ex-husband, Charles. 'Oh my God! I remember that picture,' she said, pointing at it. 'We all look so young.'

'That's because we were. It's probably the last time you wore anything other than black, navy or grey too.' Jackie laughed. 'Now stop stalling and tell me what's going on.'

Andréa took a deep breath and told her about the phone call with Diane…

'I don't understand,' Jackie said, after she finished. 'Detective Parsons has had officers watching his building the whole time. And there's been a patrol car driving by Diane's every night too. He'd have to be some kind of Houdini to avoid all that.'

'I'm only telling you what she told me.'

'So why did you come here?' Diane's made it perfectly clear she doesn't want anything to do with me, or the police by the sounds of it.'

'Because she's scared and she's not thinking straight. We need to go and talk some sense into her. Together.'

'I've already tried helping and look where it got me.' Jackie made a face and took a sip of her drink.

'Just come with me, please.' Andréa sighed. 'I'll be useless if I go on my own. You know that.'

'That's true.' Jackie's expression softened. 'Okay, I'll come. As long as you understand if Diane gets angry, I'm blaming everything on you.'

'Thank you.' Andréa smiled.

'We'll have to get a taxi though. This is my third rum of the day.' Jackie shook the empty glass. The leftover ice tinkling inside.

'It's not even two-o-clock yet!'

'And?' Jackie stood up and stretched. 'I'm going to go and get dressed. Help yourself to anything you want in the kitchen. Although there's probably none of that fancy healthy stuff you like,' she added, disappearing upstairs.

9

Anaïs sat in her bedroom, curtains drawn, door locked, the dim glow from the phone screen the only light visible as she scrolled through endless messages of support from Jenny and the rest of her friends. Why couldn't they just leave her alone? Nothing they said could change what had happened. Her life was ruined. And this man still wouldn't stop. She dropped the phone on the bed and flipped onto her stomach.

She squeezed her eyes shut, trying to block out the negative thoughts swirling around inside her head, but the sound of the automated gates opening made her look up. Who could it be? Her mother hadn't mentioned any visitors.

Since the tube had been removed a few days ago she'd barely spoken to anyone. She preferred to stay in her room, only venturing out when she needed food or the bathroom. But curiosity got the better of her and she went over to the window. She peeked through the curtains and watched Jackie and Andréa walking up the driveway with Chewie in tow.

What were they up to?

Suddenly the front door burst open, and her mother came marching out, remonstrating angrily with her arms. Anaïs couldn't hear what was being said, but from the look on Jackie's face it clearly wasn't a warm welcome.

They shouted back and forth, Andréa desperately trying to get between them. Anaïs thought they might actually come to blows. Then, to her surprise, they all stopped and hugged.

She watched them enter the house a moment later and crept out onto the hallway landing, peering over the banister as they disappeared into the kitchen.

She thought about going back inside her room. Then she changed her mind and tiptoed down the stairs.

When she got to the kitchen, the door was pulled shut, the blinds lowered. She hovered outside, unsure what to do. What were they up to? Something didn't feel right. Her mother wasn't usually so private, especially at home.

Crouching down, she eased open the door and spied through a small gap.

The blinds to the garden were pulled down too, and her mother walked around the gloomy room lighting candles while Jackie and Andréa sat at the island counter, Chewie sleeping at their feet.

'I'm glad your both here.' Diane lit the last candle, and then took some glasses from the cupboard. 'There's something I wanted to discuss with you.'

'So what was all that shouting and arm-waving about just now?' Jackie asked.

'I'm still mad at you, but this is more important.'

'Are all these candles really necessary?' Andréa glanced around nervously. 'It's like a witches' coven in here.'

'I'm just creating some ambience.' Diane put the glasses on the table and went over to the fridge, pulling out a bottle of white wine and a jug of water.

'Ambience for what? A séance? You're not going to sacrifice a goat or something, are you?' Jackie chuckled.

'Not quite…' Diane smiled, the flickering light contorting it into a wicked sneer.

'I don't like the sound of this.' Andréa shuffled on the stool, making Chewie stir, and Anaïs leant back a little.

'Hmm, me, neither. What are you up to?' Jackie asked.

'I assume Andréa's already updated you on what's been happening the past few weeks?' Diane filled the glasses and passed them around.

'She has,' Jackie replied. 'You should have come to me. I could have spoken to Detective Parsons and got more officers out here. I could have got them watching the pharmacy more closely too, and monitoring your calls–'

Diane dismissed her with a wave of her hand. 'It's pointless. They wouldn't have found anything. They didn't before, and they won't now. This man's like a ghost. He'll never get caught. He's too clever. He ran rings around your detectives and one day he'll get in here and there'll be nothing anyone can do about it. Unless we stop him ourselves, that is...' She picked up her glass and twirled it between her fingertips.

'What do you mean?' Andréa asked.

'Yes. What are you getting at, Diane?' Jackie's eyed narrowed.

'I think you know what I'm saying. We kill him. Together. The three of us. I've thought about it a lot, and you turning up today, saying you want to make amends. It's a sign—'

'I said make amends. Not murder someone! Jeez, Louise!' Jackie let out an incredulous laugh.

'Jackie's right,' Andréa added. 'Do you hear what you're saying? It's madness!'

'I do. And I've never been more certain of anything in my life. This man needs to be punished, and if nobody else will do it, I will.'

'You do remember I'm a police officer, right?' Jackie spoke up. 'This goes against everything I stand for. Not to mention it's completely illegal. Even if he is guilty.'

'If?' Diane's voice rose, cutting her off.

'You know what I mean – if we get caught, we go to prison, regardless of what he's done. And we won't get any special treatment, either. Haven't you ever seen *Bad Girls*? Or what's that American one... *Orange is the New Black*? People like us aren't made for life behind bars. Especially Andi, she'd get eaten alive. Let me speak to Detective Parsons again—'

'No. It's too late.' Diane cut her off. 'I've made up my mind. I'm doing this with or without your help.'

Andréa threw up her hands. 'I can't listen to any more of this. Think of Anaïs. She needs you. If you went to prison, it would destroy her. Hasn't the poor girl been through enough already, without losing her mother too?'

'Who looked after you when your mother had cancer a few years ago?' Diane's eyes bored into her. 'And who was there for you when Charles ran off with that girl half his age?' She turned her fierce gaze on Jackie.

'That's completely different,' Jackie said.

'Yes. Not to mention completely unfair,' Andréa added. 'I value our friendship above everything. You know that. And you know I'm always there for you. But this... this is too much. I just can't. I'm sorry.'

'What about you?' Diane looked at Jackie.

'I'm sorry, Diane. You're like a sister to me. But there's other ways of doing this.'

'Very well. You can both leave now. There's nothing left to discuss.'

'I'll help you, maman.' Anaïs stood up and pushed open the door.

'Ah! Ma puce. How long have you been listening?'

'Long enough.' Anaïs glanced at Andréa and Jackie, who both looked down guiltily. 'We don't need their help, anyway. We can do it without them.'

'Hey! Don't be like that, Ani.' Jackie frowned. 'I know you want revenge, but we need to be serious here. You can't just go around killing people.'

'My darling girl.' Diane wrapped her arms around Anaïs, hugging her tightly. 'I didn't want you to hear this conversation. I can't put you at risk again. You're too important to me.'

Anaïs pushed her away and stared defiantly. 'There's nothing he can do to me that he hasn't already done. I'm tired of being scared. I just want this nightmare to end. And I'm never going to be able to move on completely if I know he's still out there. Please, maman, let me help you.' Tears filled her eyes, but she refused to back down.

Jackie downed her drink and slammed the empty glass on the countertop.

'Okay! I'm in. Lord help me if I let you two do this without me. It'll be like the blind leading the blind. And you, little missy!' She looked at Anaïs. 'You've got less meat on you than a Nando's chicken wing. You'd struggle to beat an egg let alone a full-grown man. Now get over here and give your Auntie J a hug.'

'Are you with us too?' Diane asked Andréa.

'Do I have a choice?' She let out a sigh of resignation. 'I'm outnumbered as usual. Even Chewie's on your side.'

'You're always on my side, aren't you, boy?' The dog leapt up on Anaïs, and she stroked his head.

'So, what's the plan?' Jackie asked. 'I assume you have one?'

'I do...' Diane smiled, her eyes sparkling with mischief.

10

Lexie walked through Brick Lane in the late afternoon sun and stopped outside a busy nail parlour, checking her reflection in the window. She pursed her lips, cocking her head to one side, and opened her denim jacket a little further. Still not satisfied, she pulled back the straps on the lowcut floral dress underneath, lifting it higher to show off her delicate curves and long slender legs, which were accentuated by sheer black tights and bright-white Converse trainers.

'I look about fifteen,' she muttered in a soft Liverpudlian accent. 'I can't remember that last time I went anywhere without my mascara or some lippy.'

'Don't worry, Lexie, darling. You look divine,' Diane's voice crackled through a tiny speaker lodged inside the girl's ear. 'Just go in there and do exactly what we told you. There's no way he'll be able to resist your angelic charms.'

'Thanks, Ms Dubois. My mam would be so happy to see me right now.' Lexie bowed her head and spoke into a microphone hidden inside the decorative necklace she wore, along with a tiny camera designed by Andréa's company.

'We're not at the agency now. Just call me Diane.'

'And don't look down when you speak, honey,' Jackie spoke up. 'You'll blow your cover straight away, and then we'll be in all kinds of trouble. Just act naturally, okay? Oh, and try to sound a little less Scouse if you can. You want to seduce the man. Not make him think you're going to rob the place.'

Lexie almost gave a snarky comment in reply, but they were paying her more than she got for a whole year's worth of modelling work, so she bit her tongue.

'Okay, got it. I'm just a little nervous.'

'That's completely understandable. But we'll be right around the corner, watching and listening the whole time,' Diane reassured her.

'Diane's right. And if he tries anything funny, we'll be out of this van like the *A-Team*, don't you worry your pretty little self. I pity the fool who messes with you.' Jackie let out a loud laugh, which reverberated around Lexie's head like a gunshot in a barrel.

'Okay, I'm ready.' She gave herself one last look in the window, tightening her ponytail and tucking the loose strands of her usually wild blonde hair behind her ears. Then she took a deep breath and entered the pharmacy.

A tall, gaunt-looking man was upon her in an instant, taking her by surprise with his litheness, and she had to fight the urge to take a step back.

'Good afternoon, my dear. How can I help you today?' He smiled down at her, standing so close she could feel the heat of his breath.

'Wow! That was fast.' She laughed nervously.

'I like to provide a swift service. I'm sure you're a busy young lady. Now! Did you come for something in particular or just to peruse?' His smile grew wider as he clasped his long fingers together.

'I came for my prescription, actually.' She rummaged through her bag, nervously fumbling for the slip Diane had given her in the van. 'Ah, here it is.' She pulled it out and handed it over.

'Nicole. What a lovely name,' he said, reading the fake name. 'And I see you live in Whitechapel. That's very close.'

'Yeah, I've got a little studio there. I'm studying Fine Art at UEL, so it's very convenient. The place is a mess though. Full of clothes and canvases. And pretty much everything is covered in paint.' She let out a playful giggle, her confidence growing as she reeled off the backstory she'd rehearsed.

'Ha! That sounds wonderful. I'd love to see some of your work. I'm sure you're very talented.'

'I'm not sure about that. But thank you, uh, Victor.' She glanced at his nametag and twirled her ponytail, their eyes locking together for a moment. 'Soo… could I get my medication, please? Sorry, it's just that I've got an essay due tomorrow, and I haven't even started it yet. Story of my life.' She rolled her eyes in mock exasperation.

'Of course, that's perfectly fine, my dear. Studies are very important. Let's see… Salbutamol. You poor thing, asthma is no joke.'

'I know, and it gets worse when I'm stressing about stuff.' She frowned, biting her lip.

'You should try eucalyptus oil. Massage it into your chest after a nice hot bath. It does wonders for your airways. It's good for the skin too.' He leered down at her for a moment, and then turned away.

'What a fucking creep,' she muttered as he disappeared into the back room.

'Okay, plant the tracker, and then get the hell out of there,' Jackie spoke up.

'You don't need to tell me twice,' she whispered, quickly slipping behind the counter and looking for somewhere to hide the penny-sized device.

'Is there a jacket or something you can put it in?' Diane suggested.

'I can't see one.'

'There!' Jackie exclaimed, the noise piercing her eardrum. 'Put it in his wallet.'

'Where? I can't see it.' Lexie scanned the shelf, her panic rising with each passing second.

'On your left. Behind the stapler.'

'Got it!' She grabbed the wallet and flipped it open, gently sliding the tracker into an empty compartment and jamming it down as far as it would go–

'I'm sorry for the delay. It's almost ready.' The man's voice boomed out from the backroom and she dropped the wallet in surprise.

'Shit, shit, shit…' she hissed, quickly scooping it up and replacing it, before leaping back around the counter.

'Everything okay, my dear?' He reappeared with a small paper bag in his hand. 'You look a little flushed.'

'Uh, yeah, sorry, I had a bit of a funny turn and dropped my phone. I'm such a klutz sometimes.'

'Do you want to sit down? I can take you upstairs if you like and make you a nice cup of herbal tea.'

'No, no, that's fine. Honestly. But thank you.'

'It's no bother. I'll be closing soon anyway. It would be nice chat a little longer.'

'Next time, I promise. How much do I owe?' she asked, quickly changing the subject.

'The first one is free. Just make sure you come back again soon.'

'Thank you. That's very kind.' She took the bag from his hand and smiled demurely.

'Does that mean we have a deal?'

'Yes. I'll be back in a few weeks, I promise.' She gave him a little wave and left as calmly as possible.

When she got outside, she took a few steps along the pavement, making sure she was out of sight, and then raced around the corner, back to the main street.

'I'm never going back there ever again!' she panted, collapsing against a wall and breathing heavily.

'Good job, Lexie,' Diane spoke up. 'I'm proud of you.'

'Yes. Well done, honey,' Jackie added. 'Now hurry up and get back here. We've still got lots to do.'

*

Victor stepped over to the window and watched the young girl walk away. Her short dress billowed in the soft breeze, revealing even more of her slim, stockinged thighs, and his body ached with anticipation, wishing he could follow her.

'What a delightful little creature,' he murmured, stroking the prescription, which was folded neatly in his pocket. He lingered a moment longer until she disappeared from view. Then he flipped the sign and locked the door.

A few minutes later, he rang up the cash register, turned off the lights and went upstairs, hanging his white coat in the hallway and entering the living room.

He went straight over to a long glass tank that ran along the backwall and reached inside.

'Hello, Kinga, my dearest, did you miss me?' he cooed, stroking under the chin of a large, bearded dragon. 'Are you hungry? What a silly question. You're always hungry, aren't you? Just like me. But we need to be patient, don't we?' He picked up a plastic container, prising off the lid, and pulled out a fat cockroach. 'Yes. Good things come to those who wait...' He dangled the squirming insect above the tank for a moment before dropping it inside. 'There you go, my lady. Dinner is served.'

He stepped over to an old-fashioned record player and kicked off his shoes, letting out a long sigh. 'Ah, yes, that's much better. Let's put some music on, shall we? Do you have any requests?' He glanced at the lizard, half a cockroach jutting from its mouth, and raised his eyebrow. '*Chopin*, you say? Good choice. I was thinking the same thing.' He slid a vinyl out of its sleeve and balanced the disc on his fingertips, gently blowing on the surface. Then he placed it on the turntable and lowered the needle.

After a short, scratchy pause, soothing piano music filled the air and he eased himself into a comfy old armchair, his tired eyes falling shut.

He stayed that way for a while, floating through a melodic nebula, his body sinking deeper and deeper into the soft fabric but, try as he may, he couldn't get the girl out of his mind.

Soon the cosmic clouds parted, and he stood beside a moonlit pond. He recognised it instantly from Epping Forest and approached the water's edge, gazing at the silvery surface.

Beams of light danced and pirouetted on top, like characters in a Tchaikovsky ballet. The ethereal figures moved in time with the music, and he saw all the other girls he'd preyed upon, before Anaïs, lying amongst the reeds below, their pale bodies glowing softly in the murky depths. She should have been there with them. He balled up his fists, still angry at letting her get away and the lights faded. Why didn't he get rid of her body when he had the chance instead of going back to the van and dillydallying about?

Suddenly his mind went back to the empty clearing in the woods, the car headlights disappearing into the distance and his eyes popped open.

'Her time will come again, but I have other matters to attend to first...' He sat up and took out the prescription, unfolding the paper and stroking the girl's name. 'Nicole, Nicole, what a beautiful soul...' he murmured, glancing outside at the slowly darkening sky.

11

The front door clicked open and Anaïs leapt up from the couch, startling Chewie who had been sleeping peacefully beside her. 'Sorry, handsome.' She patted his head as his long ears pricked up in attack mode. 'It's okay. It's just your mamma and my mamma. Although you can bite mine if you like,' she added, still angry at being left behind.

'Hi, darling. Sorry we're so late. It took a little longer than expected.' Diane breezed into the living room, followed by Jackie and Andréa.

'I still don't know why I couldn't come too,' Anaïs replied.

'We've already been through this. And we all agreed that it was best for you to stay behind and look after Chewie.' Diane sighed. 'You're still fragile and I'm not putting you at risk again.'

'You can't wrap me in cotton wool forever!'

'True. But I can keep you away from that man until we've taken care of him.'

'*Taken care of him.* Huh! You make us sound like the Mafia.' Jackie slumped down in a vintage, olive-coloured Chesterfield armchair. 'By the time we're finished with him, he'll be sleeping with the fishes.' She chuckled.

'This isn't a joke.' Andréa crouched beside Chewie and scowled.

'Don't you start.'

'Does anybody want a drink?' Diane asked. 'I doubt very much he'll risk doing anything tonight, or at least until later.'

'I'll have whatever you're having, as long as it's alcoholic.' Jackie kicked off her shoes and stretched her toes, letting out a contented sigh.

'I'm okay,' Andréa said. 'I'm going to take Chewie for a walk, and then give him some food. How does that sound?' She scratched behind his ears and rubbed his belly. 'Did you miss me? Because I missed you. Yes I did.'

'Where is he now?' Jackie asked.

'He's right here.' Andréa looked confused.

'I meant Farkas, not the bloody dog!'

'You should be a little more specific then, shouldn't you?' Andréa opened her phone and checked an app, which was connected to the tracking device inside the man's wallet. 'He's still at the pharmacy.'

'Okay, good. I'm beat–'

'Wait a second!' Andréa's brow furrowed. 'He's moving...'

'He can't be going there now. It's too early,' Diane said.

'Which way's he headed?' Jackie asked.

'Towards Whitechapel. And he's moving fast. Look...' Andréa showed them the screen.

'Okay, let's go.' Diane strode towards the hallway. 'I'll call Lexie on the way.'

'Lord, give me strength. I'm starting to hate this man more and more.' Jackie lifted herself up, grimacing with the effort. 'Can I at least get some wine to go?' she said, slipping back into her shoes.

'Wait! I'm coming too.' Anaïs followed them into the hallway and grabbed her coat and trainers.

'No, you're not!' Diane spun around and lifted her hand. 'You're staying here. And that's final.'

'Your mother's right,' Jackie added. 'Let us deal with this, honey. You just concentrate on getting yourself better. By tomorrow this'll all be over.'

'This is such bullshit!' Anaïs threw her trainers across the floor. 'I'm the one who got raped. I should be there too. I want to see the bastard suffer. Just like I did. Like I still am every fucking day!' Tears welled up in her eyes and she looked at her mother pleadingly. 'Please, maman. Don't leave me here again. It's not fair.'

'I'm sorry, ma puce.' Diane's face softened. 'But I'm not changing my mind. I'll see you in a few hours.' She turned and followed Jackie and Andréa outside.

'Argh! I hate you!' Anaïs called out.

She stayed there for a moment, shaking with anger, part of her spitefully wishing they would fail. Then she felt Chewie licking her bunched-up fist and a wave of guilt rushed over her.

'I didn't mean it,' she muttered, looking down at his innocent brown eyes. Sensing that he could read her nefarious thoughts. 'Come on, let's go upstairs.'

12

Victor parked on a quiet, low-lit street around the corner from the address on the prescription, and glanced around, making sure the coast was clear.

'Okay. Just take a quick look around. See if you can catch a glimpse of her. Then straight back home. This is just a little reconnaissance mission. Is that understood?' He grabbed a wide-brimmed hat off the passenger seat with a black-gloved hand. Then he got out of the car and crossed the road, stopping in front of a block of high-rise flats. Where are you, lovely Nicole? He glanced up at the third-floor, where her apartment was located, before scurrying into a nearby bus shelter to avoid a group of lairy teenagers passing by.

This was a bad idea. He was about to leave when a light came on in the building's foyer and a girl approached the entrance. It couldn't be, could it? He watched in disbelief as Nicole breezed outside in a light-blue sports jacket and skin-tight black leggings.

She crossed the road and turned down the quiet side street where his car was parked, and he followed her over, taking cover behind a wall.

While he stood there, he reached into his pocket and fingered a small glass vial filled with liquid LSD and a folded switchblade.

'Oh well, I guess it's fate. You could always resist everything except temptation, couldn't you, Victor?' He smiled to himself, and then stepped out into the street. He planned to sneak up on her from behind and bundle her into the back of his car. But he was surprised to find her standing in the middle of the road, waiting for him.

'Hello, Victor, fancy bumping into you here.' She smiled.

'Oh, hello, my dear. This is quite the coincidence. I was just doing some deliveries in the area. I like to help out my more elderly and immobile customers,' he added, thinking fast.

'How very noble of you, Mr Farkas.' Someone else stepped out from the shadows and stood beside her.

'Ms Dubois, to what do I owe this pleasure?' He recognised the woman straight away and took out the knife, holding it by his side as discreetly as possible.

'Cut the games, Victor. You've been caught red handed, and this time we're going to make sure you're punished.'

'*We.*' He smirked. 'All I see is a broken old woman and a foolhardy little girl.'

'You forgot me,' a voice emerged from behind him, but before he could react, an excruciating pain spread through his entire body, his nerve-ends exploding like a million overcharged lightbulbs, and he crumpled to the floor in a writhing, convulsing heap.

'Ch-Chief-N-Njoku.' He looked up at the woman. His eyes peeled back so far he thought they were going to pop out of his head. 'Y-You-c-can't-d-do-th-this!' He tried to continue, but the words came out like coins being shaken from a piggybank.

'I think you'll find I can.' She knelt down in front of him and held out a yellow-coloured taser, the high-voltage wires glowing ominously in the gloom.

'No, please–' he shook his head. But before he could say anything else, she shot the wires into his solar plexus. The shock sent his body into another bout of uncontrollable spasms and his eyes rolled back in his head.

As he lay on the floor, barely conscious, he heard the women talking frantically above him, their voices merging into one:

'Okay, we need to be quick. You two grab his legs, and I'll take his arms.'

'Jesus! He weighs a ton!'

'Where the hell's Andréa?'

'Here she is.'

'Come on! Come on! Hurry up–'

Bright lights illuminated the blurred shapes hovering above him, and he felt his body being dragged along the pavement.

'He's coming around. Zap him again.'

Suddenly there was another explosion of pain. His jaw clenched so tightly he thought the bones would shatter and turn to sand.

He tried to breathe, but the sound of metallic doors swinging open made him panic.

'Quick. Get the rope.'

'Here, I've got it. Let's get him inside.'

The women rolled him onto his front and pinned him down.

'Try anything and I'll blast you right between your shoulder blades.'

He felt the hard plastic of the weapon pushing against his back. Staring at the dark tarmac, he tried to focus.

'Must you tie it so tightly?' He grimaced. 'You're not going to get away with this. Surely you must know that. I haven't done anything wrong. If I was guilty, I'd be in prison right now, wouldn't I?' He tried to struggle free as the women dragged him up a metal ramp, but it was no use.

'By the time this night's over, we'll get a confession out of you. Believe me. But you won't be going to any prison.'

Another jolt of pain tore through him. This one seeming to last for an eternity. And the doors slammed shut, plunging him into darkness.

*

Diane tapped her fingers on her thighs and stared straight ahead, turning up the radio to drown out the muffled grunts and shuffling coming from the back of the van. The thought of the man alone in there made her feel uncomfortable. Although, knowing what they had to do next made her even more anxious as they drove through the Rotherhithe Tunnel and passed under the Thames.

Soon they emerged onto the south side of the river and Andréa navigated through a labyrinth of quiet little side streets until they reached a derelict warehouse on the waterfront.

'We're here.' She pulled into a rubble-strewn courtyard and turned off the engine. 'I guess there's no turning back now.'

'Let's just get this over with,' Jackie said, uncharacteristically terse.

'She's right.' Diane opened the passenger door and climbed out. 'The sooner we do this, the sooner we can get out of here and never come back.'

They approached the back of the van and Jackie pulled them into a huddle.

'Wait a second,' she said, lowering her voice. 'I know you're both scared. I am too. But we need to be strong right now. Is that understood?'

Diane and Andréa nodded in reply.

'Good. Then follow my lead...' She stepped forward and threw open the doors, revealing the man who sat in the middle of the floor, smiling serenely.

'Ah... have we arrived already?' he asked, his face sending a shiver through Diane's body, although she was relieved to see that his wrists and ankles were still bound.

'Yes, we are. And I wouldn't be smiling if I was you.' Jackie scowled at him.

'How terribly exciting. And where, may I ask, is the lovely Nicole? Please don't say she's left us so soon.'

'You'll never bother her, or any other girl ever again,' Diane spoke up, her anger rising.

'I have to admit it was an ingenious plan. Enticing me with a beautiful young girl and then luring me to her flat. I'm impressed. How did you know I'd go there tonight? Did you plant some kind of tracking device on me? I bet that's what you did, didn't you? Such clever ladies—'

'Do you ever shut up?' Jackie snapped.

'Maybe we should tie something around his mouth,' Andréa suggested.

'Let's just get him inside before anyone sees us.' Diane walked around the side of the building and retrieved a flatbed trolley from the shadows while Jackie and Andréa pulled out the ramp and slid it into place.

They dragged him down and bundled him onto the trolley. Then they took a moment to catch their breath.

'You sound a little tired, my dears. Would you like a quick tea break? I wouldn't want you to do yourselves a mischief on my account.'

'Oh, there's going to be plenty of mischief,' Jackie replied. 'Now stop talking or I'll zap you again.'

'My lips are sealed.' He closed his mouth and sucked in his lips. But his silence only lasted a few seconds. 'What is this place, if I may ask?' He looked around as they wheeled him into a dark cavernous room. The rotten floorboards creaking with every step.

Speckles of moonlight seeping in through the filthy cracked windows. 'It's so gothic. I love it.'

'Watch him for a second.' Diane stepped forward and lit a row of candles, bathing the room in a soft flickering glow and illuminating a lone wooden chair.

'Bring him over.' Her voice echoed through the gloom and a rat scurried along the exposed wooden beams above.

'How are we going to get him on the chair?' Andréa asked.

'You're going to help us, aren't you, Victor?' Jackie took out a small handgun and pointed it at the man.

'Of course, I'd hate to be a burden.'

'Right. After three.' Diane looked at Andréa. 'One... two... three...' They both lifted and he popped up like a Jack-in-the-box, swaying unsteadily on his bound feet.

'Now turn and sit,' Jackie commanded.

He hopped around in a circle, and then dropped down elegantly onto the chair.

'Shouldn't we tie him to the chair as well?' Andréa asked.

'Good idea.' Diane nodded. 'There's more rope in the van.'

'I'll go get it.' Andréa raced off.

'So who's going to kill him?' Diane approached Jackie and lowered her voice, momentarily turning her back on the man.

'I thought we agreed you were. This was your idea.'

'I know, but you have the gun. And you are a police officer. You have more experience in this field than I do.'

'My job is to stop people getting killed. This is literally the opposite of what I do. Anyway, the gun will be too loud. I only brought it as a last resort. I thought you had a knife.'

'I do. It's in here.' Diane patted the front of her jacket.

'Got it.' Andréa came running back, holding the rope.

'Okay. You go behind him, and I'll take the front,' Diane replied.

'How is young Anaïs doing? I do hope she's well.' The man smirked as Diane wrapped the rope around his chest. Their faces just inches apart.

'Don't you ever mention her name again!' She glared at him.

'Her body felt amazing by the way.' He whispered in her ear. 'Such immaculate skin. So soft and supple. Maybe next time I'll take you both to the forest together. You're not so bad yourself, for an older lady.'

'How dare you!' She slapped him and reached for the knife, but before she could take it out, he leapt up and rammed his shoulder into her face. Knocking her to the floor and making his escape.

The next few seconds went by in a dizzying blur as he shuffled awkwardly towards the door. The rope dangling loosely around his ankles. His hands still tied behind his back.

Jackie shouted at him to stop. Then she let off a series of wild shots that reverberated around the room with a deafening roar. The walls exploded in clouds of dust and splinters. But none of them hit their intended target, and he disappeared with a parting grin.

Diane watched him go and her head dropped. 'What have I done—'

But she was cut short by the screech of tires and a loud bang.

*

Anaïs let out a weary groan and eased her head up from the airbag.

What had happened? The last thing she remembered was coming around the corner too fast and seeing a dark figure run out in front of her. She'd slammed her foot down on the brake pedal and tried to swerve out of the way, but it was too late; she'd hit him with a sickening thud before coming to a stop in front of the entrance to the warehouse.

She squinted out of the cracked windscreen and saw a crumpled body lying motionless on the bonnet.

For a moment she thought the person was dead. Then they slowly lifted their head, and she saw it was Victor. His face was stained with blood, and he looked around wearily, but when he saw her, his eyes lit up and he flashed the same wolfish grin that had plagued her dreams for the past few weeks.

Suddenly the door swung open and she gasped in terror, until realising it was her mother standing there.

'Oh my God! Ma puce! Are you okay?' Diane reached in and hugged her tightly.

'He's still alive!' Anaïs struggled free and looked at the man, but he was lying face down again.

'He can't hurt you now. It's over.' Diane stroked her hair, and Anaïs saw that she had a deep gash on her forehead.

'Maman! What happened to you?'

'Oh, it's nothing.' Diane reached up and gingerly touched the wound, inspecting her bloody fingers. 'I'm just glad you're okay.'

'I'm sorry about the car.' Anaïs glanced down guiltily.

'I don't care about the car.' Diane hugged her again. 'You're all that matters to me. Don't you ever forget that.' She sniffed, both of them breaking down into tears.

'Chewie!' Andréa opened the passenger door and undid his seatbelt. 'Come here, my beautiful boy.' She gave him a big hug, and he licked her face excitedly.

'So what are we going to do about him?' Jackie stood in front of the car and looked down at the motionless man.

'Let's get him back inside and finish what we started,' Diane replied. 'After the racket we've made, we don't have much time.'

Straightaway the women went to work, quickly retrieving the trolley and wheeling the man back into the warehouse. They lifted him onto the chair as his head lolled about listlessly and retied the ropes.

Once he was secured, Jackie and Andréa went out to the van while Diane blew out all the candles. Apart from one.

'You might want to take a step back,' she said, joining Anaïs at the entrance and shielding the flickering flame.

Jackie and Andréa came back a moment later with two jerry cans and doused the whole place in petrol.

'Okay, we're done,' Jackie said, shaking out the last few drops.

'You two should get going,' Diane replied. 'Take the van and Anaïs and I will meet you back at mine.'

'Are you sure?' Jackie asked.

'It's okay, we won't be long.'

'Thanks for saving our behinds back there,' Jackie said to Anaïs. 'Lord knows what would have happened if you hadn't shown up when you did. You did good, honey.' She squeezed Anaïs' arm, then climbed into the van.

'Go and wait in the car, ma puce.' Diane gave her a solemn look. 'I don't want you to see this.'

'Let me do it.' Anaïs stood her ground.

'I don't think that's a good idea. You don't want something like this on your conscience for the rest of your life.'

'Please, maman, I want to.' She clenched her fists by her side. 'I need to see him die, otherwise the nightmares will never stop.' Her eyes filled with fresh tears, but her gaze remained unwavering.

'Okay.' Diane sighed, handing her the candle.

Anaïs took it and faced the still unconscious man.

She closed her eyes and took a deep breath, but when she opened them again, he was sitting up, his deep blue eyes boring into her.

'Hello, my dear.' He grinned. 'So nice to see you again. I'd give you a hug, but I'm a little tied up right now.' He let out a high-pitched giggle and Anaïs shuddered. Her mind transported back to the forest. His masked-face looming over her...

'We need to hurry.' Diane touched her arm, bringing her back to the present.

Anaïs crouched down holding the man's gaze, the candle hovering just inches above the petrol-soaked floor.

'You don't have the guts.' He sneered.

'Don't I?' She dropped the candle and fire spread through the room in an instant. The whole place erupted in flames and fiery tendrils climbed the walls and snaked across the beams, like an army of ants devouring a rotting carcass.

'Come on, ma puce.' Diane tugged her arm.

'Just a few more seconds...' Anaïs watched as the fire surrounded the man. The flames licking at his feet.

'You can't beat me!' he roared above the rising inferno. 'I'll never die. I'm going to haunt you forever–' But before he could say anything else, there was an almighty crack and one of the beams crashed to the ground between them, causing the whole building to shake.

'It's going to collapse!' Diane shouted above the din, shielding her face against the searing heat.

Finally Anaïs relented, and they drove away as the building crumbled behind them and sirens wailed in the distance.

PART II

PRESENT DAY

13

Siobhan leant forward and stared into the monitor at the stricken man. His blood-spattered body lay motionless in the oversized crib. The knife still protruding from his gaping mouth. His lifeless eyes glowing eerily in the reflection of the slowly-rotating nightlight.

She was about to zoom in, transfixed by the macabre scene, when she noticed Angela leaving the room.

'Shit!' She quickly got up and went to meet the woman, finding her in the corridor.

'Hey! Hey! Miss A, that was insane! I bow down to your bad-assery,' she called out. 'How you feeling? Pumped, I bet.'

'I guess so. It feels like I've been struck by lightning. My whole body's tingling.'

'That's the adrenaline. You'll be grand. Just relax and enjoy the buzz. We can go to my office for a brandy if you like?'

'Thanks, but I'd just like to go home and take a long hot bath.'

'Your wish is my command.' Siobhan led her back up to the restaurant and stopped in the middle of the gloomy dining room. 'Before you go, just remember, if you need to talk to somebody, we're here for you. You did a great thing tonight. Your donation is going to help so many women and children who've suffered at the hands of sick criminals, like the guy you got rid of tonight.'

'Thank you. That means a lot.'

After saying their goodbyes, Siobhan ushered the woman outside and smoked a quick cigarette in the doorway.

The street was empty. She scrolled through her phone idly and came across an article that caught her eye.

'Sneaky little fucker...' she murmured, blowing smoke into the chilly night air and scanning through the text. This wasn't good. She flicked the cigarette butt away, the glowing embers extinguishing on the damp pavement, and went back inside.

A few minutes later, she reached the boardroom and pushed open the heavy double doors. Bursting into a vast, dome-shaped room, where a small group of women sat at a long glass table. 'Did you guys see that?' she called out. 'Talk about a show! That's got to be one of the best yet. I didn't think the old bird had it in her. She went from Mary Poppins to Sweeney Todd in the blink of an eye.'

'Hey! Less of the old.' Jackie replied. 'She's the same age as us.'

'And Sweeney Todd used a razor, not a knife,' Diane corrected. 'How was the client when she left? Was everything okay? We don't want another incident like before.'

'Yeah, yeah, everything's grand. Smoother than a dolphin's vagina, you might say.'

'Nobody has ever said that.' Jackie shook her head. 'Remind me why we hired her again?'

'Because, despite her lack of etiquette, she's very good at what she does. And we can trust her.' Andréa spoke up.

'That's right. You tell 'em, Andi-Pandi. Now, do you want the good news or the bad news?'

'Just tell us what's going on,' Diane said impatiently.

'Okay, the good news is the five-hundred-thousand buckeroos from tonight's client is safely in our account. The bad news is I came across another article from that eejit reporter, Liam Patterson. It's only been online a few hours and it's already got over two-thousand hits...' Siobhan held up her phone for the others to see.

Vigilante Vixens Strike Again!

Just a few weeks after I broke the *exclusive* story of a highly-secretive group of rich, middle-aged women running an underground vigilante club in the heart of London, four more men, wanted for sexually-related crimes, have mysteriously vanished without a trace. Is this a coincidence or are these women performing weekly rituals to cleanse our city of *bad guys*?

And, in a *sensational* new twist, it is rumoured one of the women is a high-ranking officer in the Metropolitan Police! If true, the city's police force, as well as our nation's government, will have a lot of explaining to do.

After all, as citizens, isn't it our right to know who is protecting us? Whatever happens, you can rest assured, I will keep investigating this shocking story as it continues to unfold and post any updates as and when I get them.

*

Do you agree with what these women are doing, or are they wrong to take the law into their own hands? Vote below and click on the button to see the results:

YES
NO

Written by L. Patterson

*If you have any more information regarding this story or you have any other stories about what's going on in our weird and wonderful capital then email me at: **Liam@Capitalconspiracies.com**. And remember, if we publish, we pay! *T&C's apply**

'Oh my God!' Andréa looked aghast. 'How does he know so much?'

'Isn't it obvious?' Siobhan replied. 'Out of all the clients we've dealt with, only one has ever caused us any problems—'

'Let's just stay calm.' Diane waved the phone away dismissively.

'That's easy for you to say. I'm the one he's talking about!' Jackie exclaimed. 'Although *Vixens* does have a nice ring to it. Nobody's called me that in a long time.'

'And if they really wanted to expose us, they would have gone to *The Times* or *The London Beacon* or, God forbid, *The Sun*. Not some young boy working at a little online magazine. They just want to scare us,' Diane added.

'Lady D's probably right. As always. And anyways, look at this…' Siobhan pressed the 'Yes' button on the screen. 'Boom! Eighty-six percent of people agree with what we're doing. And the other fourteen are probably perverts themselves, or liberal snowflakes who think we should rehabilitate these guys with hymns and hugs.'

'So what are we going to do?' Andréa asked.

'Leave it with me,' Diane replied.

'So what's Nay-Nay up to tonight?' Siobhan asked.

'She's busy with her studies. And please don't refer to her that way. She's my daughter, not a horse.'

'If she was a horse, she'd be a prize-winning filly, so she would.' Siobhan grinned.

'Yes, well, on that note I think it's time to go home. I'll be in touch during the week, unless anyone else has something constructive to add?'

'I'm flying out to Berlin in the morning,' Andréa spoke up. 'It's going to be a hectic few days, so if you need me, I'll get back to you as soon as I can.'

'Okay, thanks for letting us know.'

'Before youse all leave me. Is there any chance I can get someone to help with all the admin stuff?' Siobhan asked. 'I'm drowning in paperwork lately. Kinda takes the fun out of killing bad guys if I'm being honest with you.'

'I suppose that would be okay,' Diane answered. 'As long as you can find someone trustworthy and they understand what they're getting into.'

'Great. Don't worry, I'll make sure I find someone suitable. Also, before I forget, Queeny messaged and said we're running low on the old tranquilisers.'

'Very well. I'll speak to my contact tomorrow.'

Diane led Jackie and Andrea towards the lift while Siobhan went back to the Treatment Room, where the Operations Team were busy cleaning up.

'You guys almost done?' she asked Carla, the supervisor of the small team.

'Yes, Ms Whelan, we just need to mop and then take the remains to the incinerator.'

'Ooh, I love that bit.' Siobhan stepped over to a discreet one-way mirror at the back of the room and checked her reflection. 'Do you want to go for a beer after we've toasted him? I'm buying.'

'But it's very late. Where would we go?'

'There's a late-night sports bar not too far from here – you know how to play pool?'

'Of course. I'm from Poland. I know pool, vodka, beer, all these things.'

'Then it's a date, my little Polish princess.'

'Okay, I come. But just for one hour. I have a husband and children at home. I can't party all night like some teenager.'

'Urgh! Husband, shmusband.' Siobhan rolled her eyes. Then she followed Carla and her team down the corridor.

They went through a set of swinging doors at the far end and loaded the dead man and all his belongings into a customized waste-disposal unit. Siobhan watched, her eyes glued to the machine, as it whirred into action, incinerating everything inside and releasing the remains into the river via a sophisticated filtration system to feed whatever lurked in the murky depths.

A little while later, she flung open the doors of a neon-lit bar and entered a dingy room. It had blacked-out windows, garish red carpets and lines of tattered old booths on either side, which were empty apart from a smartly-dressed couple kissing passionately in one, and a white-bearded old man drinking a beer in another. He stared vacantly at one of the big TV screens hanging on the wall, which was showing a football match from somewhere in South America, and Siobhan gave him a friendly nod.

'Isn't it great?' She smiled.

'It's a dump,' Carla replied.

'Ah, come on. It's not that bad. I mean, look at all these...' Siobhan spread her arms and gazed at the old sporting memorabilia and framed pictures of sports stars from yesteryear. 'This is history right here. You can almost smell it.' She took in a deep breath. 'History smells like shit.' Carla scrunched up her face. 'Aye, you're not wrong there. Come on, let's get a drink.' Siobhan approached the bar where a bored-looking woman in an oversized white shirt leaned on the counter, staring at her phone.

'Evening, evening,' she called out.

'What can I get you?' the woman asked, without looking up.

'Ah, don't be like that. Give us a smile, at least.'

The woman tilted her head and smiled sarcastically.

'There we go. That's better. I'd like two bottles of your finest beer, please. And a couple of cues when you're ready – hold the balls. I'm kidding. We're going to need some of them too. Needs must and all that.'

After paying for everything, Siobhan took the equipment through to the backroom while Carla carried the drinks.

The room was full of men, young and old, playing pool on American-style tables, each one laid with red baize and illuminated by individual spotlights. But they all stopped when the two women entered.

'It's like they've never seen a woman before.' Carla walked through, glancing around nervously.

'Just ignore them,' Siobhan replied, her head bopping to the high-tempo eighties rock music that blasted from the speakers. 'Let's take this one.' She stopped at the last table on the left.

After a few games, and a few more beers, Siobhan noticed two men from a nearby table glancing over and snickering as she mishit a shot.

'Which one of youse two is up for a challenge then?' she asked, slurring her words and swaying a little unsteadily.

'Nah, you're alright, love. I'd hate to upset such a pretty little thing,' the taller one shouted back in a brash south London accent.

'What's wrong? You scared of losing to a girl? Come on, we'll make it interesting. Here's twenty-quid.' She took out a note and placed it on the side of the table.

'Okay, but don't say I didn't warn you.' The man strutted over and placed a note on top, giving Siobhan a little wink as he did so. 'There you go, sweetcheeks.'

'Orite, guvnor. You can break. Age before beauty and all that.' She stood aside, and the man smashed the balls apart.

'Boom! Somebody's been hitting the gym,' she exclaimed, stepping up to take her shot.

'You're a funny one, aren't ya?' He grinned, but the smile quickly disappeared when she potted a striped ball and screwed the white back perfectly to set up her next shot.

'Would you look at that?' She glanced up, and then potted five more balls in quick succession before finally missing a difficult long one.

'Right then. Here we go. No more messing about...' The man crouched down, taking his time to line up the shot, tongue out, eyes squinting; but when he finally hit it, the ball rattled in the jaws of the pocket and ricocheted away to safety.

'Ooh! I can't believe that stayed out.' Siobhan threw back her head in mock despair while the man skulked back to his friend.

She returned to the table and potted her last remaining ball before knocking the black into the middle pocket with a flourish.

'Talk about the luck of the Irish, aye.' She grinned. 'You know, in Belfast, the loser has to run around the room in their keks if they get seven-balled.'

'It's a good thing we're not there then,' the man replied, stony-faced. 'Let's go again.' He finished his drink and slammed down the bottle. 'Double or nothing.'

'Sounds good to me.' Siobhan re-set the table and smacked the white ball into the pack.

The balls burst apart and a spotted one disappeared into the bottom left-hand pocket. She potted three more, the man's frustration growing with each shot, before finally missing.

The man stalked over to the table, taking aim and potting his first ball.

'Get in there!' he shouted, clenching his fist.

Four more balls quickly disappeared, and he looked over at Siobhan with a smirk.

'Looks like that luck's running out. Maybe you want to give your little leprechaun a rub.' He leered at Carla and potted his last two balls, leaving him with just the black to win.

Luckily for Siobhan it was tight against the cushion and his attempt stopped in the jaws of the pocket, hanging precariously over the edge.

'Fuck!' He slammed his cue against the table in frustration. 'How did that stay out?' He walked away, shaking his head.

Siobhan sauntered over and quickly cleared her remaining balls, leaving just the easy black.

She lined up the shot, drawing back the cue. Then she glanced up at Carla and potted it without looking.

'I think you'll find that's two-nothing,' she said, reaching for the money.

'Not so fast, little lady.' He pinned her hand to the table. 'You're not really going to take a man's last few pounds, are ya? We was just having ourselves a little bit of fun. I need that cash to get a taxi home and feed me family.'

'Cry me a fucking river, Fagin. You should have thought about that before you started betting, shouldn't you? Now, kindly let go of my hand. Didn't your daddy ever teach you not to mess with a crazy redhead?'

'Listen here, you dirty little tinker–' but before he could finish the sentence, Siobhan hit him across the head with the cue, and then kicked him between the legs with her Doc Martens.

'I just can't miss a ball tonight,' she exclaimed as the man fell to his knees with a high-pitched cry. 'And this is for calling me sweetcheeks.' She kicked him in the ribs, and he crumpled to the floor.

'Lookout!' Carla cried as the other man approached Siobhan from behind.

Instinctively she smashed an empty beer bottle against the side of the table and spun around, holding the jagged edge to his throat.

'You better think long and hard about your next move, pal.' She stared straight at him, her green eyes a calm meadow, but there was a wildness behind them, a fire burning on the dark horizon. The man backed away, holding his hands up in surrender. 'Good choice. Now, help your buddy up, and then get the hell out of here.'

'Oh my God! That was crazy!' Carla said, after the men had left.

'They were just a couple of eejits.' Siobhan got rid of the bottle and picked up the money. 'You want another beer? I'm rich!'

'Okay. One more. Then I go. I've had enough excitement for one night.'

'In that case, let's have a quick smoke first.'

'Good idea. I need a cigarette too.' Carla followed her outside.

14

Liam sat inside a little café in Peckham and sipped coffee, his laptop open, a tattered copy of Jack Kerouac's *On the Road* beside it, which he'd bought at a second-hand bookshop in Russell Square when he first moved to the city. He'd been reading the book for almost six months, barely making it halfway through, but he liked the way it looked on the table and the air of well-read intellectuality it gave. He secretly hoped that one day, someone, preferably a beautiful girl, maybe an English Lit graduate, or fellow writer, would spot it and strike up a conversation. Although, if they did, he probably wouldn't have a clue what to say. But he still liked the idea.

He put down the coffee and opened the article he'd posted the previous day. It was up to almost four thousand hits now, which was already over double what the previous article had managed.

He refreshed the page every few minutes, his excitement growing as the number rose steadily with each click. At this rate he'd hit ten thousand, maybe even twenty by the end of the week. He let his mind wander, dreaming of working for a big national newspaper and seeing his story on the front page, his name up in lights, or at least a bold-printed by-line.

He scrolled through to the comments, revelling in all the praise and positive replies. He'd clearly captured people's imagination with this story. But what now? He needed another follow up. His anonymous source clearly knew more than they were letting on. Maybe next time they would give him an actual name or an address. They still hadn't replied to his last message though. He checked his junk folder. Then he opened his personal account. But they were both empty.

Frustrated, he closed the laptop and picked up the book, but his phone rang before he could start reading.

He glanced at the screen, but the number was withheld.

He hesitated for a moment, thinking it was probably a telemarketer or some weirdo who'd found his number on the Capital Conspiracies website; then the thought struck him that it might be the source, and he accepted the call.

'Hello…' he said guardedly.

'Oh, good afternoon. Is this Liam Patterson?' A well-spoken woman answered.

'It is… Who's this?'

'Fantastic! I wasn't sure if I had the right number. My name's Caroline Burnett. I'm the Chief Editor at *The London Beacon* newspaper. You might have heard of us?'

'Yeah – I mean, yes. Of course. You're the biggest newspaper in London.' Liam sat up, gripping the phone a little tighter.

'We like to think so. I hope you don't mind me calling unannounced, but I came across your article this morning. It's quite the read. Great traction too. You're definitely trending right now.'

'Uh, thank you.' He shuffled in the seat, barely able to breathe, his chest tightening with anticipation.

'Let me cut to the chase, Mr Patterson. You have a lot of potential. A little rough around the edges maybe. But with the right guidance, I think you could do well. I'd like you to come and work for us. We could do with some fresh talent around here. Is that something you might be interested in?'

'Yes! Definitely. That would be amazing!' His eyes lit up, the tension disappearing, replaced by a kaleidoscope of butterflies in his stomach, which threatened to lift him off the seat.

'Great. I need an article by Thursday morning. That gives you two days. Do you think you can manage that?'

'Hundred-percent. I'll make it my number one priority.'

'I like your attitude. I'll get my assistant to send over the details ASAP.'

'Thank you so much for this opportunity, Ms Burnett. You won't regret it, I promise.'

'I'm sure I won't. Oh! One last thing. I'm curious, who's your source for these articles? After all, a story that fantastical needs a reliable witness, otherwise it may as well be written by Stephen King, or that *Killing Eve* girl. What's her name again, Phoebe Waller-something?'

Liam squeezed his eyes shut and rubbed his temples. If he told her it was just some random stranger who'd probably made the whole thing up, she'd take the job offer right back. But if he gave a fake name, she'd probably see through that too…

'Mr Patterson? Are you still there?'

'Yes, uh, sorry.'

'So, are you going to answer my question?'

'Well, the thing is, they, uh, want to remain anonymous. And to be honest with you, I'd like to respect that. I kinda promised them. I hope that's okay? They're definitely legitimate though,' he quickly added, settling on a white lie.

'Of course. Integrity is thin on the ground in this business. Very well. Bring the article into our offices on Thursday and we can chat more then. Goodbye, Mr Patterson,' the woman added curtly before ending the call.

'Yes! Get in there, you beauty!' He threw his head back and thrust his hands into the air.

A few people glanced over, curious about the spontaneous outburst, but he didn't care. It was really happening. He put his hands down and sat in silence for a few minutes, basking in the moment and envisioning his article in the paper. His name printed below for all the world to see.

He wondered what it would be about. Hopefully it would be something juicy, like a murder mystery or a new terrorist threat, or maybe even something political…

He continued to imagine the possibilities when suddenly his phone pinged, bringing him back to reality. He looked at the screen and saw that it was an email from Caroline Burnett's assistant.

'That was quick!' he muttered, quickly opening the message, eager to see what it said. But when he started reading, his heart sank.

15

Anaïs entered an old, Victorian-style pub on Lower Sloane Street, a short walk from her mother's modelling agency, and spotted Siobhan sitting by the window. She wore a sheer-black sleeveless top and matching skin-tight jeans, and Anaïs walked over to her.

'Hey, hey, Nay-Nay.' Siobhan stood up to greet her. 'It's great to see you.'

'Hi, Shiv. I love the top. Where did you get it?'

'It was on sale in Zara. I'm glad you like it. There's only so many heavy metal t-shirts a girl can wear, right?'

'I don't know. You look good in them too.' Anaïs stared into her bright-green eyes, which were accentuated by the dark eyeliner and mascara she wore.

'Are you flirting with me, Ms Dubois?'

'You wish.' Anaïs took off her jacket and sat down.

'Damn right, I do. So how you been? I feel like I haven't seen you in ages.'

'Yeah, I've been a bit of a hermit lately. Just lots of sitting at home doing uni work and helping out with my mother's agency. You love these old man pubs, don't you?' Anaïs glanced around at the rustic décor and mature patrons.

'Is there any other kind?' Siobhan shrugged.

'Uh, yeah. There's a nice cocktail bar around the corner, actually, that does the best espresso martinis.'

'I didn't take you for a snob. Please don't tell me you're turning into your mother.'

'Very funny.' Anaïs gave her a sarcastic smile.

'Ah, come on! I'm just teasing ya. What do you want to drink? I doubt they have espresso martinis, but I could ask the old fella behind the bar to stir a little Nescafe into your vodka.'

'I'll just have a small white wine. I can't get too drunk. I've got an assignment to finish later.'

'Aw! Seriously? I thought we were going to hit the town tonight.' Siobhan scowled. 'I've got so much free time since I finished at Sterne-Tec and went full-time in the revenge business.'

'Sorry, but I need to get it done.' Anaïs shrugged. 'Oh, and make it a sauvignon, please, darling. Preferably a New Zealand. Chop, chop,' she added, mimicking her mother.

'You're lucky you're so pretty, otherwise you'd be in trouble.' Siobhan gave her a playful nudge and went to the bar.

While she was alone, Anaïs took out her phone and read an email from the catering company she'd hired for an event at the modelling agency the following week. After sending a quick reply, she glanced up and caught Siobhan gazing at her from the bar. She knew the other girl lusted after her, and she wondered what it would be like to give into her constant advances and flirting. She'd never been with another girl, but there was something about Siobhan's confidence that appealed to her. She was very attractive too. Anaïs glanced at her bare arms and arched back as she leant on the bar. The sheer fabric gave a tantalising glimpse of her delicate spine, and Anaïs followed the little indents all the way down before quickly looking away. What was she doing? This was crazy.

'Here ya go, my lady.' Siobhan came back a moment later and put the drinks on the table.

'Thanks.' Anaïs picked up the wineglass and took a sip. 'So, why did you want to meet tonight? It's a long way to come from Stoke Newington on a wet and gloomy Wednesday evening.'

'Aren't I allowed to come visit my favourite girl just for the hell of it?'

'With you there's always a reason. Usually a nefarious one.' Anaïs gave her a disapproving look.

'Well, if you really want to know, I have a proposition for you.'

'I knew it.' Anaïs rolled her eyes.

'It's not what you think. Although feel free to share your nefarious thoughts any time.' Siobhan took a sip of beer, leaving a little white moustache above her lip.

'Nice *tache*.' Anaïs smirked.

'You like that, do you? Come on, love, give us a kiss, will ya,' Siobhan put on a gruff voice and leant forward, puckering her lips.

'Just tell me what you're up to.'

'I'm not sure it's such a good idea anymore.' Siobhan leant back and wiped the froth away. 'You seem pretty rammed already. And not in a good way, if ya know what I mean.'

'You're disgusting.' Anaïs shook her head

'Whoa! I was just kidding.'

'Well, it's not funny.'

'You're actual upset with me?' Siobhan looked confused.

'I'm sorry. It's not you. It's just two-years, this week, since *it* happened. And the nightmares have been worse than ever. Sometimes it feels like they'll never go away.' Memories of Epping Forest came flooding back and she looked down at the table.

'Oh shit! I'm sorry, Ani, I didn't realise.' Siobhan reached out and squeezed her hand. 'You know you can talk to me anytime, right?'

Anaïs felt a strange tingling sensation spread along her fingers and up her arm. Soon it spread through her entire body and she pulled away, nervously running her hand through her hair, which was now back to its natural dark-auburn colour.

'So, what's this proposition?' she asked, eager to change the subject.

'We can talk about it later. There's no rush.'

'No, tell me now. I could do with a distraction.'

'Okay... it's nothing major. I was just going to ask if you wanted to help me with some admin stuff in the office. It'll only be a few hours a week, but I'm swamped at the moment and the paperwork keeps piling up. We've got another client booked in on Monday too, so I'll be rushing around like a blue-arsed fly, as usual.' Siobhan rolled her eyes. 'Your mother said I could get an assistant, but by the time I find someone, do the security checks, and then train them up, it'll be more hassle than it's worth. And I know you're always keen to get more involved.'

'I'd love to,' Anaïs said instantly. 'But I don't think my mother would approve. She doesn't like me going down there, as it is. She still thinks I'm this fragile little bird who needs constant protection from the world. I think that's part of why I'm still getting these nightmares. It feels like I'm living this weird half-life, locked away in that big house in Strawberry Hill, almost twenty-four-seven, like Rapunzel.'

'Well, I'm more than happy to be your Prince Charming. And what your mother doesn't know won't hurt her.' Siobhan winked.

'You can come Monday, if you're free. I'll sneak you in before the others arrive. Then, when you're all done, you can watch everything on the big screen – front row tickets to the carnage.' She grinned. 'It's gonna be a good one too. The client has made some very interesting requests.'

'Like what?' Anaïs leant forward.

'You'll see...' Siobhan raised her eyebrows, glancing around conspiratorially, but she didn't say anymore.

'Tease.' Anaïs smiled, her mood suddenly brightening.

'Soo... how about we get drunk and celebrate your new job.'

'Nice try, but I still need to get that assignment finished later. Even more so now.'

'Then I rescind my offer.'

'Nuh-uh, too late.'

'Fine. Just remember, when you come down that lift next week, I'm the boss. And I can be very demanding. Especially if you don't do as I say.'

'Hmm, we'll see about that.' Anaïs took a sip of her drink, and then went to the bathroom.

16

Liam glanced at his watch and saw that it was almost eight am. This wasn't good. He was meant to be leaving now; not running around his cramped apartment in his socks and underpants.

He squeezed into a pair of snug-fitting chinos, hitching them up with a grunt, and put on his best brown brogues. Then he unpacked a white shirt he'd bought the day before.

'I thought this was meant to be non-iron,' he grumbled, buttoning it up and smoothing down the creases, before stepping over to the mirror and struggling to do up a red-striped tie he'd found in the bottom of his sock drawer. 'Oh well, that'll do.' He delicately touched-up his blonde hair, which was immaculately coiffed on top and neatly-trimmed on the back and sides, and then slipped on a navy blazer.

'Okay, looking good.' He checked his hair one more time and threw his laptop bag over his shoulder.

When he got outside, he scurried down the leafy pavement that ran alongside the vast green expanse of Burgess Park and reached the bus stop on Old Kent Road just as the bus pulled up.

He arrived at London Bridge a little while later and fought his way through the rush hour crowds, making his way to the riverside, where the offices of *The London Beacon* were located inside an ultra-modern, glass office block.

He went through the revolving doors, almost doing a three-sixty, as he gawped at the huge open-plan lobby with its marble floors, stylish seating and private café; there was even a full-grown tree in the middle of the room, its leaves almost touching the high ceiling.

'Hi, sir, can I help you?' a receptionists asked.

'Oh, hi, yes. Sorry. I'm here to see Caroline Burnett at *The London Beacon* newspaper.'

'What's your name, please?'

Liam gave his name, and she told him to go and wait on a cream leather sofa.

He perched on the edge, inspecting his tie, turning the soft fabric over in his hands, and he imagined what it would be like to work in a place like this every day.

'Liam?' A girl around his age with a blonde bob suddenly appeared, and he dropped the tie, almost falling to the floor.

'Yes. That's me.' He popped up like a Jack in the box and held out his hand. 'Nice to meet you.'

'You too.' She shook it limply. 'Sorry to startle you. I'm Hannah. I'm Ms Burnett's PA. If you follow me, I'll take you up to our offices.'

He followed her into the lift and they went up to the eighth floor.

The doors opened onto a panoramic view over the sprawling, sun-drenched city and sparkling river below, and he gazed out at all the famous landmarks and buildings that spread out before him.

'Pretty great view, right?' she said, leading him towards a spacious open-plan office.

From the outside it seemed quiet, but there was a rush of noise when she opened the door. All around him people spoke loudly on handheld phones and headsets while others shouted across the room, everyone in motion, gesticulating animatedly, the whole place a frisson of nervous energy and excitement. Suddenly he felt very out of his depth.

'Hey there, how do you doo-doo?' A tall red-headed man with a strong Welsh accent stopped in front of him. 'I'm Rhodri, but most people just call me Rhod. I'm the head of the Sports Department here. You must be Liam?' He held out his hand and smiled.

'Uh, yes, nice to meet you.'

'Hey, mate, how ya going?' A good-looking Aussie guy with long messy hair joined them. 'I'm Pete. Good to meet ya.'

'You too,' Liam replied.

'I'm one of the feature writers here so if you need any help or advice just hit me up.' He gave Liam a pat on the shoulder.

'Thanks.' Liam nodded.

'No worries, mate. Doo-doo you want a coffee? I'm just on my way to make one.'

'Uh, no, I'm good, thanks.'

'Suit yourself. Don't forget what I said – anything you need, I'm here. Oh, and watch out for this one. She's not as innocent as she looks.' He grinned at Hannah and then walked away.

'Just ignore him,' she said. 'He thinks he's a comedian.' She raised her voice loud enough for Pete to hear, and he winked over his shoulder.

'Do you know why they keep saying do-do?' Liam asked, confused.

'I *doo* not.' She quickly looked away, but Liam caught the flash of a smile on her face.

'Ms Burnett's office is just down here,' she said, walking on.

They stopped outside a smaller glass office in the corner of the room, where a slim elegant-looking woman in her mid-to-late forties sat behind a large white desk.

Hannah tapped the glass and the woman ushered them inside with a curt nod.

'Ah, Mr Patterson. Sit down, please. I was just about to sign off on the final copy of this evening's edition. I've put your article on page fourteen. Here, take a look…' She swivelled her huge iMac screen around. Liam winced when he saw the title, **'Doggy Doo-Not's'**, written in bold lettering.

That explained a lot. He wanted to say something, but he bit his tongue, keeping a straight face despite his annoyance.

'Looks great, doesn't it.' She smiled. 'Your first by-line. You should be proud. I hope you don't mind, but I decided to go with a lighter title.'

'Of course not, it's great,' he said, trying to sound enthusiastic, although inside he felt like his soul had literally been shat on by the very dogs he'd written about.

The article was about the rise in rogue dog walking companies operating in the city, leaving a trail of dog faeces and destruction in their wake. Liam had tried to jazz it up by writing a closing paragraph about how it was rumoured some of the companies were using the business as a front to sell drugs in the community, but he could already see that she'd removed it along with his original title, **'Canine Handlers Linked to Rise in Coke and Cannabis'**.

'Was there a reason why you cut the last paragraph?' he asked.

'I thought it was a little far-fetched,' she said, dismissively.

'With all due respect, Ms Burnett, I spoke to a few people in the area, and they all raised similar concerns. I have names too. One lady, called Margaret, even told me that she'd found clear plastic pouches and used joints close to where the dogs were being walked.'

'I admire your enthusiasm, Mr Patterson, but it's your first day. Don't run before you can walk. There'll be plenty more stories. Now, if you go back outside, Hannah will show you around the rest of the office and get you up to speed.' She turned the screen back and picked up the phone.

'Uh, yeah, okay. Thanks again, Ms Burnett.' Liam stood up and left.

Once Hannah finished showing him around, she assigned him a desk next to a small kitchen area, which also served as a break room, and left him to read through the company's intranet.

He scrolled through the information about how the paper was formed and its current structure, but soon got bored and opened a web browser to check his email.

To his surprise, there was a new message entitled, 'Where the Wild Vixens Roam…'

Curious, he glanced around to make sure nobody was looking, and opened it.

Inside, there was only one line, and he re-read it about four or five times:

If you want to know more, meet me tonight at 11pm, underneath Tower Bridge, on the north side of the river. William.

'Who the hell is William?' he muttered, checking the email address and realising it was completely different to the anonymous source, who still hadn't replied.

'What ya up to there, mate?' Pete glanced over his shoulder.

'Uh, nothing.' Liam quickly minimised the window and spun around on his chair.

'Bit jumpy, aye? You working on something juicy?'

'It's just a message from a girl I've been dating,' Liam replied, thinking fast.

'Women, aye? Come on, let's go get a coffee. Don't turn me down twice.'

Liam logged off the computer and followed him into the kitchen.

'How'd ya take it?' Pete tapped on the front of a fancy-looking machine. 'This thing makes a great cuppa, take it from a Sydneysider. If it's one thing we know, it's good coffee.'

'I'll have a cappuccino, please – just one shot, though.'

'Ya soft cunt,' Pete said with a laugh

'I'm not good with too much caffeine.' Liam shrugged.

'You can't call yourself a real journo unless you're a sleep-deprived, borderline drug addict, who survives on copious amounts of caffeine, coke and cold hard liquor.'

'That's not really my style.'

'I'm just pullin' ya leg, mate. Geez, you need to stop taking things so seriously if you want to survive in this place.' Pete grabbed two mugs from the cupboard and placed them under the nozzles of the machine.

'Sorry, I'm just a little nervous. First day and all that.'

'No worries, mate. We've all been there. You'll be alright.'

'I just wish Ms Burnett would give me something more interesting to write. That last article was a joke.'

'Cazza's just testing you. She's a wily old fox. Bit of a milf, too, right?'

'I hadn't noticed,' Liam lied.

'Yeah, yeah, whatever. That sweet, innocent act ain't fooling me. And don't take it so personally. We all get the shit jobs to start with – in your case literally.' He grinned.

'What was your first article about?' Liam asked.

'Ah, it was some boring-ass story about a dispute over planning permission in Hampstead.' He passed Liam one of the mugs. 'But now look at me – front page of tonight's edition.'

'Really? That's awesome.'

'What you mean, *really?* You haven't seen it yet? I thought Cazza would have shown you. It's a pretty huge scoop.'

Liam shrugged.

'Well, you're in for a treat. It's a ripper!'

'What's it about?'

'Did you hear about that rich chick, Cecilia Davenport, the one that went missing a little while back?'

'Umm, yeah, I think so. It rings a bell.'

'You'd definitely know her if you saw her: early-forties, looks like a horsier version of Angelina Jolie. Always posing in *Hello* and *Cosmopolitan* and all those other shitty magazines. Her husband's

Henry Davenport, the billionaire property tycoon…'

'Ah, yeah, isn't she a UN Goodwill ambassador too?' Liam said, suddenly remembering.

'Yep, and a vegan, animal-rights activist, and generally perfect human being,' Pete scoffed. 'Although I've heard the only goodwill she likes to give is on her knees between lines of coke and vintage bottles of Dom Pérignon.'

'Really?' Liam looked at him in surprise.

'Yep. Right goer apparently. Anyway, the rumour was she'd run off with her driver. Some young Greek guy, she'd been having an affair with. But then the vehicle turned up a few hours ago, and they found his body stuffed in the trunk.'

'Holy shit! What happened to him?'

'Poor fucker's throat had been slashed.'

'That's awful. Did they find her too?'

'Nope. Vanished without a trace.'

'Who do they think it was? The husband's got to be the main suspect, right?'

'The spouse is always the first person they look at. Especially with old Cecilia's track record. But he's got a cast-iron alibi apparently. Then again, a guy with that much money could easily pay someone to do his dirty work.' Pete raised his eyebrows. 'Although I was told that the police think it might be related to a terrorist group – some Al-Qaeda-type fuckers who want to make a big statement. Whatever happens this story is going to run for a good few weeks yet, which means lots more exposure for yours truly.'

'How do you know so much?' Liam asked.

'It's all about contacts, mate. I've got friends in high places. You'll learn. Anyway, I should get back to it. A bunch of us usually go for drinks on a Thursday night. You should come along.'

'Sounds good,' Liam replied.

'Good man. We're heading there around six-ish.' Pete picked up his coffee and walked towards the door. 'Laters, Shitboy,' he added, raising his mug and grinning over his shoulder.

'Fuck sake!' Liam muttered. 'That better not stick.'

He stepped over to the window and looked out at Tower Bridge, which wasn't much more than stone's throw away, and he wondered what this William had to say…

17

That evening Liam stood in the cobblestoned courtyard of an old medieval pub, opposite Borough Market, sipping on his fourth pint of lager, as Pete told everyone yet another story from his extensive travels. This one was about the time he got drunk with a group of Norwegian students in a hotel ten-thousand-feet above sea-level in Tanzania.

While Pete continued, Liam checked his phone and saw that it was almost ten pm. He glanced around, the throngs of people blurring together in the glow of the fairy lights that hung from the long galleried windows, and he realised he was already a little drunk.

This wasn't good. He was meant to meet William in just over an hour. For all he knew, the guy could be a psychopath or a murderer, or anything. He needed to sober up fast and be prepared for anything.

'Hey, guys, I'm going to head off. I've got a spin class in the morning,' he called out above the din, his voice a little slurred.

'Hey! Come on, mate. I was just getting to the best bit. We were about to get into the hot tub overlooking Kilimanjaro.' Pete threw up his arms, spilling beer over Hannah, who'd been stood beside him all night.

'Hey! Watch it,' she cried.

'Sorry, babe. You want me to lick it off?' Pete grabbed her hips and poked out his tongue.

'You two need to get a room.' Rhodri shook his head as Hannah squealed and wriggled, although it was clear to everyone that she was enjoying the attention.

Liam took the opportunity to leave and weaved through the crowds, back to the main street. He stopped in a fried chicken shop near the entrance to the tube station, and then found a quiet spot to eat, close to London Bridge.

When he finished, he cut down a dark stairwell, leading to the riverside, and strolled along the quiet promenade, gazing at the glittering water, its calm surface shimmering in the blaze of a million evening lights. He spotted the reflection of Tower Bridge in amongst the swirl of shapes and colours and looked up, peering across the water and wondering if William was already there.

Soon he reached the bridge and crossed over, pausing at the top of a dimly-lit stairwell on the other side. Maybe this wasn't such a good idea. He thought about leaving, but curiosity got the better of him, and he descended the stone steps.

He turned a corner halfway down and saw that the light on the wall was out. A gust of wind travelled up from the river, whispering eerily as it rushed by. He came to a stop, pulling his jacket tighter, his eyes darting around, ready to flee if anything emerged from the darkness below. But nothing came, and he crept the rest of the way down, reaching the shadowy riverside and peering around. There was nobody there either, and he checked his phone: five-past-eleven. Where was this guy? Maybe it was all just a big joke. Some elaborate ploy to make him look like a fool. He wandered over to the railings and listened to the soft rhythmic splashing of the oily water against the underside of the bridge.

While he stood there, the faint aroma of caramelised nuts wafted through the air, the sweet smell lingering enticingly from the street-sellers who'd roasted them earlier that evening. He closed his eyes, smiling wistfully, until someone grabbed his shoulder.

He whirled around and looked up at a broad-shouldered man, dressed all in black.

'Sorry, I didn't mean to startle you.' The man smiled through a thick unruly beard. His long dark hair peppered with strands of grey. 'It's me, William.'

'If you don't want to startle people, try saying hello like a normal person, instead of sneaking up on them like Jack-the-fucking-Ripper!' Liam shot back, his heart still racing.

'I'm sorry, but we need to be discreet. You don't know who you're dealing with. It's safer for both of us this way. Trust me.'

'If you want me to trust you, you better tell me who the hell are you?' Liam demanded, his voice growing louder.

'I'll explain everything. Just calm down.'

'I am calm,' Liam snapped. 'Now start talking.'

'Okay…' The man sighed. 'Like I told you, my name's William. I'm from the US originally. Pennsylvania. But while I was serving in Afghanistan a few years back, I met a British nurse, called Karen, and we fell in love.' He smiled briefly, but Liam could see the sadness in his eyes. 'We moved here together when it was all over. Karen got a job at Guy's Hospital, and I worked as a delivery driver and security guard. Everything was great. Then she got involved with *them* and it all changed.'

'The women?'

'Yes. Your mysterious Vixens.' William let out a bitter laugh. 'Great name by the way.'

'Thanks,' Liam replied. 'So, how did you find out? Did she tell you?'

'Not at first. But the more she went out at night, the more suspicious I got. I was convinced she was having an affair, so I followed her one evening to a Thai restaurant in Charing Cross, after she'd told me she was working late. When she got home, I confronted her, and she told me everything: how the women would trick the men into coming to the restaurant, drug them, and then kill them. At first, I didn't believe her, but then she showed me the medication she'd hidden in the back of the closet.'

'What kind of medication?'

'Diazepam… Rohypnol… Ketamine… pretty much anything you could use to knock someone out. She told me she was just their supplier and that she didn't get involved in anything else. I asked her to stop. I told her it was still wrong and if they got caught, she'd be an accomplice. But she wouldn't listen. She said we needed the extra money. She even tried to blame me, saying I wasn't earning enough and that I'd gotten lazy since I left the military.'

'So what happened?'

'I got angry and threatened to go to the authorities. The next thing I know, she'd drugged me and I woke up gagged and blindfolded. They were there too. And they told me that if I tried to expose them, they'd kill me.'

'How long ago was this?'

'About three months. Give or take.'

'So are you the one who sent me the other emails?'

'No. I don't know who sent those. Probably some other poor soul who crossed them. These women are dangerous. They pretend they want to rid the world of bad guys, but what they really want to do is kill all men. They're sadists – far right feminists with a death wish – and they need to be stopped.'

'So why are you only coming to me now?'

'Because, despite everything, I still love her.' His voice caught for a moment, his eyes welling up. 'I thought if I gave it time, she'd eventually come to her senses. But I haven't seen or spoken to her in almost two months now.'

'How do I know you're telling the truth?' Liam asked, still unsure.

'If you go to The Sacred Lotus restaurant in Charing Cross on Monday night at seven-thirty, you'll see a beautiful young girl going inside with a plain-looking man. Probably older. But only the girl will leave. What I want you to do is follow the girl and find out where she goes. Hopefully she'll lead us to them.'

'Why can't you just do it yourself? It seems like you've done pretty well so far.'

'I told you – they threatened to kill me last time. If I'm going to bring them to justice, I need your help. I can't do it alone.'

'Okay. So say I do this for you, and I find out where this girl goes. Then what?'

'We meet here the following night. Same time. Same place. And I tell you everything I know. Then we come up with a plan to stop them once and for all. Oh, and when we do, the story's all yours... I should go. It's important we don't spend too much time together. They have spies everywhere. I'll see you Tuesday. Goodnight, Mr Patterson.' He turned and left.

'Wait!' Liam called out.

He still had so many questions. But the man strode away, his long hair billowing in the wind before disappearing into the darkness.

18

Anaïs followed Siobhan into her office and noticed the dimmed lights and wine on the coffee table.

'I thought you said you wanted help with admin stuff.' Her eyes narrowed.

'I do. I just thought it'd be nice to have refreshments for the show later. There's snacks in the cupboard too, if you get hungry. I like to be an accommodating boss.' Siobhan grinned.

'How about being an actual boss and showing me what you want me to do.'

'Ooh, I love it when you're feisty. Bring that cute little arse over here, and I'll show you exactly what needs doing.' She dragged two carboard boxes out from under the desk.

'What's all that?' Anaïs asked.

'It's the paperwork for our clients: terms, conditions, invoices, contracts, etcetera, etcetera ... I need you to sort through it all, type it into a database, and then file it in here.' She tapped the metal filing cabinet behind her.

'There's so much!'

'Yep, I've been meaning to do it for a while. It doesn't help that your darling mother keeps adding more and more shite to the pile.'

'Is it because of the articles that guy wrote?'

'Yep. That and a few other things—' But before Siobhan could answer, the phone rang. 'I should get that.' She pressed the loudspeaker button.

'They've just arrived, darling.' Queen Bea's languid voice filled the room.

'Already!' Siobhan tapped the keyboard and brought up the CCTV footage inside the restaurant.

'It's seven-thirty, so get off Tinder or Bumble, or whatever it is you lesbians use and do your job. Buh-bye.'

Siobhan hung up and zoomed in on a couple waiting to be seated.

'So he's the one who's going to get tortured?' Anaïs shuffled uncomfortably, memories of Victor and that fateful night in Epping Forest suddenly flooding back.

'Yep. His name's Benjamin Tomey. Don't let the plaid shirt and dad-jeans fool you though. This guy's raped at least three girls – that we know of – all under sixteen. He's currently on bail while the police carry out their investigations. Luckily, we managed to get to him before he's given some weak arse sentence, or he gets away with it altogether.'

'How did it take them so long to catch him?' Anaïs grew more anxious, her nails digging into her thighs. She'd been inside the underground complex before, but that was always in the daytime when everything was quiet. Now that the man was on the screen it felt different. More real. And the dark memories swirled around her brain like spiderwebs in a creepy old attic.

'He's a teacher,' Siobhan replied, bringing her back to reality. 'Poor things were probably too terrified to say anything. Thought nobody would believe them. But a few weeks ago, someone finally spoke up. And, one-by-one, the others have come forward too. Who knows how many more he's abused over the years – fucking sicko!' She grabbed a tablet off the shelf and switched it on. 'Right. I need to go and sort everything out. Will you be okay down here on your own?'

'Yeah, I'll be fine.' Anaïs forced a smile. 'What's that for?' she asked.

'Andie gave it to me the other day. It's linked up to my computer. Some remote access thingymajig. I just need to login using an online program, then I can see everything on here, including you.' She showed Anaïs the CCTV feed of her office on the small screen. 'So you better behave. Or not…' She winked.

'Just go.' Anaïs shook her head.

*

Queen Bea sashayed through the empty dining area in a purple-sequined gown and led Alessandra, a Spanish model from Diane's agency, and a shorter older man, towards the bamboo curtain at the back of the room.

'Come this way, my delectable darlings.' She passed by a young waitress, giving her a discreet nod as she opened the curtain with a delicate twirl of her wrist and ushered them inside. 'This is the best table in the house. A private paradise for star-crossed lovers.' She motioned for them to sit down and watched out of the corner of her eye as the waitress changed the sign on the door to 'Closed'.

'Thank you so much. It's perfect.' Alessandra smiled. 'And I love the cat.' She gave Queen Bea a knowing look.

'Ah, yes, Sheba, she's my pride and joy.' She stroked its gold-plated head. 'I got her specially-made for my thirtieth birthday – I know, I know, I don't look a day over twenty-five. But it's true. Even a Queen must age. Gracefully, of course.' She touched up her immaculate beehive hairstyle, and then handed them the menus.

'Can I get you both something to drink while you decide?'

'I'll have an Aperol Spritz, please,' Alessandra replied.

'Ah, good choice, a lady after my own heart. I love the black dress too.' She looked Alessandra up and down. 'Timeless, darling. You have the most exquisite figure. If I could feel envy, I'd be so jealous right now. Luckily, I can't. I keep myself busy with other sins.' She purred. 'And what can I get for the handsome gentleman?'

'I'll just have a beer.' The man stared at the menu, not even bothering to look up.

'Which one would you like, my darling? We have a wide selection from both the East and West: Asahi, Tiger, Chang, Amstel, Heineken…'

'Heineken's fine.' He gave her a dismissive look.

'As you wish.'

'Oh, and bring us some water for the table,' he called out.

'Of course. I'll get the waitress to bring you a jug.' She fluttered her long eyelashes and slipped back through the curtain.

'Would you like me to prepare the drinks, Ms Queeny?' the waitress asked.

'It's okay, Loulou. Just take the water and see if they're ready to order. I'll do the rest.' She bent down awkwardly in her snug gown and opened a small safe under the counter. She took out a clear plastic pouch filled with white powder and emptied it into a pint glass. She was about to pour the beer when she decided to add another pouch. Let's see how smug you are after this. She filled the glass, stirring it discreetly. Then she made the Aperol Spritz.

'Here you go, my darlings.' She glided into the room a moment later, carrying the drinks on a silver tray and placed them on the table.

She lingered for a moment, watching with glee, as the man took a long sip of beer. Then she slipped back through the curtain.

About five-minutes later, she heard the loud metallic clang of cutlery hitting the tiled-floor, and she went to investigate.

'Everything okay?' She peered inside. 'I hope you're not up to any funny business in here,' she added with a grin.

'No Fuzzy Bishness.' The man giggled, his eyes like saucers.

'Are you okay, sir?' She entered the room and approached the table.

'I'm more than okay, I'm poshitithly fantashtic… fantathtic… fantastic!' He swayed on the chair unsteadily.

'I can see.' She stepped over to the cat and rested her hand on its paw.

'What are you waiting for?' Alessandra asked.

'What's wrong, darling? Are you in a rush?' She watched as the man bent down to pick up the fork before losing his balance and crumpling to the floor, flailing about helplessly.

'Not really.' Alessandra shrugged.

'Whath the hell did you gith me?' He tried to stand up, but instantly fell back down.

'Okay, I've had my fun.' Queen Bea pulled the paw down and the wall slid open, revealing Siobhan, who was flanked by Carla and another woman from the Operations Team.

'Have no fear, the cavalry's here.' Siobhan stepped out of the lift while Carla and the other woman wheeled out a metal gurney. 'What the hell did you give him?' She glanced down at the man who sat on the floor rambling incoherently and dribbling all over himself. 'He's a right fucking mess!'

'Just the usual,' Queen Bea lied. 'He is quite small though.' She smiled innocently.

'Hmm, if you say so.' Siobhan gave her a dubious look. 'Okay, ladies, let's load him up.' She took out a taser and shot it into the man's chest. For a moment he came to life, flapping about like a ragdoll. Then he passed out, a puddle of urine spreading across the floor.

'Was that really necessary?' Queen Bea glanced down in disgust.

'Better safe than sorry,' Siobhan winked. 'Nobody likes surprises. Just ask the last guy that got into your pants.'

'Believe me, darling. Whatever man I allow inside my pants is bewitched for eternity. I dread to think what kind of unkempt monstrosity you're hiding inside yours.'

'I'm perfectly maintained, I'll have you know – tell her, Ale.'

'You wish.' Alessandra raised an eyebrow and smirked.

'Too right I do, you sexy senorita.'

'Can you help us, please?' Carla looked up, straining to lift the man.

'Yeah, yeah, sorry, my bad.' Siobhan helped them load him onto the gurney. Then they pushed him into the lift.

19

Liam stood across the street from the restaurant and peered out from behind a wall as a man and woman strolled towards the dimly-lit entrance. This had to be them. He gazed at the tall olive-skinned woman. Her long dark hair flowing enticingly in the wind. Her unzipped jacket revealing a figure-hugging black dress underneath.

Tearing his eyes away, he lifted his phone and took a few pictures, zooming in as much as he could before they disappeared inside.

He took out a small notebook and pen, flipping to a new page. But he stopped when a young Thai girl appeared in the doorway and changed the sign to 'Closed'.

Were they just going to kill him there and then? Suddenly it all felt very morbid and gratuitous. He thought about calling the police, but he knew he couldn't do that. He was already in too deep. And, despite his reservations, he still wanted to find out what was going on.

He glanced around, making sure the coast was clear. Then he crossed the street and stopped at the window. He crouched down, using the wall to conceal himself, and peered through the glass. But it was empty inside.

Where was everyone? He edged towards the entrance, tempted to sneak inside and investigate, when a shadowy movement behind the bamboo curtains at the back of the room caught his eye.

Quickly, he took out his phone and started filming.

Soon the shadows grew longer, spreading out into the dining room, like an oil slick polluting the clear ocean, and the curtains parted.

He ducked lower, his eyes barely above the windowsill, and watched as a glamourous Thai lady appeared. She was joined by the olive-skinned girl. But the man was nowhere to be seen.

Gotcha! Liam smiled to himself before scurrying away and ducking into a doorway across the street.

A few seconds later, the girl left and strode along the pavement towards Charring Cross station. Liam waited until she had gone a safe distance, then followed.

She entered a side entrance up ahead, and he scurried after her, tapping his Oyster card and rushing through the turnstile as she disappeared down the escalator.

When he got to the platform, it was surprisingly busy. He peered around, trying to spot her amongst the late-evening crowds, but she was nowhere to be seen.

He glanced up and saw that the next train was due in less than a minute. Panicking, he jumped up and down. Come on, come on. Where are you?

Finally he spotted her, hidden amongst a group of weary-looking commuters a little further down, and he breathed a sigh of relief.

He edged closer, but a low rumbling sound brought him to a halt. The noise built to a thunderous roar and two yellow dots pierced the blackness as a train came hurtling through the tunnel. It blasted into view like a herd of stampeding rhinos, and Liam took a step back.

A few seconds later, it came to a screeching halt and a horde of passengers piled out, an avalanche of bodies spreading over the platform.

For a moment he lost her again in the maelstrom of activity. Then, to his relief, he caught a glimpse of her sitting in the middle of the carriage, and he jumped on, just as the doors slid shut.

The girl changed trains at Oxford Circus, and he continued to follow her, until she finally got off at Holland Park and stepped into a busy lift.

He thought about going up the stairs, worried that she might start to get suspicious, but the doors beeped, and he decided to take his chances. He tried to keep his distance, but a few more people crammed in at the last second, and he found himself standing right behind her. She was slightly taller than him and her wavy hair tickled his nostrils, the subtle floral aroma intoxicating him. He glanced down, trying to focus, and spotted a burgundy-coloured scarf hanging from the top of her bag. Suddenly an idea struck him. He glanced around, making sure nobody was watching, and subtly pulled it out, quickly stuffing it into his pocket.

The doors opened and his head popped up like a meerkat as everyone piled out onto the quiet leafy street.

He planned to hand the scarf back outside and pretend she'd dropped it. Then he could strike up a conversation and find out a little more about her. But before he could build up the courage to put his plan into action, she crossed the road.

Shit!

He tried to follow her, but a double-decker bus hurtled past, stopping him in his tracks.

'Come on, come on,' he muttered, as a procession of vehicles followed.

Finally he saw a gap and raced across, catching a glimpse of the girl as she reached the entrance to one of the identikit pristine-white Victorian villas that spread out before him in either direction. Maybe this was where the Vixens lived. His source did say they were rich.

'Hey! Wait!' he called out, waving the scarf in the air.

She took out her earphones and looked at him in confusion.

'Sorry, I didn't mean to startle you.' He stopped in front of her. 'You dropped your scarf when you came out of the tube. I tried to call a few times, but I guess you didn't hear me.' He held it out and gave her the friendliest smile he could muster.

'Ah! Thank you so much. My grandmother gave me that scarf for my birthday. I'd be devastated if I lost it.' She broke into a smile, and Liam's heart skipped a beat.

'It's okay, I'm sure most people would have done the same.' He shrugged, noticing a subtle Spanish accent. 'Is this your place? It's very fancy.'

'I just share a flat on the top floor with a friend. It's not all mine unfortunately. Do you live around here too? You look familiar for some reason.'

'I wish. I'm in south-east London. Far less fancy.' He let out a little laugh. 'I'm just here to meet a friend for drinks.'

'Ah, right. That's cool. Well, have a good night. And thanks again. Honestly, I'd forget my head if it wasn't screwed on.' She stepped towards the door and took out her keys.

'So, uh, what's your name?' he blurted, eager to keep her talking and find out a little more.

'Sorry, I'm Alessandra. And you?'

'I'm Liam.' He gave his real name without thinking and cringed inside. 'So, what do you do here – for work I mean?' he quickly added.

'I'm a model,' she replied, although he could see she was getting a little uncomfortable with his questioning, her arms folded in front of her.

'Really? I actually work for *The London Beacon* newspaper,' he said, deciding that it didn't really matter if she knew his real identity or not. Maybe it could actually work to his advantage. 'Here…' He gave her one of the business cards he'd gotten printed over the weekend. 'We're always looking for models to feature in our supplements. We can help with advertising your company too. Which agency do you work for?'

'Oh, thanks.' She took the card and smiled politely. 'It's the Dubois Agency in Chelsea. Although you're best off speaking to my boss, Diane Dubois. You can find her details on the website. Anyway, I should go. I've got an early start in the morning. Goodnight, Liam.' She unlocked the door and slipped inside.

20

After taking the man downstairs and making sure he was ready for the evening's client, Siobhan went to the boardroom and sat down, putting her feet up on the table.

'Come on, come on… where is everyone?' she muttered, eager to get the formalities out of the way and get back to Anaïs.

She was about to go look for Diane and the others when they breezed through the door.

'Can you get your feet off there, please,' Diane called out. 'That table's worth more than your salary.'

'Then youse lot clearly ain't paying me enough,' Siobhan swung her feet down whilst the others took a seat.

'Right, let's get started,' Diane announced. 'Andi, would you do the honours.'

Andréa tapped on the table and the whole surface came to life, LED sensors lighting up in front of each woman, giving them access to the main operating system via individual touch-screen displays, while a huge holographic screen floated above them.

'Okay, bring us up to speed.' Diane looked at Siobhan.

'I thought you'd never ask.' Siobhan tapped the table, and a picture of the man, taken from the Metropolitan Police's criminal database, along with his personal details, crimes and warning indicators appeared on the screen: 'Tonight, ladies and, uh, ladies, we have Benjamin Tomey, a forty-three-year-old Physics teacher from Birmingham, who's been living in Harringay, north London for the last eight-years. As you can see, he's a pretty normal-looking fella, but don't let that fool you. He's currently under investigation for the rape and sexual assault of three of his former students, although that number is likely to rise to at least double that. Thankfully, after tonight, that's the only thing that'll be rising for ole Mister Tomey.'

'Has the client arrived yet?' Diane asked.

'Not yet. She messaged a little while ago to say she's on her way.'

'I know this isn't work-related, but has anybody heard from Anaïs this evening?' Diane looked around the table. 'She hasn't replied to any of my messages, and her phone keeps going straight to answerphone.'

'Uh... yeah, she's in my office,' Siobhan replied sheepishly.

'What do you mean?' Diane glared at her.

'You told me to get some help for all this extra paperwork.' She shrugged.

'I didn't mean my daughter!' Diane's voice rose. 'You know I don't like her being down here, especially when we have a client in.'

'Don't you think it's time you stopped mollycoddling her?' Siobhan replied. 'She's not a kid anymore.'

'How dare you tell me how to raise my own child!' Diane exploded.

'Whoa, overreact much?' Siobhan raised her hands.

'Let's all just take a breath,' Jackie cut in.

'Jackie's right. This isn't helping anyone,' Andréa added.

'Will you look at that. The client just arrived at the station.' Siobhan glanced at her phone. 'Talk about saved by the bell. I better go collect her...' She stood up and walked towards the door.

'Take Anaïs with you on your way out. And tell her to go home,' Diane called out. 'I'll speak to you both about this tomorrow.'

'Yes, boss.' Siobhan left the room and went back to her office, throwing open the door in frustration.

'Hey, everything okay?' Anaïs looked up from the file she was reading. 'This stuff is so interesting–'

'Your mum knows you're down here, and she wants you to go home,' Siobhan interrupted.

'What? How?' Anaïs looked confused.

'I told her.'

'Why would you do that?'

'Because she's been trying to call you, and she was worried. What was I supposed to do?'

'Just lie.' Anaïs rolled her eyes.

'Well it's too late now. I need to collect the client from the station. We can leave together.'

'This is such bullshit!' Anaïs threw down the file. 'I've got as much right to be here as anyone.'

'Hey, you're preaching to the choir here. But my hands are tied.'

'Just tell my mum I went home and I'll sneak out later. Nobody will ever know.'

'Fine. But if she finds out, I took you out, and you snuck back in by yourself – Okay?'

'Deal.' Anaïs smiled

'Dammit! How can I resist that angelic little face?' Siobhan shook her head. 'Right, I need to go. I'll get the client to fill the paperwork in upstairs. Then I'll stay with your dear mother and the rest of the three amigos. I don't want them to get suspicious that we're hiding in here together. And, FYI, you owe me for this – big time!' She grabbed the forms she needed and left.

After collecting the client and going through the contract and the rest of her usual spiel, Siobhan took her downstairs and joined Diane and the others in a soundproofed booth, hidden behind the one-way mirror at the back of the Treatment Room.

'You guys are going to love tonight's show,' she exclaimed. 'This gal's sense of humour is so dark–'

'Has Anaïs gone?' Diane cut her off.

'Yes, yes. She's gone. Vamoose. You don't need to worry – oh, look, it's starting…'

A light came on inside illuminating the room, which had been transformed into a children's classroom. Then a woman walked in wearing dark-rimmed glasses, her hair tied up in a neat bun.

She stopped in front of a blackboard and picked up a piece of chalk while the man hung limply from a metal-framed contraption, his wrists and ankles bound by sturdy shackles, which were attached to metal runners that ran vertically and horizontally.

'Good evening, Benjamin, my name is Miss Reeves.' The woman's voice came through the speakers as she wrote her name on the board, the chalk screeching with every movement, like a pair of alley cats fighting over a can of leftover tuna.

'Do we really need the sound on?' Andréa winced.

'Just wait…' Siobhan grinned.

'Good Lord, what is that thing?' Jackie stared in confusion. 'It looks like he's about to be crucified.'

'That's not too far from the truth,' Siobhan replied. 'I got some of our guys at Stjerne-Tec to make it – it's an ingenious little invention, so it is.'

'Did you know about this?' Jackie asked Andréa.

'I've given up asking why anyone does anything anymore.' Andréa let out a weary sigh.

'Any reason why he's dressed like a schoolgirl?' Diane looked the man up and down, her expression unchanging.

'It's the theme. You know how all these women love a good theme,' Siobhan replied.

'Well the blonde wig and the pigtails are an improvement, at least. George Clooney, he ain't.' Jackie chuckled.

'Shush.' Siobhan glared at her. 'We're getting to the good bit.'

'Don't you shush me, missy!' Jackie shot back.

While they bickered, the woman strutted over to the man and stopped in front of him.

'I must say, Benjamin, you're looking very fetching. Or maybe I should call you Benjamina.' She smiled. 'I love the long socks, they really compliment those knobbly knees, and that pink lip gloss is just the cutest.'

'What's going on?' he mumbled. 'Where am I?' He squinted around, still dazed.

'We're going to have a private lesson this evening. It's called: *How not to be a perverted piece of shit*. It's pretty straightforward. I'm going to ask you a question. If you get it right, I'll give you a gold star. But if you get it wrong, I press this little red button here.' She held up a small remote control.

'Wait a second. Don't I know you?' The man looked at her more closely, his eyes becoming lucid. 'Shit! You're Annabelle Reeves, the actress!'

'Correct. Here's your first star.' She took a sticker and placed it on his ill-fitting white blouse.

'Is this some kind of practical joke?' He glanced around the room, his pigtails flicking through the air. 'If this is some crappy reality TV show, I'm not interested. You can't hold me against my will. I know my rights. I haven't signed anything.' He tried to struggle free, but the shackles wouldn't budge.

'I'm afraid this isn't a show, or a movie, for that matter. Now, first question: What was the name of the last girl you abused?'

'This is ridiculous. When I get out of this, I'm going to sue you and everyone involved in this farce.'

'Is that your final answer?'

'Do whatever it is you're going to do. I'm not afraid of you. You're just some over-the-hill actress—'

But before he could say anything else, she pressed the button and his whole-body spasmed uncontrollably as …*Baby One More Time* by Britney Spears blared out of the speakers.

'Woo! I told you this would be a good one,' Siobhan shouted above the din as the man danced and jerked like an out of control marionette, his arms and legs sliding up and down the runners while his eyes rolled into the back of his head.

'Turn it down!' Andréa covered her ears.

'Okay, okay…' Siobhan was about to adjust the volume when the music suddenly stopped, and the man slumped forward, murmuring unintelligibly, urine gushing down from his frilly skirt and splashing to the floor. 'Oh, man, that's so gross! That's the second time this guy's pissed his pants tonight. He must have a bladder like a fucking hippo!'

'Your levels of vulgarity never cease to amaze me.' Diane gave her a disapproving look.

'I just say it as it is.' Siobhan shrugged.

'Now, Benjamina' The woman spoke up again. 'Let's try another question, shall we? How many poor innocent girls have you abused since you became a teacher?'

'I haven't abused anyone,' he mumbled.

'Now, now, we both know that's not true.' She stepped closer. 'Don't make me ask again.'

'You think I'm going to cave into your pathetic attempt at an interrogation?' He lifted his head and spat in her face.

'You're going to regret that.' She slapped him, then wiped her face with a tissue. 'Now, where were we? Ah! Yes…' She pressed the button again, and he let out a cry of pain as Britney's voice filled the room.

'Lord, please, put us all out of our misery and stop this awful racket.' Jackie grimaced. 'Listening to this song over and over again is enough punishment for anybody.'

'How dare you!' Siobhan said indignantly. 'Britney is a Goddess! I won't have a bad word said about her in my presence.'

'Honey, please! Aretha Franklin was a Goddess. So was Dinah Washington, Etta James, Nina Simone, and Whitney, God rest her soul. This is trash.'

For the next few minutes, the woman repeated the same process over and over...

'That's enough of that.' Diane finally turned off the speaker.

'Aww... What you do that for?' Siobhan sulked before looking up in confusion as the lights began to flicker. 'Uh, guys, I don't think that's supposed to happen.'

'There must be some kind of electrical surge from the machine he's attached to,' Andréa replied

'Should we tell her to stop?' Diane asked.

'It's okay,' Andréa assured her. 'My team wired this whole place. We have a backup generator in case of an emergency. There's no need to worry.'

But before anybody else could speak, the lights went out completely and the whole place was plunged into darkness.

'Okay, that's it. I'm putting a stop to this,' Diane spoke up. But her mouth fell open when the lights came back on and the woman lay sprawled across the floor, the door hanging open, the man nowhere to be seen.

21

Liam got back to his flat and kicked off his shoes. Then he grabbed a bottle of beer from the fridge and slumped down on the couch. 'Ah, that's better.' He turned on the TV and sunk deeper into the worn old cushions.

'Okay, let's try to make some sense of all this...' He took out his notepad and read through everything he'd written on the tube ride home.

Once he'd finished, he turned to a new page and wrote 'VIXENS' in the middle, circling the word. Then he scribbled Alessandra's name underneath, along with Diane Dubois'. Maybe the modelling agency had nothing to do with it, but the woman seemed to fit the bill: rich, successful, middle-aged... he pictured the attractive older lady with the shiny blonde hair and wrinkle-free face on the agency's website.

He added William's name too, along with Karen's, and Beatrix Bannarasee, the woman who owned the restaurant.

He connected the names to the circled word in the middle, jotting down questions and theories as he went. The last thing he wrote was 'Who is the source!?', underlining it twice. Then he took a sip of beer and paced around the room.

'If I can just find out who sent those emails, maybe I can find out what they know about this Dubois woman and the other people involved. They clearly know more than they're letting on. The same goes for William. He's definitely holding out on me.'

The more he found out, the more questions he had. One thing he knew for sure, there was some seriously shady shit going down, and he was determined to get to the bottom of it.

He turned on his laptop and opened the last message he received from the source, cutting and pasting the email address into the web browser.

'Okay, let's find out who you really are…' He hit 'Enter', but nothing came up. Undeterred, he searched through Facebook, Twitter and all the other social media platforms he could think of, but they were all dead-ends too.

'Jesus! This person's like a ghost. There must be some way of finding out who they are.' He typed 'How to find an anonymous email address' into the search engine and read through the results.

'What the hell's an IP address?' He saw the same two words pop up over and over.

After skim-reading the top article, he learnt that it was a unique number assigned to a device while connected to the Internet. He continued reading until he figured out how to locate the number. Then he followed the instructions and cut and paste it into a free IP tracking program.

'Why the hell is someone from Ontario, Canada messaging me?' he stared at the screen in confusion. 'That's got to be some kind of mistake.' He read through the rest of the information, but it was all gibberish to him.

He was about to give up when he remembered his old uni friend, Doug, who worked at a private cyber security firm in central London. He was also one of the most annoying people Liam knew, with a penchant for cheap vodka, suicidal drinking games and starting fights wherever he went. There had to be someone else? But try as he might, he couldn't think of anyone. He's probably calmed down by now, he told himself, taking out his phone and calling Doug's number–

'Liam-fucking-Patterson! Well, fuck me sideways with a wooden stake! How you doing, you handsome, Twilight-looking bastard?' an enthusiastic voice boomed down the line after barely a ring.

'Oh, hey, mate,' Liam replied sheepishly. 'I'm good, thanks. Sorry to call you out of the blue like this, but–'

'No need to apologise, bro. It's great to hear from you.' Doug cut him off. 'I saw on Facebook that you're living in London now too.'

'Yeah, I've been here a while. I just got a new job at *The London Beacon* newspaper actually.'

'No shit, that's awesome! My offices are in Farringdon. We should get together for a beer soon.'

'Sounds great,' Liam said as enthusiastically as possible.

'How about Saturday? There's a great little rock club in Camden that plays killer *chunes* and is always full of fitties. We can go and cause some carnage, like the good old days. What you say?'

'Uh, I can't do this weekend. I'm already slammed with work and stuff. But maybe we can get some of the other Loughborough boys together soon and arrange a proper reunion.'

'Yes! Fucking A! That's a great idea. I'll set up a WhatsApp group, pronto.'

'Great,' Liam said, wondering what he was getting himself into, before quickly changing the subject: 'To be honest, I actually called to ask a favour.'

'Course, mate. What can I do for you?'

'Well, I've had some emails recently from an anonymous account and I want to try and find out who sent them.'

'Hmm, okay.' Doug's voice turned serious. 'What have you tried so far?'

'Just Google and Facebook, and a few other sites... I searched their IP address too, but it said they were located in Canada, which is weird. Whoever sent these messages seemed to know a lot about what's going on in London at the moment. And not just normal, everyday stuff. I'm talking top secret information that only someone with connections would know.'

'Hmm, it sounds like they're using a VPN.'

'What's that?'

'It's a software program that gives the user a temporary IP address – in your mysterious friend's case, one in Canada – then it hides their real address, making them invisible. Which means they can surf the web to their heart's content, without being seen.'

'So, if this person is using a VPN, does that mean we can't find out who they are?'

'It's tricky. But there's always a way. That's what I get paid the big bucks for. Give me the details, and I'll see what I can do.'

'Really? Thanks, mate, I owe you one.'

'No worries, bro. I'll drop you a message when I find something. It shouldn't take too long. And don't forget our night out in Camden.'

'You get me a name, and the drinks'll be on me all night.'

'In that case, I'll get straight on it. Laters, bro.'

Doug hung up and Liam sent him the details. Then he went to the fridge for another beer.

Less than an hour later, his phone beeped, and he snatched it up.

'That can't be right,' he murmured, reading the message from Doug and staring at the familiar name on the screen.

22

Anaïs sat in the office, watching the drama unfold on the screen. Her mouth agape as the woman tortured the man on a weird machine that made him look like some kind of Jesus/Britney hybrid. She leaned back for a moment and took a sip of wine, the intensity of the onslaught exhausting her as the man shook and convulsed with every fresh burst of electricity.

Then, to her surprise, the lights flickered. She looked at the screen, but the woman continued, unperturbed, until suddenly the power cut out completely, plunging the room into darkness. She shuffled nervously, not sure what to do. Then, to her relief, the power returned. She took another sip of wine, waiting for the computer to restart, but she almost dropped the glass when she re-opened the camera feed and saw the woman lying motionless on the floor; the man gone.

Panicking, she scanned the other cameras and spotted him shuffling along the corridor.

To her horror, he was heading her way. She ducked beneath the desk, her eyes peeking above the edge, as he continued to get closer.

Soon he was right outside. She held her breath. Heart thumping in her chest. But he kept going, and she realised he was heading for the lift. She looked for Siobhan and the others, expecting them to give chase, but they were still in the Treatment Room, tending to the stricken woman.

There was no way they were going to get to him in time. If he escaped, they'd all be screwed! The thought stunned her into action. She swiped the wine bottle off the table and rushed towards the door. But when she grabbed the handle, memories of Epping Forest returned, and she stopped, icy tendrils ensnaring her, her whole body temporarily paralysed.

She tried to block it out, but Victor's leering face taunted her, and she crumpled to her knees, banging her head against the door in anger and frustration. She couldn't do it. She was too weak. Too afraid. Tears trickled down her face, and she squeezed her eyes shut. Ashamed.

She was about to give up when a vision of her mother and the others locked up in prison flashed through her mind. She couldn't let that happen. Breathing deeply, she climbed to her feet and forced the door open.

She poked her head out tentatively and saw the man standing at the lift doors, his back to her.

This was it. It was now or never. She stepped into the corridor and crept towards him.

Up ahead the doors slid open and without thinking she broke into a run.

The man glanced over his shoulder, pigtails swinging, and smirked when he saw Anaïs approaching.

For a moment their eyes locked, and his face morphed into Victor's, the small smirk growing into the familiar wolfish grin that still haunted her dreams. But it was too late to stop now; she swung the bottle with all her might, and it crashed into the side of his head with a sickening thud. The impact made his head spin almost 360-degrees, and he crumpled to the ground in a lifeless heap.

'Holy shit! That was awesome!' Siobhan appeared next to her a moment later.

'Is he dead?' Anaïs stared at the pool of blood gathering beneath the man's motionless body, and the colour drained from her face.

Siobhan kicked his foot, and he groaned weakly. 'Nah, he's still alive – piece of shit – he won't be for much longer though.'

'What's happening? Are you okay, honey?' Jackie stopped behind them, resting her hands on her knees and breathing heavily.

'She's better than you by the looks of it.' Siobhan smirked.

'I wasn't talking to you!' Jackie glared up at her, still doubled over.

'I'm fine,' Anaïs answered. 'Where's my mother?' Her eyes flitted about nervously.

'Her and Andi are looking after the client.'

'Is she okay? I saw her lying on the ground.'

'She's fine. Just a little shook up, that's all,' Jackie reassured her.

'Luckily the guy doesn't hit as hard as you.' Siobhan gave her a playful nudge.

'I still can't believe I did it.' Anaïs looked down, still in shock. 'I thought he was coming for me. I hid under the desk. Then I realised he was going to the lift, and I knew I had to do something. I didn't have a choice…' The words came out in a torrent, adrenaline pumping through her veins as the magnitude of what she'd done suddenly hit her.

'Breathe, honey, you did good.' Jackie took the bloodstained bottle from her hand. 'Here.' She passed it to Siobhan. 'Take this and get Carla and the team to come and clean this mess up.'

'I wasn't even meant to be here.' Anaïs frowned. 'My mother's going to be so angry.'

'Don't worry about your mother. I'll deal with her.' Jackie squeezed her shoulder and smiled warmly.

23

The following evening Liam arrived at the same spot, beneath the bridge, and found William waiting for him, his broad silhouette shrouded in shadows, his bearded face barely visible in the gloom. 'Good evening, Mr Patterson, I'm glad you could make it.' He stepped into the light and smiled. 'How did it go last night?'

'There's a few things I want to talk to you about first,' Liam replied, his face set in a determined grimace.

'Everything okay? You look a little tense.'

'What do you know about Cecilia Davenport?' Liam stared into the man's eyes, hoping for a reaction. But he didn't flinch.

'I don't know who that is.'

'She's my source. The one who sent me the emails about the women. If it wasn't for her, I would have never written those articles for *Capital Conspiracies*.'

'And how do you know it was her?'

'That's not important. I just do. And now she's gone missing. Just as you magically appear, full of information. It's all very convenient, don't you think?'

'I've already told you how I know so much. Karen was heavily involved with these women.'

'Yes. Yes. Your dear Karen. What's her surname by the way? Can I look her up? Maybe she'll talk to me.'

'Haven't you listened to a word I've told you?' William finally lost his patience, his cloak of calmness momentarily slipping. 'If these women think you're getting too close, they'll do the same to you that they did to me. Probably worse. I don't want Karen implicated in any of this either. When you publish your story, I want her omitted. That's my only stipulation. Do we have a deal?'

'Fine,' Liam muttered. 'Although that still doesn't explain Cecilia Davenport's disappearance, or the fact that it happened now while all this shit is going on.'

'It was probably the women. Think about it… they're all wealthy and successful with connections all over the city. If you managed to find out who sent those emails, I'm pretty sure they could too. And if she was a threat, it would make sense for them to silence her before she could say anymore. This thing is bigger than you can imagine. Believe me. And these women are ruthless. They're not going to let anyone, or anything, get in their way. You, me, Cecilia Davenport, Karen… we're all expendable.'

'I guess that's plausible.' Liam shifted uneasily. Uncertainty creeping into his thoughts.

'What did you see last night?' William asked.

'It was exactly like you said…' Liam hesitated for a moment. Still unsure whether he could trust the man. But he knew, right now, he didn't have a choice. '…The man and woman turned up at seven-thirty. But only one left. I got pictures too. And some video footage.' He held up his phone and showed the man. 'They're not very clear, but it's something.'

'This is really good. Did you find out where the girl went afterwards?'

'I did. I followed her back to Holland Park. Her name's Alessandra Valera, and she's a model at the Dubois Modelling Agency in Chelsea, which just happens to be owned by a rich middle-aged woman called Diane Dubois. I'd put money on her being one of the Vixens.'

'That's fantastic!' William slapped him on the shoulder. 'You really are a journalist. I knew you were the right man for the job. Karen also mentioned a woman named Diane, along with two others called Jackie and Andréa. As far as I can tell they're the ringleaders of this operation.'

'Seriously? This is huge!' Liam's excitement grew. Front-page headlines, TV interviews and big money offers flashing before his eyes. 'If we do a little digging into Diane Dubois, I'm sure we can find out who the others are too.'

'I agree. But we need to be patient. If we push too hard, we'll scare them off. And then we'll be back to square one.'

'What else do you know?' Liam asked. 'You promised you'd tell me everything if I did this for you.'

'I did. And I'm a man of my word.' William nodded. 'I know the restaurant is a front for their organisation and there's a whole underground complex hidden beneath it. I also know they've set up some kind of charity to launder the money they make.'

'How do they make money from killing these men?' Liam looked confused.

'According to Karen, they sell the experience to other rich women, who torture the men to fulfil some kind of sick fantasy.'

'That's insane! So what do we do now?'

'Those pictures and videos you took are a good start, but they don't really show anything incriminating. We need more. We also need documents, bank statements and witnesses who are willing to testify against these women.'

'But how are we going to do all that?'

'We need to get inside somehow.'

'That's going to be pretty tough, especially if it's a female-only organisation.'

'True. But there's always a way.' William gave him a knowing smile. 'The first thing I want you to do is visit the Dubois Agency in the morning and speak to Diane Dubois herself. See what you can find out. But be subtle. Try not to spook her too much. Not yet anyway.'

'And how am I meant to do that?' Liam gave him an incredulous look. 'You want me to just waltz in there and be like, "Hey, Ms Dubois, how's it hanging? You fancy going for a coffee and telling me about all the evil shit you and your gals are up to inside the Sacred Lotus restaurant?"'

'That wouldn't be very subtle, now, would it?' William leant on the railings and looked out at the water.

'Then what do you suggest?'

'Use those journalistic instincts of yours. They've served you well so far. That's enough for tonight. I have to go.' William spun away and approached the stone steps that led back up to the bridge.

'Wait!' Liam shouted.

'What is it?' William stopped and looked over his shoulder.

'When will I see you again?'

'I have to go away for a few days. I'll be in touch.'

'Care to elaborate?'

'All in good time… Goodnight, Mr Patterson.' William strode up the steps and disappeared from view.

24

The next morning Liam got off the tube in Sloane Square and made his way towards the Dubois Modelling Agency on King's Road.

The area was already busy, and he passed a long queue of people waiting to enter a new exhibition at the Saatchi Gallery before reaching the entrance to the agency a little further down.

He stopped in front of the glass doors and checked his reflection. Then he took a deep breath and stepped into a lavish hallway, lined with guilt-silver mirrors, tropical plants and white-marble sculptures of beautiful naked women.

He strolled along a red carpet, glancing around in awe at the opulent surroundings, and approached a young receptionist who sat behind a tall white desk, the company's double-D logo hanging behind her.

'Hi.' He smiled nervously, taken aback by how pretty she was. It seemed everyone involved in this agency was out of his league, even the statues.

'Can I help you?' she asked, her face blank, although he caught a hint of disdain in her dark sultry eyes, which were accentuated by black-rimmed glasses and thick, perfectly-sculpted eyebrows.

'Uh, yes, sorry. I'm here to see Ms Dubois.'

'Do you have an appointment?' She looked him up and down. Her stern expression and tightly pulled-back hair reminded him of the bitchy girls at school who used to tease him for his nervous stutter and the braces he wore until he was seventeen, and he felt his confidence draining.

'Well, not officially, no. But I spoke to one of the models that works here a few days ago – Alessandra Valera – and she told me it would be okay to pop in for a chat.'

'Ms Dubois isn't in the habit of doing *chats*.' The receptionist almost spat out the last word. 'And we rarely represent men unless they are extraordinary.' She smirked.

'No, no, I don't want to be a model. I'm clearly way too short for that.' He gave a weak laugh. 'I'm a reporter from *The London Beacon* newspaper. I was hoping to do a feature on Ms Dubois for our weekly lifestyle supplement.'

'Here's a card. Email us your details, and we'll get back to you as soon as possible.' She held out a brilliant-white business card with the Dubois logo embossed on the front in silver leaf.

'Can't you just tell her I'm here now?' he replied, desperation seeping into his voice as his plan unravelled.

'I'm sorry. But as I said–'

'It's okay, Lizzy. I can spare a few minutes to chat with – Mr Patterson, is it?' An immaculately-dressed older woman appeared from a narrow corridor on Liam's right, and he instantly recognised her from the pictures he'd seen online.

'I'm sorry, Ms Dubois. I didn't want to disturb you unnecessarily.' The smug look disappeared from the receptionist's face in an instant.

'Hi, yes, that's right, It's Liam Patterson. I'm from *The London Beacon* newspaper.' He stepped forward to greet her. 'It's a pleasure to meet you, Ms Dubois.'

'Likewise,' she replied, looking into his eyes, her chin raised with a haughty air. 'Let's go through to my office, shall we.'

Liam followed her inside and she slipped behind a long marble desk.

'Take a seat, please.'

'Nice garden.' Liam looked over her shoulder at an enclosed courtyard, which was designed to look like a Japanese garden, its narrow streams filled with koi carp, while a wooden pagoda stood in the middle, accessible by a crescent bridge.

'Ah, yes, I like to go out there sometimes when I need a break from the madness.' She smiled. 'We also use it for photoshoots on occasion. So how can I help you today, Mr Patterson? I'm sure you didn't come here to talk about gardening.'

'Ha! No, of course not. I was actually hoping to do a feature on you and your agency for our weekly lifestyle supplement. One of your models, Alessandra, said you might be interested.'

'Did she now? And where did you two lovebirds meet?'

'Oh! No, no, it's not like that.' Liam squirmed in his seat, his cheeks flushing. 'I was just in Holland Park the other night, and I returned a scarf she dropped. That's all.'

'That's very noble of you.' She laced her fingers together and rested them on the table. 'I have to say, Mr Patterson, you do look awfully familiar. Have we met before?'

'I, uh, I don't think so.'

'Hmm, maybe I've read some of your articles. Who did you work for before *The London Beacon?*'

'I was with, umm, an online magazine called *Capital Conspiracies.* I did a few other bits and pieces here and there too. I doubt you'd have seen any of it though...' His eyes flitted about nervously, not sure where to look.

'Ah, yes! You wrote about those Vixens, didn't you? One of the girls here showed it to me. I'm not very good with technology, you see. It was very entertaining, I must say. Although a little over the top for my tastes.'

'You don't believe it?' Liam asked.

'It doesn't matter whether I believe it or not. However, if it is true, then good on them, I say. Far too many men get away with committing violent crimes against women. The statistics really are quite shocking.'

'That's true. All the more reason to do something about it.' He gave her a knowing look.

'Indeed. So tell me, how does one go from writing fanciful articles about groups of women hunting criminals to doing interviews for lifestyle supplements? Seems like quite the jump, wouldn't you say?'

'I guess.' He wanted to come back with a clever reply, but she had him tongue-tied.

'So what were you doing in Holland Park on Monday evening? You never said. Do you live there too? I'd have thought it was a little expensive for a young, up-and-coming journalist.'

'No, I live near Old Kent Road. I was just meeting a friend for drinks after going for a meal in Charing Cross. I went to this great little Thai restaurant called The Sacred Lotus. Have you heard of it?' He looked into the woman's eyes, his mouth tilting up ever so slightly. Now it was his turn to go on the offensive.

'I don't believe I have.' She leaned back, unclasping her hands and putting them under the table. 'I'm not one for Asian food. It doesn't agree with me.'

'You should try it. It's an interesting place.' He smiled, his confidence growing as he sensed her unease.

'I'm sorry, Mr Patterson, but I've just remembered, I have an appointment with my chiropractor at midday. Can we reschedule for next week? I'll have more time then, and we can discuss this supplement you mentioned in more detail.' She smiled back, although Liam could see a subtle difference in her demeanour, and a hint of fear in her eyes.

'That would be great. And thank you again for taking the time to speak with me. I really appreciate it. I hope your back isn't too bad,' he added, getting up.

'Oh, it's fine. Just an old horse-riding injury. When you get to my age, everything becomes a bit of a pain.' She ushered him out of the room and closed the door in his face.

*

Diane watched the young man leave the building on the CCTV cameras. Then she pressed the intercom and buzzed through to the receptionist on the front desk.

'Lizzy, can you get me Caroline Burnett on the line, please.'

A moment later the Chief Editor of *The London Beacon* newspaper was transferred through to her office.

'Hi, Diane, this is a pleasant surprise. How are you? Is everything okay?'

'No, Caroline. Everything is not okay,' Diane answered sharply, skipping the pleasantries. 'Quite the opposite actually. I'd like you to explain to me why Liam Patterson was just in my office, snooping around and asking questions about things he shouldn't know anything about?'

'I'm not sure I understand. He told me he was going to Hackney Downs this morning to follow up on an anti-social behaviour story I gave him.'

'Well I can assure you he was just here.' Diane tapped her fingers on the table. 'You were meant to be keeping an eye on him! Do you realise what's at stake here? We can't afford to be lax. Not now—'

'Look, Diane! I did you a huge favour hiring this guy. I mean he's not exactly winning any awards for his writing skills. And I've been keeping him busy doing all kinds of mundane tasks. But I can't watch over him twenty-four-seven. I'm an editor, not a babysitter. What's he been saying, anyway?'

'He's been speaking to one of my girls, and he also mentioned the restaurant. He knows more than we thought. We can't underestimate him anymore. We need to take this threat seriously, otherwise it could blow up in our faces.'

'Yes. I understand. Who do you think told him? Do you think it was Cecilia Davenport again?'

'I don't think so. Andi's team hacked into her email account a few days ago, and she hasn't sent anymore messages. Unless they're communicating another way. It doesn't feel right though. I've tried reaching out to her numerous times to bury the hatchet, for want of a better phrase, but she hasn't replied to any of my calls or messages. And now she's disappeared off the face of the planet.'

'You did keep all her money after she got cold feet. I wouldn't blame her for being a little upset.'

'True. But five-hundred-thousand pounds is a dip in the ocean to her. And she knew what she was getting herself into. She signed the contract. I knew I should have never let her be a client. She's always been a loose cannon.'

'Do you think her disappearance has anything to do with all this?'

'I hope not. It does seem quite ominous though. Especially after what happened to her poor chauffeur.'

'So what do you want me to do about Liam Patterson? I can have a chat with him if you like. Try to find out what he's up to – I'd be discreet, of course.'

'No. We don't want to make him even more suspicious than he already is. Let him think he's in control for now – I have a better idea.' Diane spun around in her chair and gazed out of the window.

'Care to elaborate?'

'Not yet. Just leave it with me for now. I'll be in touch.' She hung up, and then wrote a group message to Jackie, Andréa and Siobhan, telling them to meet her in the underground complex at midnight, and to use the emergency entrance located on the South Bank side of the river. Now that Liam Patterson knew about the restaurant, it wasn't safe to be seen going in and out of there.

After sending it, she wrote a separate message to Anaïs. Then she put on her coat and sunglasses and walked to a little French café in Sloane Square. She sat outside and ordered a large glass of white wine.

25

It was almost midnight and Anaïs waited in the shadows of the Hungerford Bridge, hunkering down under the metal stairwell that led to the walkway above. The bridge connected South Bank with Charring Cross and Westminster on the other side of the river, and she gazed out at the promenade, the usual procession of tourists, street performers and food stalls long gone, the whole place eerily empty, until a lone figure suddenly appeared. Their slim body was silhouetted by the towering lights of the London Eye, which soared in the background, but Anaïs could tell straightaway from the distinctive swagger that it was Siobhan, and she stepped out to greet her.

'Hey, hey, Nay-Nay. What are you doing here?' Siobhan called out.

'My mother asked me to come tonight. She didn't say why though.'

They embraced, a frisson of energy passing between them as their bodies came together briefly.

'Ah, that's grand.' Siobhan's hands lingered on Anaïs' forearms. 'So, you're finally joining the inner circle.'

'I hope so. Although it wouldn't have happened if you hadn't given me the chance to come down there and show them what I can do.' She looked into Siobhan's eyes and suddenly felt an overwhelming urge to kiss her.

Siobhan gazed back, her lips slightly pursed, and Anaïs knew she was thinking the same thing.

'Let's go down. I don't want to be late to my first official meeting.' She stepped back, breaking the spell.

'Fine.' Siobhan frowned, poking out her lower lip. She stepped over to a glass lift, which was built into the side of the bridge, and tapped a plastic card against the control panel.

A moment later the empty carriage travelled up a transparent shaft to the top of the bridge, and it was replaced by an identical carriage which appeared from below.

They quickly got in, making sure there was nobody else around, and it went back down.

It opened onto a cylindrical corridor and Siobhan led Anaïs to the boardroom, flinging open the doors and striding inside.

'Ah! Nice of you to finally join us,' Diane called out.

'Sorry, maman.' Anaïs sat down quickly while Siobhan slumped into a chair on the opposite side of the table.

'Now that we're all here, we can begin.' Diane glanced around the table. 'So… I had surprise visitor to the agency today. A certain Mr Patterson. Apparently, he wanted to interview me for *The London Beacon's* lifestyle supplement.'

'What did he really want?' Jackie asked.

'He didn't say, but he knows about the restaurant. That's why I asked you to use the other entrance. He's also spoken to Alessandra. It would seem he followed her back to Holland Park on Monday evening.'

'Shit! I say we bring him in and sell him to the highest bidder,' Siobhan spoke up.

'You can't do that!' Andréa cried. 'He's an innocent man.'

'Aye, an innocent man who's going to get all of us sent to prison if we don't do something about it.'

'I hate to say it, but she's right,' Jackie spoke up. 'The boy's trouble.'

'Woo! Look at that. The two of us actually agreeing on something.' Siobhan grinned.

'You're not seriously condoning this?' Andréa looked horrified. 'Have you forgotten why we started this organisation in the first place? It's to punish criminals who've committed crimes against women and children. Not kill innocent people because they don't fit our agenda.'

'I'm just saying we have a problem that needs dealing with.' Jackie shrugged.

'What if we just pay him off,' Andréa suggested. 'I'm sure a couple of thousand pounds would keep him quiet. What do they call it in the movies, hush money?'

'Okay, Don Corle-Andi!' Siobhan let out a little chuckle. 'And what if he, ah, turns ah-down our generous offa?'

'Then we think of something else.'

'Wrong! Then our cover's blown, and we're really screwed. Unless, of course, we kill him, like I suggested.'

'We're not going to kill him,' Diane interrupted. 'Or pay him off. I have a plan much more befitting of our womanly wiles. We're ladies, after all.' She smirked. 'Let's not forget that.'

'What's your plan, maman?' Anaïs asked, finally mustering the courage to speak up.

'I thought about using one of the other girls at the agency to seduce him, but he knows too much, especially after he spoke to Alessandra. If a beautiful model suddenly showed an interest in him, he'd see it a mile off. That's why I invited you here tonight.'

'Geez. Thanks a bunch.' Anaïs frowned.

'No, no, I didn't mean it like that, ma puce. You're as beautiful as any girl who works for me. But they're all six-foot, size-four catwalk models while your beauty is much more subtle and wholesome, like the pretty girl next door.'

'Well saved, Dee-Dee,' Siobhan called out. 'You could live next door to me anytime.' She winked at Anaïs.

'Please don't call me that.' Diane glared at her.

'So what do you want the wholesome hobbit next door to do exactly?' Anaïs asked.

'Please don't be upset, darling. I thought you wanted to be more involved?'

'I do. I was just kidding.'

'Good. Because I need you to get as close to Liam Patterson as you can. Then I want to find out everything he knows and, more importantly, who he's working with. We know Cecilia Davenport sent him the original emails, but I'm convinced there's somebody else involved too. Somebody a lot more dangerous. It's time the hunted became the hunters.'

'Or huntresses.' Siobhan grinned.

'But what if he recognises her?' Andréa asked.

'I don't see why he would,' Diane replied. 'Nobody knows that Ani is involved down here, not even our closest contacts, and she's rarely at the agency either. She usually works from home.'

'And I deleted all my social media accounts after the attack,' Anaïs added. 'So even if he did somehow manage to find an old picture of me, I'd probably be super young, or have green hair in it.'

'So what are we going to do about next week?' Jackie asked. 'We have a target under surveillance, and an American businesswoman in Hampstead has already put down a very big deposit.'

'We go ahead as usual.' Diane glanced around the table with a determined stare. 'We don't want to show any weakness. Although, from now on we should only use the South Bank entrance. It's not safe to be seen near the restaurant.'

'I agree.' Jackie nodded.

'What about you?' Diane asked Andréa.

'I guess it makes sense to continue as normal. Although none of this is particularly normal...' her voice trailed off.

'Then it's settled.'

'What about me, maman? Anaïs asked. 'How am I meant to get close to this Liam guy without him finding out who I am?'

'I'll talk to you later, ma puce.' Diane gave her a warm smile. 'And I'll message the rest of you tomorrow. That's enough excitement for tonight, I think.'

Diane led them out of the room and Anaïs grabbed Siobhan by the elbow.

'You okay?' Siobhan looked confused.

'Wait for me in your office. I need to talk to you about something.' She strode off before Siobhan could reply and got in the lift with the others.

When they reached the riverside, Jackie and Andréa went their separate ways while Anaïs followed her mother to her car.

'Dammit!' she muttered, coming to a stop.

'What's wrong, ma puce?'

'I left my bag downstairs.' Anaïs rolled her eyes.

'Just run down and get it. I'll wait for you in the car.'

'No, it's okay. You go ahead. I'll get an Uber.'

'Don't be silly. It'll cost a fortune to get one all the way home.'

'It's fine, honestly. I could do with a little fresh air anyway, and I like to stroll along the river when it's quiet like this.'

'It's very late, darling. You don't know who's lurking about at this time.'

'I'll only walk as far as Vauxhall Bridge, and then I'll get a taxi from there, I promise.'

'Okay.' Diane sighed. 'But be careful. You're still my little girl no matter how many men you wallop over the head.'

'I will. And thanks again for believing in me.' Anaïs kissed her on either cheek, then went back to the bridge.

A few minutes later, she reached Siobhan's office and stopped outside. The door was slightly ajar, and she lingered for a moment, suddenly overcome with nerves, before pushing it open and stepping inside.

'Hey, I was starting to think there was some weirdo loitering out there.' Siobhan sat up on the leather couch at the far side of the room. 'I wasn't sure what you wanted, so I cracked open a bottle of wine, just in case. I mean everything's better with a little vino, right? Apart from bungee jumping. I made that mistake once in New Zealand.' She laughed, although Anaïs could see that she was nervous too.

'I think you know what I want...' Anaïs crossed the room, her hips swaying seductively with each step, although inside her heart was beating like a frightened rabbit caught in the headlights of a hurtling truck.

'Where's your mother?'

'She's gone home. It's just the two of us.'

She stopped at the edge of the coffee table and picked up a glass of wine, taking a long sip to calm her nerves. Then she lowered herself onto the couch, leaving a small gap between them.

'You seem different tonight.' Siobhan scooched across until their knees touched. 'I've wanted this for so long.' She reached out and stroked Anaïs' hair. 'You can't believe how many times I've dreamt about it. About you. You're the most amazing girl I've ever met, Ani.' She leant closer–

Anaïs pushed her away and shook her head, a mischievous smile on her lips.

'Stay there.' She put down the glass and climbed on top of Siobhan, trapping her against the back of the couch. 'I'm in charge. Is that understood?' She put her hands around Siobhan's slender hips, surprised at how soft they felt.

'Yes,' Siobhan replied breathlessly, her green eyes aflame in the reflection of Anaïs' auburn hair.

'Good.' She grinned, her confidence growing.

'Ani, I–'

'Shhh...' She put her finger to Siobhan's mouth, touching her soft pink lips. 'No more talking. And keep your hands where I can see them, otherwise there'll be trouble, okay?'

Siobhan nodded and Anaïs slid deeper into her lap, their bodies melding together. 'I've wanted it too.' She slipped her hands behind Siobhan's neck. 'I just didn't want to admit it.' She felt the heat radiating from Siobhan's jeans, and she rotated her hips softly, her body tingling with anticipation.

Siobhan groaned below her. Pushing back excitedly. Seeking out Anaïs' lips with hers.

'Not yet.' Anaïs shook her head. 'Good things come to those who wait…'

She continued to rotate her hips, grinding harder, and Siobhan matched her rhythm, both of them completely in synch, a single throbbing entity consumed by a mutual desire.

'Kiss me, please! I need it,' Siobhan murmured, her pupils dilated, a feverish longing in her eyes, but Anaïs stayed tantalisingly out of reach, squeezing her thighs tighter. 'Fuck! I want you so badly.' Siobhan's groans grew louder, more urgent.

'Me too.' Anaïs leaned closer, their lips almost touching. She wanted to prolong the agony. To make Siobhan beg. But it was too much. Her body ached for release. Needed it.

Suddenly her eyes glazed over, all the dark thoughts and inhibitions dissolving into a bright-white light, and she grabbed Siobhan's collar, kissing her with a ferociousness that took them both by
surprise.

This time there was no stopping, their bodies writhing together like wild animals, grabbing and tearing at each other's clothes with reckless abandon…

26

Liam arrived to work on Monday morning and was summoned straight to Caroline Burnett's office.

'*Meow* you've gone and done it.' Pete spun on his chair and winked as he walked by.

'What are you talking about?' Liam glared at him, not in the mood for any banter after tossing and turning all night, his frustration growing as he waited for William to contact him again. The man had seemingly vanished into thin air, and Liam wasn't sure whether he'd ditched him, or the women had gotten their hands on him.

'*Mewl* see…' Pete took a sip of coffee and leaned back. 'Ahh, that's a purr-fect cuppa.'

Liam shook his head and carried on walking, a chorus of meows ringing out in the background as the stern-faced woman beckoned him inside.

'Morning, Ms Burnett.' He opened the door and hovered nervously in the entrance.

'Stop lingering like a bad smell and come in, please, Mr Patterson,' she said, motioning for him to sit down.

He quickly closed the door and took a seat.

'So…' She picked up a small pile of papers and shuffled them until the edges aligned. 'I've been reading through your articles and you're doing very well – I'm impressed. I've had good feedback from the rest of the team too. It seems like you're fitting in very well here at *The Beacon*.'

'Really?' His eyes lit up, taken aback by her unexpected praise.

'Yes. *Really*. Don't look so surprised.'

'Thank you so much, Ms Burnett. That means a lot coming from you.'

'So how was your first week?'

'It's been great. I'm really enjoying it.'

'I'm glad to hear it.' She gave a thin-lipped smile. 'I actually have something I'd like you to do for me. It's quite an important assignment. The workload will be quite heavy, but I'm sure you can manage it.'

'Of course. Anything,' Liam stared at her expectantly, barely able to contain his excitement. His mind suddenly awash with all the potential opportunities.

'Very good. I'd like you to cover Rosie for the next few weeks. She's going overseas to visit family, and I need someone to keep our Reviews section up-to-date.'

'Reviews?' His body sagged.

'Yes: theatres, cafes, restaurants, social events… that kind of thing.'

'Uh-huh.' He forced a smile.

'Don't worry, Mr Patterson, your time will come, but right now this will be a good experience for you. I'll get Hannah to email you Rosie's itinerary. It contains everything you need. I suggest you start with the new cat café on Lower Marsh Street. I hear they do great carrot cake.'

'So that's what Pete was on about,' he muttered.

'A little advice: ignore Peter Waring and his gang of jokers. It'll only get worse if they see they're getting to you. Oh, and one other thing. We have a new intern starting today. I'd like you to take them under your wing and show them the ropes. They can help with the extra workload too. I take it that won't be a problem?'

'Of course not,' he said as enthusiastically as possible.

'Ah, here they are – perfect timing.' She glanced over his shoulder, and he followed her gaze as a beautiful, auburn-haired girl entered the office. She wore a white rollneck jumper and checked trousers, the tight-fitting outfit showing off her slim, yet curvy, figure, and he almost fell out of his chair.

The girl was smiling and chatting with Hannah, but his heart sank when Pete sauntered over to join them.

*

Anaïs listened politely to the smarmy Australian journalist as he leaned on a pillar, telling her all about his newest front-page story.

Who did this guy think he was? She glanced over his shoulder and breathed a sigh of relief when Caroline Burnett came out of her office with a young, blonde-haired man in tow.

'Good morning, Laura, it's lovely to meet you properly.' The woman smiled, using the fake name Anaïs and her mother had decided on over the weekend. 'Don't you have some work to be getting on with, Mr Waring?' She glanced at the man, who wandered off with a parting grin.

'It's a pleasure to meet you too, Ms Burnett. And thank you again for this opportunity,' Anaïs replied, the two women exchanging a knowing look.

'Please, call me Caroline. And this is Liam Patterson.' She stepped aside. 'Mr Patterson, meet Laura Miller, our newest intern. She recently graduated from Goldsmiths University and she's eager to become a journalist. Hopefully here at *The Beacon* if we're lucky enough to keep her.'

'Nice to meet you, Laura.' He held out his hand, flashing a boyish smile.

'You too, Liam.' She held his gaze for a moment, wondering how this man, who only looked a few years older than herself, could be the same man who was threatening to destroy their whole organisation. There was an innocence about him, and a gentleness in his soft blue eyes, that instantly disarmed her.

'Mr Patterson will be looking after you this week and showing you how everything works around here.'

Caroline Burnett walked away, leaving them alone, and an awkward silence descended.

'So…' he finally spoke up. How about we go and get a coffee first. Then I can show you around the rest of the place.'

'Sounds good to me,' Anaïs replied. 'Hannah mentioned something about going to a cat café later?'

'Oh, yeah, I've got to go and review it, which means you'll be coming too. Sorry, it's not something more exciting.'

'Getting paid to drink coffee and play with cats sounds pretty exciting to me.' She smiled.

'I guess it doesn't sound so bad when you put it like that.' He led her into the kitchen and turned on the coffee machine. 'What would you like?'

'Just a black coffee, please.'

'Hardcore, aye.' He pressed some buttons, and then turned to face her. 'So how long have you been in London for?'

'Uh, I think you're missing something there…' She looked over his shoulder.

He stared at her in confusion for a second, then followed her gaze and saw coffee gushing from the machine and spilling out onto the countertop.

'Shit!' He jabbed the buttons, desperately trying to stop the machine, but the coffee kept coming, cascading down to the floor like a waterfall. 'How the hell do you turn this bloody thing off?' He ran to the sink and grabbed a cloth. Rushing back as the machine finally came to a stop.

Anaïs stifled a laugh and went to help him, using some kitchen roll to mop up the spilled liquid from the counter.

'Thanks,' he muttered, glancing up from his hands and knees.

'That's okay.' She giggled. 'Maybe we should wait until we get to the café.'

They arrived an hour or so later, after taking the tube from London Bridge to Waterloo, and stopped outside the little café, which was hidden away behind the station on a pedestrianised street full of market stalls and independent shops.

'This place is so cute.' Anaïs gazed at the café's colourful ramshackle exterior, its narrow entrance overflowing with a hotchpotch of mismatched potted plants, garden ornaments and wildflowers, while a long wooden bench ran along the length of the glass-fronted facade. 'And look at the name!' She glanced up at a wonky sign, hanging above a striped canopy, which said 'Barista-Cats' in elegant lettering.

'Go and stand in front of the window. I need some pictures.' He held up his phone and she quickly stepped out of the way, worried her cover might get blown.

'Come on, I need some for the review. What's the point of having a glamourous assistant if you can't see them?'

'I think you should focus on the café. Nobody's interested in seeing me.'

'I'm sure they would be. I'd like to see you – in the paper, I mean,' he quickly added.

'I appreciate the compliment, but it's still a no,' she said, stepping aside.

'Fine. I'll let you off this time.' He took a few pictures. Then they went inside.

'Oh my God! I love it in here!' Anaïs looked around the busy room at the assortment of rickety old tables and chairs, everyone desperately trying to get the attention of the cats, who wandered around disinterestedly, or slept on the colourful cushions dotted around the floor, while jazz music played in the background and the waiting staff delivered trays filled with tea, coffee, sandwiches and cakes.

'It is pretty cool actually. And it smells like my auntie Nelly's house in the Yorkshire Dales,' he said, following her towards the counter.

'That's cute. Do you go there often?'

'She passed away a few years ago, but I used to go there every summer when I was a kid. She made the best poached eggs, and her bread pudding was amazing! Her secret was she cooked everything in lard.'

'Aww, I'm sorry. She sounded like a great lady.'

'She was. And she lived till she was ninety-five.'

'Wow! That's impressive. It must have been the lard.'

'Ha! Yeah, maybe. I love these pictures.' Liam pointed at the funny cat portraits hanging on the walls, which portrayed famous figures in feline form.

'Aww! The Charlie Chaplin one is adorable,' Anaïs replied. 'Look at that little moustache and the big hat. Do you think they'd notice if I stole it?'

'Not if I create a diversion.' He grinned. 'Make sure you get the Elvis one for me while you're at it.'

A waitress showed them to a table, next to an old piano. Two tabbies slept on top and a little black-and-white one sat on the stool in front, cleaning itself, and she handed them a menu each.

'Order whatever you like,' Liam said. 'Ms Burnett gave me the company card. There's got to be some perks to this, right?'

'There's plenty of perks if you ask me.' Anaïs held out her finger and the cat on the stool touched it inquisitively with their nose before going back to its cleaning ritual. 'Also, if we're going to review this place properly, we need to try everything. Including all those cakes on the counter,' she added with a mischievous grin.

'I agree. It would be unprofessional not to. I'll work it off in the gym later.'

'You don't need to worry about.' She gazed at his toned arms and chest, which were clearly visible through his snug-fitting shirt.

'Uh, thanks,' he replied, his cheeks flushing as the waitress returned to take their order.

'So did you grow up in Yorkshire?'

'Yep, in a little village outside Sheffield. How about you?'

'My dad was in the military,' she lied, using the fake story she'd concocted to go with the fake name, 'so we lived all over: Germany, Cyprus, Dubai. Even North Wales for a few years.'

'That must have been interesting. Did you learn any other languages?'

'Not really, I was always in International schools, although do you know what they call a microwave in Welsh?'

'Nope, what do they call it?'

'Popty ping,' she said, breaking into a fit of giggles.

'That can't be true.' He laughed.

'Google it if you don't believe me.'

'Maybe I will.' He took out his phone but put it on the table when the waitress reappeared with their order.

'Ooh, I'm excited.' Anaïs clapped her hands together, eyeing up the cakes. 'So where did you go after Sheffield?' She picked up a knife and cut off a big piece of chocolate brownie.

'I went to Loughborough Uni to study Sports Science. Then I moved to London after I graduated and got a job in the marketing department of a betting firm.'

So how did you end up getting into journalism?' She shoved the whole piece in her mouth.

'I ended up doing some copywriting and I really enjoyed it. Then it kinda just went from there.' He shrugged.

'Mmm, this is so good,' she mumbled.

'I can see.' He raised an eyebrow.

'I'm sorry. I'm not making a very good first impression, am I?' She took a sip of coffee to wash it down.

'You're not doing too badly. Although I'm not sure if I'd hire you yet.' He grinned.

'Luckily for me, it's not up to you.' She grinned back. 'So did you go straight from the betting place to *The Beacon*?'

'Uh, no, I did some freelance stuff for an online magazine called *Capital Conspiracies*.'

'That sounds like fun. What kind of stuff?' she asked casually, not wanting to push him too soon.

He was about to answer when his phone lit up and a message preview appeared from someone called William. She read the text discreetly and saw that the man wanted Liam to go to the restaurant that evening at seven-thirty, and then meet him the following night. But Liam snatched up the phone before she could see where.

'Sorry, work stuff. I won't be a sec.'

'That's okay. I need to go to the bathroom anyway.'

When she got there, she messaged her mother. Then she checked herself in the mirror, applying some lip gloss and rearranging her hair.

'All done?' she asked, returning to the table a few minutes later.

'Yep. Sorry about that. I'm always getting messages and emails about stories and stuff. It's never ending.' He rolled his eyes.

'So… you were telling me about this *Capital Conspiracies* magazine…' She leaned forward a little, hoping he might mention the stories about her mother and the others.

'Oh, yeah, it wasn't that serious, to be honest. We'd pretty much publish anything: UFO sightings, secret societies, mysterious disappearances, Government plots to control the public – people always love a good ghost story too. I remember one about a pub in Whitechapel. The owners were convinced it was haunted by Jack the Ripper. A couple of colleagues actually spent the night there, but they didn't see anything. Anyway, what about you? What made you want to be a journalist?'

'I've always loved writing. One day I'd love to be a murder mystery novelist like Agatha Christie.'

'Agatha Christie – really?'

'Yes. What's wrong with that? I love a good whodunnit, and she's the Queen.'

'Fair enough. She's just a little old school, I guess. I thought you would have been more into *Twilight* or *Fifty Shades of Grey.*'

'Ha! *Fifty Shades* was so lame. I mean what girl doesn't like a good spanking?' She grinned, revelling in his shocked expression. 'I have read all the *Twilights*, though. And I've seen all the movies too – I'm definitely team Edward. Has anyone ever told you, you look a little bit like Robert Pattinson?'

'A few people.' He gave an embarrassed shrug. 'I don't see it though.'

'Well, it's definitely a compliment. So where in London do you live?'

'I'm just off Old Kent Road. It's not the greatest area, but I'm right next to Burgess Park, which is pretty nice. Especially in the summer. And I have my own place, which is always a bonus. What about you?'

'I live with a couple of girls in Stratford,' she replied, sticking to her story.

The waitress came back over and they ordered two more coffees and another two slices of cake.

For the next hour, Anaïs subtly flirted, prying as much as she could, while Liam stared at her the whole time, hanging onto her every word. She could tell he was interested, and she liked the feeling. But every time she got a little carried away, she quickly reminded herself why she was there.

Finally they headed back to *The Beacon*, and they spent the rest of the afternoon working on the article together…

27

Anaïs arrived home just after six-thirty and raced upstairs, kicking off her shoes and squeezing out of the tight-fitting outfit she'd worn all day. There was no way she'd get back to the restaurant before seven-thirty if she used public transport, so she ordered an Uber and put on a pair of loose-fitting black cargo pants and an oversized dark-green hoodie. She completed the transformation by tying up her hair and putting on a baseball cap. Then she stepped over to the mirror.

'Okay, I officially look like a teenage boy.'

She grabbed a pair of Converse trainers from the wardrobe and went downstairs.

The taxi arrived a few minutes later, and she got in the back, reading a text from Siobhan:

Hey, Ani, just checking in after your first day at the new job! Hope it went well and you learnt something useful? I still can't stop thinking about last week in my office. It was so amazing! I was just wondering if you wanted to come and watch the show again tonight? No pressure if you can't. It would be nice to see you though. And I have more wine. Obvs ;) Shiv X

When she finished reading, her mouth turned up ever so slightly. She knew that Siobhan only ever called her Ani when she was trying to be sincere, which wasn't very often, and a vision of the night they spent together flashed through her mind. She'd never been touched like that by a woman before, or anyone for that matter, and she'd enjoyed every moment of it. Although she was still confused about what it all meant. She knew she wanted to do it again though. The memory turning her on as she shuffled discreetly on the backseat.

She thought about replying but decided to wait until later. Instead she put her phone away and gazed out the window.

Soon the taxi reached the city, and she got out opposite the main entrance to Charring Cross station. She glanced around, making sure the coast was clear. Then she headed towards the restaurant.

When the building came into view, she pulled up her hood and lowered the cap, but there was still no sign of Liam.

Where was he? She checked her phone and saw that it was almost seven-thirty.

Maybe he was running late. She carried on walking and almost jumped out of her skin when she spotted him crouched behind a wall. Luckily, he was writing in a little notebook and didn't notice her.

Thinking fast, she shoved her hands in her pockets and hunched forward, passing by as casually as possible.

She ducked into the back entrance of an office block a little further along the street and hid in the doorway.

A moment later Alessandra strolled along the pavement in a flowing white dress, cropped denim jacket and brown-leather cowboy boots, while an older man strode confidently beside her in a tailored suit, his dark hair slicked back, like a character from *The Wolf on Wall Street*.

Anaïs watched them enter the restaurant and, even though she couldn't see him, she knew Liam was watching too.

A moment later the waitress changed the sign on the door, and he emerged from his hiding place and crossed the road. He peered through the glass and took out his phone, but Anaïs stayed where she was, curious to see what he did next. Then, to her surprise, he approached the door and casually slipped inside.

Panicking, she raced across the road, ready to burst in there and distract him somehow. But when she got closer, she saw him talking to Queen Bea in the middle of the dining room. The woman blocked his way in a figure-hugging red evening gown, and Anaïs slowed down, crouching beside the door and peeking inside.

'I ask you 'gen. What you doing here? Sign say closed!' Queen Bea put on a strong Thai accent, jabbing her finger in the air. 'Can't you read?'

'I, uh, yes, I know. I'm sorry, I just really needed to use the bathroom.' Liam gave an embarrassed smile. 'I'll be quick, I promise.' He tried to sidestep past her.

'No payee, no pee-pee!' She cut him off. 'This is business. Not bathroom. And we cu-lu-osed. You no understand English?'

'I don't mind buying a bottle of water or a beer to go.'

'Bathroom back that way.' Queen Bea pointed over his shoulder. 'Hurry! Chop, chop, pretty boy.' She waved him off impatiently, and he turned away in defeat.

With the situation seemingly under control, Anaïs crept away and hid behind a parked van on the adjacent street. She peered over the bonnet and watched as Liam left the restaurant a few minutes later and went back to his original spot across the road.

Alessandra breezed outside shortly after and Liam followed her towards the station.

Anaïs waited a moment, and then scurried after them. Making sure to keep her distance.

Up ahead Alessandra reached the main street and jumped into a waiting taxi, leaving Liam to stare in disbelief, while Anaïs grinned in the background.

Now what are you going to do, Mr Patterson? She watched as he jotted something in his notebook, then entered the station.

She definitely needed to get her hands on that book at some point. She followed him inside, and they both got on the next train that came along.

A few stops later, Liam got off at Waterloo and jumped onto the 172 bus to Brockley. He went up the stairs, and Anaïs leapt on at the last minute, taking a seat below.

At the next stop, two teenage boys got on and strutted along the aisle, flopping down opposite her and spreading their legs wide. She could see them eyeing her up and down, but she tried to ignore it.

'Hey, girl, where you going?' The taller boy on the right rested his elbows on the back of the seat and smirked.

'Just going to meet some friends,' she said curtly, keeping her eyes on the stairs.

'They as cute as you?'

Anaïs looked at him but didn't bother replying.

'You got some serious Billie Eilish vibes going on there, girl. Anyone ever told you that? I bet you thicc under those baggy clothes too.' He slid forward, his knees almost touching hers. 'You hiding some funky hair underneath that cap too?'

'Not anymore.' She resisted the urge to move back. Not wanting to show any weakness. 'How old are you?' she asked.

'I'm sweet sixteen, baby.' He winked at her, licking his lips. 'You and your cute friends should come and kick it with me and my boys. We heading there now, and we got us some of the ole *good good*. You feel me?' He tapped his pocket.

'The what what?' She looked at him in confusion.

'Cannabis, baby.' He laughed. 'How old'a you anyway?'

'Twenty-one,' she said, peering out the window as the bus drove down Old Kent Road.

'Wow! You old, girl. I swear you were like fifteen or something.' He laughed, nudging his friend.

To her relief, Liam got off at the next stop, and she ran down the aisle, leaving the two boys behind. Thankfully, they stayed in their seats, and she followed him across the road and into the park on the other side.

The dark tree-lined path reminded her of Epping Forest and the memories came flooding back like a dark torrent. Not now. She admonished herself. Although she couldn't help momentarily slowing down as the familiar visions engulfed her.

Taking a deep breath, she glanced around and saw that the park was still busy despite the fading light, with plenty of dog walkers, runners and groups of kids roaming about. The crowds soothed her, and she spotted Liam approaching a large lake up ahead.

He crossed the narrow bridge running through the middle of it, and she gave chase, pursuing him right through to the other side of the park, where he entered a rundown block of flats.

A few seconds later, a light came on in one of the first-floor windows, and she saw a figure crossing the room.

'There you are,' she murmured, watching in surprise as he took off his shirt, revealing a smooth chiselled torso.

She looked away in embarrassment, feeling like a voyeur, but she couldn't help stealing a furtive glance. A thrill of desire passing through her as he continued to stand there, bare-chested. Then, without warning, he stepped forward and looked straight at her.

Shit! She stood rooted to the spot, not sure what to do, her eyes darting around, looking for the best escape route. Then she saw him turn away, and she sprinted towards the main road, jumping on the first bus that came along. Thankfully it pulled away before he appeared, and she slumped down onto an empty seat, breathing heavily.

She got off at Waterloo station and took the short walk to South Bank, using the lift to access the underground complex. She snuck through the winding corridors unseen and went straight to Siobhan's office, knocking on the door and slipping inside.

'Hey, sorry for coming unannounced, but I didn't want my mother and the others to know I was here.'

'Hey, Ani. What's wrong? You okay?' Siobhan came around the desk and gave her a hug.

'I think I've messed up, Shiv.' Her voice wavered and tears filled her eyes.

'Hey!' Siobhan lifted her chin and wiped them away. 'Whatever's happened, we can fix it.'

'Liam saw me spying on him,' she blurted, taking a step back.

'When?'

'Just now. I followed him back to his flat after the restaurant, and he caught me red handed,' she replied, leaving out the part about him being topless.

'Did you have that cap and hood on the whole time?'

'Yeah.'

'Then you're grand. There's no way he would have recognised you in that get up. Especially in the dark.'

'Are you sure?' She sniffed.

'Hundred-percent. He was probably wondering why Justin Bieber was wandering around south-east London.'

'Ha! Very funny.' Anaïs forced a smile.

'I'm glad you came here.' Siobhan pulled her closer and kissed her delicately on the lips.

'Me too.' Anaïs gazed up at her. 'Do we have time?' Her eyes widened, and she bit her lower lip.

'The client's not due to arrive for another hour or so.'

'Perfect.' Anaïs took off the cap and shook out her hair.'

'There's my beautiful girl.' Siobhan took her hand and led her to the couch...

When they finished, Anaïs stood up and quietly put her clothes back on.

'You okay, Ani?' Siobhan asked softly.

'Yeah, I'm just a little overwhelmed. It's been an intense day.'

'You don't have to stick around. Just slip back out the way you came, and nobody will ever know you were here.'

'But what about the show?'

'Ah, don't worry, you won't be missing much. After last week's shambles and everything else that's going on at the moment, Jackie and your mum want to keep things simple. The client didn't have any elaborate requests either, so it's going to be a pretty boring one – in, out, shake his little dead body all about.' Siobhan let out a little chuckle.

'You sure?'

'Would I lie to you?'

'Probably.'

'Aye, you're right.' Siobhan grinned. 'But this time I'm telling the truth, I promise.'

'Who's the guy in the suit anyway?' Anaïs stood up and put the cap back on.

'Some piece of shit lawyer at a big American law firm in St Paul's. Apparently, he's raped two of the girls working there. He's one of the partners though, so they're terrified of saying anything.'

'So how did we find out about it?'

'We got some intel from one of our trusted contacts.' Siobhan gave her a knowing look but didn't say anymore.

'Okay, I'll go home then. Tomorrow's going to be another big day.'

'Wait a sec…' Siobhan got up, and they kissed again by the door.

'Good-night, Shiv.' Anaïs pulled away with a tired smile and made her way back up to the riverside.

When she got outside, she took out her phone, wishing she could call Jenny or another friend and talk to them about Siobhan and Liam, and all the conflicting thoughts whirring about in her head, but she'd pushed them all away after the attack; the last she'd heard, Jenny was in Paris doing an internship at a big fashion house.

She'd have to figure it out herself somehow. She put in her earphones with a weary sigh and made her way home.

28

The next morning Anaïs rode the lift up to the offices of *The London Beacon*, her heart racing, a large knot developing in her stomach. Despite Siobhan's reassurances the previous evening, she was still worried that Liam had recognised her outside his flat, and she prepared herself for a potential showdown. But when she went inside and saw his beaming smile all her worries dissolved.

'Morning.' She smiled back. 'Someone's in a good mood today.'

'I was just looking at the list of potential places to visit today. We don't have to do them in any particular order, so the world's our oyster, or the city, to be more accurate.'

'Can I see?' She pulled a chair over and sat next to him.

'Aw, isn't this cute.' Pete stood over them. 'Can I get you lovebirds a coffee? Maybe a little partition to give you some privacy too? We have some in the storeroom for meetings and interviews.'

'Maybe you should get one for you and your ego,' Anaïs shot back.

'Ha! I like this one. You're a little firecracker, aren't ya? You're going to fit in well here. You could teach Patterson, here, a thing or two about banter. So… coffee?'

'We're good, thanks. We're about to go to the Tate Modern to review a new exhibition,' Anaïs replied.

'Are we?' Liam looked at her.

'Yes, I decided for us. Is that okay?'

'Fine by me.'

'Well, we know who wears the trousers in this relationship.' Pete grinned. 'I'll leave you guys to it. I don't want to distract you from your important work,' he added, wandering off.

'That guy's such a prick.' Anaïs rolled her eyes.

'You get used to him. So, shall we go?'

'We shall indeed.'

They walked along the river to the gallery, grabbing a takeaway coffee on the way, and sat on a bench outside, taking in the early-morning sun and waiting for it to open.

'Everything okay?' Anaïs asked. 'You've barely spoken since we left the office. If you didn't want to go to an art gallery, you should have said.' She smiled, trying to cheer him up.

'It's not that. I'm just tired, that's all. I didn't sleep very well last night.'

'How come?'

He let out a long sigh. 'Have you ever felt like you're being followed?'

'I guess so,' she said, her panic rising. Maybe he'd seen her after all, and he was just waiting until they were alone to bring it up.

'You're going to think I'm crazy, but I swear someone followed me home last night.'

'Really? Where did you go?'

'Uh, I just went for a beer with some mates in Camden,' he said a little sheepishly.

'Maybe someone took a liking to you in the bar.' She grinned. 'Was it a girl?'

'Ha! I don't think so. They were wearing a baseball cap and a hoodie so it could have been anyone.'

'Hmm, that is strange,' she said, relief flooding over her. 'Why do you think somebody would want to follow you?'

'God knows. It was probably some nutjob from *Capital Conspiracies*. I still get emails from people about all kinds of crazy stuff, but I haven't had time to reply since I started at *The Beacon*. Maybe they're pissed off at me for ignoring them. Or maybe it's somebody I wrote about.'

'Like who?' She hoped he would open up and mention the article about her mother and the others. But before he could answer, the doors to the gallery opened, and he stood up.

'Someone's eager all of the sudden.'

'I thought you wanted to see this thing?'

'I do. Come on, let's go. You're going to love it. Dorothea Tanning is amazing. Her stuff is so strange and surreal, but it's really beautiful too,' she added, leading him inside.

'Seems like we don't need to go in. You've already reviewed it. How about we go to the pub instead?' He grinned.

'Nuh-uh, you're not getting out of it that easily. I need to educate you, you uncultured Northman!'

'That's true, I am a bit of a Wildling when it comes to art.'

'Wildling?' She looked confused.

'Yes. *Wildling*. Haven't you ever seen *Game of Thrones*?'

'I'm not really into fantasy stuff.'

'Please tell me you've seen *Lord of the Rings,* at least?'

'Nope. I have watched all the *Harry Potters* though. And *Narnia,* of course.'

'I mean, I can't lie, I do love *Harry Potter* too, but that's beside the point.'

'How about we compromise? I show you some amazing artwork, and then you can show me *Lord of the Thrones,* deal?'

'That's not what it's called!' He scowled at her.

'I know. I'm just teasing.'

They walked through a narrow foyer and into a huge hallway which ran the whole length of the cavernous building. She'd been here many times before, but it was still one of her favourite places in London, the vast space reminding her of a futuristic aircraft hangar with its exposed metalwork crisscrossing the towering glass ceiling above.

'This place is amazing, isn't it?' She craned her neck and pirouetted on the spot, taking it all in.

'Yeah, it's cool. Imagine sneaking in here after it closes with a skateboard or a BMX. You could have so much fun.'

'I didn't have you down as a skateboarder.' She stopped and faced him.

'I don't do it much anymore. I've still got my board though. I think it's tucked away under my bed somewhere. Maybe I'll dust it off again one day.'

'Can you teach me? I've always wanted to do one of those little flippy things.'

'It's called a kickflip.' He smiled. 'And I'd be happy to give you some tips. Not that I'm that great myself. Maybe we can go to the park one weekend?'

Why did he have to be so cute? A wave of guilt suddenly washed over her. It would be so much easier if he was a dick, like Pete, or most of the guys in London, for that matter.

'I'd like that.' She gave him the most cheerful smile she could muster before quickly turning away. 'Come on, the lift's down this way.'

They got out on the third floor and Liam approached the two uniformed gallery assistants standing at the entrance.

'Hi, I phoned earlier. My name's Liam Patterson. I'm a journalist at *The London Beacon* newspaper, and this is Laura Miller.' He motioned to Anaïs who took a moment to register, almost forgetting the fake name she was using. 'We're here to do a review of your new exhibition,' he continued, not seeming to notice. 'I was told there would be someone here to meet us.'

One of the assistants glanced at their clipboard.

'Ah, yes, here you are. Let me just go and tell Ms Wermuth that you've arrived.'

They returned a moment later with a blonde-haired woman in her early-to-mid-thirties.

'Hallo! Hallo! Liam and Laura, right?' she said in a strong German accent.

'Yep, that's us,' he replied.

'Great. It's so nice to meet you both. I'm Monika. I'm one of the curators here at the Tate. I'll be showing you around today.'

She wore thick dark-rimmed glasses and a black trouser suit, which Anaïs thought would have looked authoritarian on most people. But she had a big smile and a round-yet-pretty face, which instantly softened her.

'Thank you so much for doing this, Monika,' Anaïs spoke up. 'We're really excited to see it.'

'Super! I'm excited to show you. This is one of my favourite exhibitions. Come, let's get started…' She led them inside, gliding past the fast-forming queue.

'I feel like a VIP,' Anaïs whispered as they entered the first room and gazed around in wonder at the myriad of surreal and dreamlike paintings adorning the walls.

'This one is so creepy.' Liam stared at a painting of two strange young girls, who stood in a gloomy dilapidated hallway. One of them had long curly hair that rose impossibly into the air, like she was possessed by some kind of evil spirit; whilst the other leaned in a doorway half naked as a giant sunflower lay wilting nearby, its oversized petals tumbling down the stairs.

'Ah, yes, this one is great.' Monika smiled. 'It's called *Eine Kleine Nachtmusik.*'

'What does it mean?' Anaïs asked.

'*A Little Night Music* – it's named after one of Mozart's compositions. It's one of her most famous works.'

'It's like something out of a horror movie.' Liam kept staring.

'Ya. That's not too far from the truth actually. She was heavily influenced by gothic novels and fairy tales that she read as a child. Come, let's keep going. If you think this is weird, just wait...'

'Can I take a picture first?' Liam took out his phone and directed Monika to stand beside the painting.

'Wait! Let's get Laura in too.'

'No, you're fine. Nobody wants to see me. You're the curator.' Anaïs waved her off.

'Please, I insist. I won't do it without you.'

Anaïs shuffled over reluctantly and stood on the other side of the painting.

'You're cutting me out of that later,' she whispered to Liam after he'd taken it.

For the next thirty-minutes or so, Monika guided them through the rest of the rooms, which were filled with a mixture of paintings, along with life-sized fabric sculptures of strange human-like creatures, entwined in a variety of sensual and erotically-charged poses that had Anaïs and Liam exchanging sly glances and smirking at each other like a couple of naughty schoolchildren.

'Come, there's one more thing I want to show you.'

Monika led them into a dark room where a jittery old film was being projected onto the wall. All the benches were taken so Anaïs stood next to Liam at the back. It seemed to her like everyone was holding their breath collectively as the nightmarish imagery played out on the screen in front of them, each scene cutting jaggedly from one weird scenario to the next.

Soon it showed a frightened woman trapped inside a dark dungeon while an evil-looking man spied on her from the shadows. He crept ever closer, like *Nosferatu* in the old black-and-white vampire movies from the 1920s, and Anaïs shuffled uncomfortably.

'Jesus! This is super freaky!' Liam let out a little chuckle as sinister music played in the background, building the tension even further. But Anaïs ignored him, her body rigid, her chest tightening with every step the man took. Suddenly she was transported back to Epping Forest, and she reached out, clasping Liam's hand like her life depended on it.

'You okay?' he asked, looking at her with a mixture of shock and confusion.

'Uh, yeah, sorry, I…' She let go of his hand and looked down at the floor.

'It's okay. I think we've seen enough anyway.' He led her out of the room and she breathed a sigh of relief.

'That was intense, ya?' Monika joined them outside.

'Just a bit,' Anaïs replied, still feeling a little unsettled.

'If you like, I can take you up to our members' café on the sixth floor. The views are amazing, and the coffee isn't bad either.'

They took the lift up and Monika flashed her ID at the uniformed woman standing at the entrance to the café.

Once they were inside, she led them to a free table close to the panoramic windows that overlooked the river and the rest of the city below.

'I have to go back down to my office, I'm afraid, but I hope you both enjoyed.'

'It was great,' Liam replied. 'Thanks for showing us around.'

'Yes, thank you so much, Monika. It was amazing,' Anaïs added.

'I'm so pleased. Enjoy the coffee and the views and, most importantly, make sure you give us a glowing review.' She let out a little laugh and then walked away.

They put their jackets down and stepped over to the windows, looking out at the London Eye, Big Ben and the Houses of Parliament.

'I'll go and get the coffee,' Liam said. 'Do you want anything else?'

'What do you think?' She grinned.

'Don't tell me. You want cake, right?'

'Correct. Get me the biggest, most chocolatey thing they have. That was too intense!'

'I thought you liked it?'

'I did. It was just a lot to process. Kinda like stepping into the mind of a deranged and beautiful genius, and then getting lost in their imagination. I wouldn't want to rush back in a hurry.'

'I like that. Maybe you should write the review this time.'

'Let's do it together.' She smiled. 'But first things first – Cake!'

'Okay, okay, I'll go and order before you turn into one of those freaky-haired little girls.'

'If you don't hurry up, I'll be scarier than all those girls put together.' She narrowed her eyes and scowled at him before breaking into a fit of giggles.

'Can I go to the bathroom first?'

'Hmm, I'll allow it. Just this once.'

She waited for him to disappear. Then she rifled through his jacket, which hung on the back of the chair.

Suddenly she found the little notebook in the breast pocket and she flicked through the pages, stopping on some kind of messy spider-diagram.

'What's this…?' she murmured, seeing the word 'VIXENS' circled in the middle of the page along with a bunch of other names, including her mother's, Cecilia Davenport's, Alessandra's and a full list of models from the agency. She also saw Jackie and Andréa's first names along with William's and someone called Karen, with 'Nurse' written in brackets beside her. But there was no sign of herself or Siobhan.

Wary of the time, she scanned through the next few pages, but they were just filled with notes about his surveillance of the restaurant along with lots of doodles and what looked like potential headlines for when he exposed the women.

There had to be something else… She kept searching, her eyes flitting about nervously, until she finally found what she was looking for on the back-page:

Meet William at Tower Bridge. Tuesday night. 11pm.

'Gotcha,' she muttered. But what side of the bridge did he mean?

Suddenly she caught a glimpse of him returning, and she shoved the notebook back in the jacket and quickly sat down.

'You okay?' He arrived at the table a few seconds later and gave her a quizzical look.

'Yeah, I'm fine,' she said as calmly as possible. 'Why'd you ask?'

'You just look a bit flustered, that's all.'

'I've just been looking around. Aren't you forgetting something?' she said, subtly changing the subject.

'What do you mean?'

'I mean where's my coffee and cake?'

'That's why I came back here. I forgot my wallet.' He reached into his jacket and took it out.

'Shall we get it to go?'

'That's probably a good idea. If we stay here any longer Caroline Burnett will be sending out a search party.'

'Oh! I just remembered. I'm meeting some friends for drinks later near the office. It won't be until nine-ish, but I thought I'd stick around and get a pizza or something first. You're welcome to come join. If you don't have any plans, that is.'

'Nope, I'm free.'

'Great. You can choose this time,' she said, deciding to keep him close until he went to meet the mysterious William.

29

When they got back to *The Beacon*, the office was a hive of activity after it had been leaked that the funeral of Cecilia Davenport's driver and apparent lover, Yannis Constantinou, would be held the following morning, somewhere in north London. The family of the deceased man wanted to keep the location a secret, but Pete was determined to get an exclusive, and he had everyone running around, barking orders, as the clock ticked.

Finally Anaïs and Liam left together just after seven-thirty, both of them exhausted.

'You still want to grab something to eat?' she asked.

'Yeah, I'm starving. I thought you were meeting friends at nine though.'

'I cancelled earlier when Pete had us ringing every cemetery and funeral directors in north London. I thought we were going to be spending the whole night there.'

'Me too. You've got to give it to him though, he might be a bit of a dick sometimes, but when he gets a whiff of a story he really goes after it. I guess that's why he's on the front page every day while I'm buried in the middle doing mindless reviews and writing stories about dog shit.' He let out a sardonic laugh.

'Hey! Don't be so hard on yourself. You're a good journalist. And one day you'll be a great one. I've got no doubts about it.' Anaïs smiled. 'Now, where do you want to go? It's your turn to choose, remember?'

'Okay. Let's get pizza. There's a good place near the station.'

'Perfect. Lead the way…'

When they got there, a waiter sat them down and they ordered two beers.

'What topping you going for?' Liam asked.

'Hmm, probably the mushroom and truffle,' she replied, scanning through the menu.

'Very fancy.'

'I'm a sophisticated lady, I'll have you know.'

'I don't doubt it. I think I'll go for the double pepperoni and spiced honey.'

'That sounds good too. Maybe I'll try some of yours.'

'Will you now?'

'You can have some of mine too. Fair's fair. Ooh! Have you seen the Nutella pizza ring with ice cream?' Her eyes lit up.

'Really?' He shook his head as the waiter brought over the beers and took their order.

They spent the next few hours eating, drinking and chatting like two old friends who'd known each other a lifetime; not a couple of strangers that only met the day before.

When they finally left, Liam walked her to the station entrance.

'Well, here we are,' he said, stopping outside and gazing down at her. The harsh light from inside bathed one side of his face in a warm glow, giving his blonde hair a rich golden hue, while the other was cloaked in shadow.

'Yep, here we are...' She stared back.

'I really enjoyed tonight–' He started to say, when a burly guy with a backpack barged past, almost knocking them both off the curb. 'Whoa! Watch where you're going, mate!' Liam shouted, reaching out instinctively and wrapping his arm around Anaïs' waist.

'Thanks,' she said, putting her hand on his shoulder to steady herself.

'You okay?' The fire in his eyes faded as he looked down at her.

'Uh, yeah, I'm fine,' she said nervously, suddenly realising how close they were. It had been a long time since she'd felt safe in a man's arms. Not since she was a little girl with her father, and she melted into his embrace.

'Laura, I–' He leant closer, their mouths hovering inches apart.

Anaïs felt his grip tightening and she pulled away, his lips brushing against her cheek for a tantalising moment before disappearing.

'I'm sorry, but I should go. I'll see you in work tomorrow.' She smiled sadly, then rushed off before he had a chance to reply.

She walked through the station and glanced over her shoulder, surprised to see that he was still standing in the same spot, staring at her like an abandoned puppy, his hands thrust in his pockets, as people rushed by in either direction.

She hesitated for a moment, a big part of her wanting to go back, but she tore her eyes away and carried on walking.

She planned to double-back and follow him, but when she looked again, he'd disappeared.

Panicking, she rushed back and peered through the crowds, trying to spot him. To her relief she caught a glimpse of him walking on the other side of the road in the direction of Tower Bridge, and she crossed over.

Soon he reached the riverside and sat on the long stone steps that ran along the edge of the manicured lawns of Potters Fields Park. Anaïs circled around and hid in the shadows of the trees that lined the pathway behind.

She watched as he sat motionless, seemingly deep in thought, while people walked along the promenade in either direction, the area still busy despite the late hour. She wondered what was going through his mind. A big part of her wished she could go and sit next to him, like the other couples cosied up nearby, but she knew that would never be possible.

Finally he stood back up and approached the bridge.

She waited a moment then stepped out from the cover of the trees and followed him up the stone steps that led to the walkway above.

He crossed over, descending the dark stairwell on the other side, and she hesitated at the top, making sure he'd disappeared, before creeping down.

This side of the river was much quieter and she heard muffled voices coming from below. She edged closer, the voices becoming clearer with each careful step, and listened intently from behind the wall as a man with a deep American accent spoke:

'...I'm sorry, but I told you I had to go away for a few days. It couldn't be helped...'

'Well, when you've been off gallivanting, God knows where, I've been running around the city, trying to keep track of everything by myself...'

Anaïs recognised Liam's voice, and she peeked out, trying to catch a glimpse of them. But it was even darker under the bridge and the man had his back to her. She could see that he was taller than Liam though, with long unruly hair that cascaded down over his broad-looking shoulders. She guessed from the flecks of grey and the gravelly tone in his voice that he must have been in his mid-to-late thirties, maybe older. She willed him to turn around so she could get a better look at him

'So what did you find out?' the man asked, seemingly unperturbed by Liam's outburst.

'Not much. The girl disappeared before I could follow her.'

'What do you mean, *disappeared*?'

'I mean she jumped in a taxi and zoomed off before I had a chance to do anything.'

'Hmm, interesting... Was it the same girl?'

'Yes. But there's something else...' Liam paused for a moment.

'What is it?'

'I'm pretty sure someone was following me.'

'What makes you say that?'

'I saw someone in a dark-green hoodie and a baseball cap at the restaurant. Then I saw them again outside my flat when I got home.'

'Did you get a look at them at all?'

'Nope, it could have been anyone.'

'I guess it would make sense for them to have you followed. This is good though–'

'How the hell is this good?' Liam snapped.

'Because it means they're worried. They know you're onto them and they're running scared. And when people are scared, they make mistakes.'

'I'm the one who's fucking scared! Last night they were outside my window. Tonight they could be inside my flat! This isn't what I signed up for.'

'I told you from the beginning they were dangerous. But we're close. You just need to stay strong and keep doing what you're doing.'

'That's easy for you to say. You're not the one being followed by a potential assassin. I think we should just write the story now before something bad happens. With all the names we've got and everything else it should be enough to expose them.'

'I don't want to just expose them. I want to destroy them! These women are parasites. They're a threat to mankind as we know it. Haven't you learned anything?' The man raised his voice for the first time and Anaïs cowered a little, his words sending a shiver down her spine.

'Isn't that a bit extreme?' Liam replied, his voice a little shaky.

It was clear to Anaïs now that the bigger, older man was in charge and not Liam.

'Maybe. Maybe not...' The man's voice returned to normal. 'Do you have anything else?'

Liam took out his phone and held it up.

'I got this picture of them entering the restaurant. Now we have evidence of two men going inside with the same girl. If we can find out their names, these women are screwed. This one looks like some kind of hotshot businessman. I'm sure there'll be plenty of people wondering why he's suddenly disappeared. I got a few others inside the restaurant too.'

The man took the phone off Liam and swiped through it. The soft light from the screen illuminated his face, and Anaïs could see that he had a thick black beard, speckled with grey, but she couldn't make out anything else.

'These are really good. Who are these two?' he asked, turning the phone to Liam.

'I took that one in the Tate Modern earlier. It's for a review.'

'Review?'

'Yup, my editor wanted me to cover for someone while they're away.'

'Are these women your colleagues?'

'The blonde lady in the glasses is one of the curators, but the other girl is an intern at *The Beacon*.'

'She's very pretty.'

'Yeah, her name's Laura. I only met her yesterday, but it feels like we've known each other for years. I know it sounds stupid, but I've never felt this way about a girl before.' Liam let out a long sigh and Anaïs couldn't help smiling, a warm glow spreading through her body despite the situation she was in.

'It's not stupid,' the man replied. 'I felt the same way about Karen. Time is immaterial. When you know, you know.'

Anaïs' ears pricked at the mention of the woman's name, but before he could say anything else, her phone started to ring. The harsh sound cut through the still air like an air raid siren, and she jabbed at the screen, desperately trying to turn it off, as Siobhan's name flashed up on the screen.

Suddenly she heard footsteps approaching, and she thrust the phone into her pocket, scurrying up the steps as fast as she could and side-stepping around the railings at top.

She raced up the hill, passing the Tower of London on her left and heading towards the tube station behind it.

Soon the brightly-lit entrance came into view and she glanced over her shoulder. Luckily there was no sign of Liam or the other man, and she finally slowed down, putting her hands on her hips and breathing heavily.

'Jesus! When did I get so unfit?' She took one more look around and then messaged her mother. This William was clearly out to get them, and they needed to act fast.

30

The women shuffled into the boardroom the following morning just before six am and took a seat around the table.

'What's that big furball doing here?' Jackie glowered at Chewie who sat on the floor beside Andréa, panting loudly. 'I thought we said no pets.'

'He usually goes for his walk at this time. If I left him at home, he'd be howling the house down and terrorising poor Artoo and Deetoo.'

'If I don't get some caffeine soon, I'll be the one howling.'

'He can wait in my office if you like,' Siobhan spoke up. 'He's always welcome.'

'Why are you being so helpful this morning, missy?' Jackie eyed her suspiciously.

'Because Chewie's the only boy I'd ever invite into my boudoir.' She winked.

'Now that's just plain wrong.'

'Okay, let's get started.' Diane interrupted. 'First of all, thank you all for coming at such short notice. I appreciate it's very early, but Anaïs has some grave news which we need to discuss right away. Ani, would you like to tell everyone what you told me last night?'

'Are you sure you want me to do it?' she asked, expecting her mother to relay the information for her.

'Yes. Go ahead, darling.'

She cleared her throat, glancing nervously around the table, then told them everything, from following Liam on Monday night, to looking through his notebook at the Tate Modern and seeing all the names and information written inside, including the mysterious nurse, Karen, right through to his meeting with William under the bridge and the man's threat to destroy them...

155

'Motherfuckers!' Siobhan slammed her fist on the table when Anaïs finally finished. 'I've had enough of this shite. We need to stop these fucking pricks once and for all!'

'Whoa, whoa, whoa. Hold your horses!' Jackie raised her hand. 'If we go in all guns blazing, it'll end badly for everyone.'

'Jackie's right. We need to think very carefully about our next move.' Diane's eyes moved slowly around the table. 'Whoever this William is, he seems to have a vendetta against us for some reason. We need to come up with a plan to deal with him as discreetly as possible. To begin with we need to suspend all our operations. That means cancelling all upcoming clients and ceasing surveillance of all future targets. And we need to pull you out of *The Beacon* too, ma puce.'

'But I'm so close. And I've found out so much over the last few days. You can't make me stop now.'

'I'm sorry, Ani, but my mind's made up. This isn't a game. This man could be a serial killer or a rapist, or some kind of deranged madman for all we know. I'm not going to risk you getting hurt. Not again. I'd never forgive myself.'

'Look, I know things are pretty shitty right now, but we can't just sit back and do nothing and hope this all just blows over,' Siobhan spoke up. 'Think about it for a second... Ani said he knows all your names, but not mine, right?' she glanced at Anaïs.

'Right. I didn't see mine or yours.'

'Okay, if we take this little notebook of your man's for gospel, then he doesn't have a clue that I exist. Which means I can do whatever I want...'

'What are you suggesting?' Jackie asked.

'It sounds like these two jokers are having regular meetings underneath Tower Bridge in the wee twilight hours, which is a pretty dark and secluded spot. I know because I've frequented it on a few occasions, myself, if you know what I mean?' She grinned.

'Just get to your point,' Jackie shook her head.

'Okay, okay, so instead of shutting everything down, how about we keep it all going as normal, and we get Ani to find out when their next meeting is scheduled. Then I go with her and take out Big Willie when he's least expecting it.'

'We've been through this already,' Andréa spoke up. 'We don't just go around killing innocent people. We only target men who've done unspeakable things, and then its only to raise money to support women who need it. Otherwise we're no better than the monsters we're trying to stop.'

'With all due respect, Andi, this guy is talking about destroying us. He doesn't sound like an upstanding citizen to me. Also, I don't know about youse lot, but I can't help thinking it's a little bit dodgy that right after Cecilia Davenport disappears, this William fella suddenly shows up on the scene.'

'That's a pretty big leap,' Diane spoke up. 'But I can't say the thought hasn't crossed my mind too.'

'Okay. Say we go with your idea,' Jackie replied. 'How are you going to take out a guy who's six-foot-something and built like a rugby player all by yourself?'

'I've dealt with bigger guys before.' Siobhan gave her a smug look. 'And anyway I'll have the element of surprise. He'll be at the bottom of the river with a knife in his back before he knows what's happening.'

'What about Liam?' Anaïs asked.

'I can wear a balaclava or something and just rough him up a bit. Tell him to back off. As long as he doesn't try anything stupid, there's no need to kill him too.'

'It's risky, but it could work,' Jackie said. 'Although what's to stop Liam going to the authorities later? From what Ani says, he has plenty of evidence. Maybe not enough to get a conviction, but definitely enough to drag our names through the mud and damage our reputations irreparably. Especially Diane's. And once the police and the press do some digging, it won't take them long to find out mine and Andi's full names too.'

'So, what do you suggest?' Diane asked.

'I think if we're going to do this, we have to kill them both. I don't see what other choice we have—'

'No!' Anaïs shook her head vehemently. 'Liam's innocent. He's just ambitious, that's all. This William is just using him to do his dirty work. I've spent the last few days with him and he's one of the nicest people I've ever met. He's just blinded by the thought of getting a front page exclusive and being a famous journalist. That's not a crime, is it?'

'I know you're fond of him, honey. But as the Lord says, pride cometh before a fall. And this boy's ambition will be the downfall of us all, unless we put a stop to it now. I don't take any pleasure in saying this, but what other choice do we have? Right now our future is in his hands, and I for one am terrified.'

Anaïs expected Andréa or her mother to disagree, but they remained silent.

'Isn't anybody going to say anything?' She looked around in desperation. 'You can't all think this is a good idea?'

'Why do you care so much?' Siobhan asked, her eyes narrowing. 'You barely know the guy. He's probably putting the nice-guy act on to try and get in your pants.'

'I don't need to know him. Sometimes you can just tell. And what you're all suggesting is just wrong, plain and simple. Andi! Surely you don't agree with this?' Anaïs stared at her, hoping she'd offer some support.

'I'm sorry, Ani...' She looked away, her voice trailing off.

Anaïs slumped down in her chair, deflated, angry, desperately trying to think of a way to solve the problem without harming Liam, but she was stumped.

'Wait! I've got an idea.' She suddenly leaped up.

'What is it, ma puce?'

'Okay, hear me out... Liam and I have this list of events and places to review for the paper. One of them is a new Spanish restaurant on St Katherine's Docks. I could get him to go there Friday night, and then get him drunk and take him back to his flat – I'm pretty sure he wouldn't take too much convincing – and he lives alone, so there wouldn't be any flatmates to worry about. Then when we get there I could drug him like Queeny does to the men upstairs and search through all his stuff. He must have an address for William somewhere, or a phone number or email address. We could find the guy that way, couldn't we?' She glanced at Jackie and Andréa. Her expression full of hope.

'It's definitely possible.' Jackie nodded.

'I agree,' Andréa added. 'I'm sure one of my team could do it if we gave them enough information.'

'See...' Anaïs looked at her mother. 'If we can find out who this William is. Then we can go to where he lives and deal with him there. Far away from Liam and anyone else who might get hurt. And if he disappears without an explanation, maybe Liam will think the guy was just a fraud and he'll lose interest in the story.'

'I don't know, ma puce. It all seems so dangerous–'

'And do you really think Liam will just give up? If you do, you're more naïve than I thought.' Siobhan let out a contemptuous huff.

'You said a few minutes ago that we didn't need to kill him.'

'I was just trying to be polite. Not to hurt your fragile feelings. I always thought we should kill them both.'

Anaïs glared at her for a moment, then looked away in disgust.

'Think about it...' she said to the others. 'With William gone and Cecilia Davenport still missing, Liam would be all on his own and there'd be nobody to corroborate his story.'

'What about all the pictures and videos he took?' Siobhan asked. 'Not to mention the notebook.'

For a moment, Anaïs fell silent. Then an idea struck her: 'That's easy. When I'm at his flat, I can delete everything on his phone and laptop. Then I can steal the notebook and destroy it. That way if it ever comes down to it, it would be his word against ours.'

'That's a good idea, I like it. It'd be a lot cleaner too.' Jackie spoke up. 'I think it could really work. Good job, honey.'

'Thanks,' Anaïs replied, suddenly feeling much more positive.

'How are you going to get into them?' Siobhan persisted. 'He's bound to have passwords and stuff.'

'I'll figure it out. And if worse comes to worst, I'll just take everything and we can wipe it here, then return it to him later. Anything else you want to bring up?' She smiled through gritted teeth but Siobhan remained silent, her face set in an angry grimace.

'Okay...' Diane let out a heavy sigh. 'We'll try it your way, but I'd prefer you did it tonight. The sooner we do this, the better. Do you think that's possible?'

'It's a little short notice, but I don't see why not. I just need to check that Liam doesn't have any other plans. Although I'm sure I can persuade him to rearrange if he has.'

'Okay, good. But if this doesn't work, we go with our initial plan. Is that understood?'

'Yes, maman.'

Liam's life was in her hands now. The thought weighed heavy on her chest, like a free-diver sinking deeper and deeper into a dark underwater trench not knowing what awaited them on the other end, and she took a deep gulp.

'Very well. I have to learn to trust you. You're not a little girl anymore, I can see that.' Diane smiled. 'Well, ladies, we have a lot of work to do.' She glanced around the table. 'Once this meeting's over, I'll speak to my contact at the hospital to see if they know anything about this Karen woman. Jackie, take Ani upstairs to get some of the tranquilizing pouches from Beatrix and give her your taser just in case. And, Ani, as soon as you've spoken to Liam, let us know.'

'Yes, maman.' She nodded.

'Okay, good–'

'What about me?' Siobhan asked.

'Right now, there's not much you can do apart from keep your phone on and be ready for anything. That goes for you too, Andi. This is unchartered territory. Anything could happen. But if we stick together, we'll get through it. Like we always do.' Diane straightened her back and thrust out her chin defiantly. 'Right, if nobody else has any questions, let's get on with it.'

Anaïs followed Jackie out of the room, heading for the restaurant, but just as she was about to leave, Siobhan pulled her back.

'Hey, Nay-Nay, can I talk to you for a sec?' she asked quietly, keeping hold of her arm.

'What do you want?' Anaïs glared at her.

'I don't know what you're looking so pissy about. I'm the one who should be annoyed.'

'What are you talking about?'

'You know what I'm talking about – What the hell's going on with you and this Liam fella? And don't tell me nothing. It's so fucking obvious! We all saw it. Even Chewie!' She let out a sardonic laugh.

'I'm just doing my job. Maybe you should try doing yours a little better. You almost got me caught last night with that stupid phone-call. You're lucky I didn't tell everyone.'

'You should have. I don't care. And if they had caught you, we could have stopped this stupid plan and just killed them both like I suggested.'

'Nice,' Anaïs replied, shaking her head and smiling sarcastically. 'Oh, and another thing, if anything did happen between Liam and me, it would be none of your damn business. I can see whoever I like.' She yanked her arm away.

'Ani, why are you being like this?' Siobhan's voice softened, her eyes filling with tears. 'I thought we had something special.'

'Look, Shiv, I'm sorry, but I can't do this right now. We've got more important things to deal with if you hadn't noticed.'

'I don't give a shit about the other stuff. I want to talk about you and me.'

'You're being ridiculous. I need to catch up with Jackie.'

Anaïs tried to step past her, but Siobhan grabbed her arm again.

'Fuck Jackie, fuck your mother and fuck Liam Patterson too. You're not going anywhere until we've sorted this out.'

'Let go of me.' Anaïs' voice went cold.

'But I love you.' Tears streamed down Siobhan's face, black eyeshadow staining her freckled cheeks. 'Can't you see that, for Christ sake?'

The words pierced through Anaïs' defences, stabbing her in the chest, and she looked down at the floor, the anger seeping out of her.

'Look at me.' Siobhan tried to lift her chin, but Anaïs shrugged her off. 'Please, Ani,' she tried again, her voice barely above a whisper.

'I've got to go. We can talk tomorrow,' Anaïs mumbled, eager to end the conversation.

Siobhan kept hold of her for a moment longer before finally releasing her grip.

'Okay, be careful tonight.' She smiled through the tears and Anaïs walked away.

31

Liam leaned on the railings bordering the enclosed marina of St Katherine's Docks and gazed out at the multi-million-pound yachts anchored inside. The weather was mellow and the bars and restaurants lining the water hummed with activity: throngs of people sitting outside, eating, drinking, and socialising in the dying embers of the fast-descending sun while music drifted out from the open windows.

Yet, despite the din, Liam remained lost in thought. His mind replaying the previous night with Laura over and over. They'd come so close to kissing, until she'd run off. And then she'd called in sick today. It felt like she was avoiding him. Although she had invited him here tonight, so she couldn't be that upset. Or maybe this was just her way of letting him down gently. Why were girls so confusing?

He was also troubled by his last conversation with William and the man's fascination with destroying these women. For Liam it was a chance to write a frontpage story and become a famous journalist. But for William it seemed like a deadly obsession. One that could get them both killed if things continued the way they were going.

Despite his worries, his mind soon drifted back to Laura, as it always seemed to do recently, and he daydreamed about escaping the city together on one of the nearby yachts and sailing down to the Mediterranean. Just the two of them, lying on the deck, feeling the gentle sway of the ocean below them and the warming rays of the sun on their bare bodies…

'Hey!' Someone called out, jabbing him in the back and bringing him back to reality.

He spun around and came face-to-face with Laura. She wore a lowcut black dress, the sheer fabric accentuating her delicate curves and giving him a tantalising glimpse of her toned chest and thighs, and his jaw almost hit the floor.

'Wow! You look amazing,' he murmured.

'Thanks. I'm glad you approve.' She leaned forward and kissed him on the cheek. 'Sorry for running off last night. I guess it was all a little overwhelming. I mean with work and everything,' she quickly added.

'That's okay. Are you feeling better now?'

'Much better, thanks. I had a killer migraine this morning, but it's pretty much gone now.'

'Are you sure you want to go to the restaurant? We can just go for a walk instead if you like.'

'No, I want to go. I've been looking forward to it all afternoon, and I'm starving!'

'Well, that's nothing new.' He grinned.

'Ha-ha, very funny. Did you come straight from work?' She glanced down at his white shirt and chinos.

'Do I look that bad?'

'I mean, you could have ironed the shirt, but it's fine.'

'I've got a jumper in my bag. I can put that on.'

'I'm just teasing. If you give it, you've got to be able to take it.'

'Don't worry, I'm a big boy, I can take it.'

'You sure about that?' She straightened her back and looked down at him. 'I'm pretty sure I'm taller than you now.'

'That's because you're wearing six-inch heels.'

'These are not six inches. They're two inches max.'

'Whatever. Two can play that game.' He went up on his tiptoes and puffed out his chest.

'Hey! Watch it, mister!' She pushed him away playfully.

*

Siobhan stood across the way in gym clothes and a baseball cap, watching angrily as Anaïs and Liam reached the restaurant and were seated on a table beside the water.

A moment later the waiter came back with a bottle of red wine and she took the opportunity to move closer, leaning on the nearby railings and pretending to look at her phone.

She peered over the top of the screen, her anger turning to sadness as they raised their glasses and gazed into each other's eyes.

This was all her fault. She'd pushed Anaïs too hard. Why did she always have to be so intense? She glanced out at the water, but when she looked back, Anaïs was laughing at something the man had said.

'I bet that handsome, Prince Charming-looking prick isn't even funny!' She muttered, her anger rising again.

She tried to tell herself that it was all an act; that Anaïs was just doing what she had to, to get the information they needed. But the way she'd defended him in the meeting that morning, and the way she looked at him now made her think differently.

What the hell was she doing here? This was a mistake. 'Eejit!' she hissed, admonishing herself. If Diane and the others knew what she was up to they'd have a shit fit.

She thought about leaving, but curiosity get the better of her, and she decided to stay a little longer.

*

Anaïs and Liam continued to drink and chat as the waiter brought out their food, piling the seemingly endless dishes onto the small table. A phantasmagorical feast of fried squid, chorizo, bean stew, giant prawns, mussels, croquettes, tortillas, patatas bravas, meatballs, stuffed peppers, grilled halloumi, olives, fresh bread and a variety of oils and sauces.

'Wow! This looks amazing.' Anaïs eyed it hungrily, and then took in a deep breath. 'It feels like we're in Barcelona or Palma with all the pretty lights, and the water, and the boats... I can't believe we ordered so much though.'

'It's your fault,' Liam replied

'I wasn't complaining.'

'Good! Because we're going to eat it all.'

'Challenge accepted.' She stabbed a piece of chorizo with her fork and thrust it into her mouth. 'Oh my God! This is so, so good!' She rolled her eyes as she chewed the spicy meat, revelling in the way the juices exploded on her tongue. 'Here. You've got to try this.' She picked up another piece and held it out in front of him.

He opened his mouth tentatively and she thrust it inside.

'Wow! You're right. This is really good,' he mumbled.

'Wait a sec...' Anaïs picked up a napkin and dabbed his chin. 'You're getting it everywhere, you messy little piggy!'

'You're the one that just shoved it in there. What do you expect?'

'I expect you to receive my offering gratefully and then close your mouth. Even a dog can manage that when you give them a treat.'

'Okay, you can stop talking now.' He picked up an empty mussel shell and held it aloft.

'What's that meant to be?' She looked confused.

'It's my conch. Only the person holding it may speak. You know, like *Lord of the Flies*.'

'That's not a conch, that's a mussel shell.'

'A shell's a shell. It still counts.'

'And stupid's still stupid.'

'That's two strikes. One more and you're banished from the island.'

'You know that book is the perfect example of why girls are better than boys.'

'How'd you figure that one out?'

'Because look how quickly they resorted to violence. They'd barely been on the island a few days before it descended into anarchy. It's always the same story with men – two much testosterone and not enough tolerance.'

'And how would a group of girls have done it better? Don't tell me – they'd have opened a beauty parlour and given each other seaweed facials and mud baths, then started a petting zoo and lived off nuts and berries and happy thoughts till somebody came to save them.'

'No. We would have created a democratic and peaceful community: allocating jobs, growing vegetables and working together to make sure everybody was taken care of. And if we had to kill any animals, we would have done it as humanely and sustainably as possible, making sure we gave as much back to the environment as we took from it. It would have been a eutopia. And yes, we would have had facials and mud baths too. As my mother always says, "we're not savages, dear." Now, let's get another bottle, shall we?' She emptied the last of the wine into Liam's glass, filling it to the brim.

'Are you trying to get me drunk?'

'Maybe,' she said, a mischievous glint in her eye. 'Is that such a bad thing?'

'No. Although you do know we have work in the morning, right?'

'Just shut up and drink.'

He picked up the glass and finished it in one go. 'There!' he said, wiping his mouth. 'Happy now?'

'Wow! I'm impressed.'

'Your turn.' He nodded at her glass.

'I'm a lady. I don't down drinks like some kind of macho rugger bugger.' She gave him a haughty look.

'Rugger bugger?'

'Yes. It's what we call rugby boys down south.'

'I'm more of a footballer.'

'That's even worse.'

'Wow! You're mean tonight.'

'I'm just playing.' She reached out and placed her hand on top of his. 'Some would say it's a sign of affection.' She felt a current of electricity pass between them and quickly stood up. 'I need to go to the bathroom. I'll order us another bottle while I'm inside. Don't eat everything while I'm gone.' She gave him a playful nudge on the way past.

*

Siobhan watched Anaïs disappear inside. Her eyes filled with tears. Her hands gripping the metal railing so tightly her knuckles turned white. She wished she could snap it off and hit the man across the back of the head with it, then throw his lifeless body into the water. It was obvious that there was a connection between them. One you couldn't fake. And it tore through her chest like a dagger.

'What the fuck is she playing at?' she suddenly exclaimed, causing an elderly couple walking by to look at her in surprise before scurrying off.

Then a thought struck her: what if she snuck inside and spoke to Anaïs while she was alone. She could tell her she was sorry, and they could put this stupid fight behind them and move on.

She found herself drifting closer to the entrance, her body floating along the walkway, like a ghost drawn to a beautiful white light. But before she'd gone more than a few feet, Anaïs reappeared, and she quickly retreated back to the railings.

With no other options, she took out her phone and sent a short message:

Sorry again about this morning, Nay-Nay. Hope it all goes well tonight. Give me a call tomorrow. Shiv. X

She looked over at the table, waiting for a reply or some kind of reaction, but Anaïs and the man continued to stare into each other's eyes, oblivious to their surroundings, lost in their own little world. Finally she gave up, slinking off into the dark night alone.

32

Siobhan left the waterside and went into the first pub she found. She took of the cap and wiped her face discreetly. Then she headed straight for the bar.

'Get me a beer and a shot of tequila, and don't give me any of the cheap shite. I want the good stuff.' She stared at the young, dark-haired bartender. 'Grab me some peanuts too. It's hungry work getting your heartbroken.' She took off her jacket and slumped onto a tall stool in front of the counter.

He came back a moment later with her drinks and she downed the tequila in one.

'Oof! Burns right down to your loins, am I right?' She gave him a leery grin, and then took a long swig of beer to wash the taste away.

She quickly finished the rest of it and ordered the same again.

'You fancy joining me this time for a shot, uh, what's your name?'

'Freddy.'

'Where you from, Freddy?'

'Italy.'

'Nice. So, whaddya say, Freddy, the Italian Stallion?'

'I'm sorry, but the manager doesn't like us drinking on shift.'

'Ah, come on. One shot won't kill ya. I promise I won't tell.' She held a finger to her lips, but he gave an apologetic shrug in reply before walking away.

'Ah! You're such a disappointment! Typical man,' she muttered, opening the peanuts, and then checking her phone to see if Anaïs had replied. But there was still nothing.

'Hey, Freddy! Make it a double this time, will you?'

'You sure?'

'To be sure, I'm sure. Don't worry about me, Fredster. I'm Irish. It's what we do. Now, less talking and more pouring, please. There's a good boy.'

He brought over the drinks, and she finished them just as swiftly as the first two. She was about to order the same again when a man appeared next to her.

'Mind if I sit down?' he asked.

'Knock yourself out, pal,' she said, barely acknowledging him.

He eased himself down with a sigh and rested his elbows on the counter.

'Hey, Freddy! Keep em coming,' she called out, already starting to feel a little tipsy.

'I'll get these.' The man took out his wallet. 'Whatever the lady's having, and a beer for me, please – sorry, what's your name?'

'Look, pal, I appreciate the offer, but I've had a pretty traumatic day, and I'd prefer to get pissed alone, if you don't mind. Also, you're wasting your time here. We play for different teams. I'm not into ball sports, or bats for that matter. I just want a nice clean wicket to play on, if you catch my drift?' She grinned, her words a little slurred.

'That's okay. I'm more of a middle stump man myself.' He glanced at Freddy who was busy preparing the drinks. 'If you catch my drift.'

'In that case, the name's Siobhan. Nice to meet ya.'

'Max,' he replied.

Freddy brought over their drinks and Siobhan picked up the shot glass. 'You need a tequila too,' she said to the man.

'I'm good with the beer, thanks. I only popped in for a quick one after work. I've got to drive home soon.'

'Ah, that's no fun. Leave your car here and get wasted with me. We can hit up a club later. Maybe go to G.A.Y – whaddya say? They'd love you in there with that cute little hat.' She glanced up at the grey flat cap he wore. 'Not to mention the beard. Gay guys love a beard. You're like a big fancy grizzly bear. We could get young Freddy here to join us too. Hey, Freddy! You wanna come party with me and old Maxy boy here later?'

'I'm on till close, and then I'm back in tomorrow morning for a delivery at seven.'

'That sounds like a maybe to me.' She winked at Max and then downed the shot. 'Ooowee! I must have some hairs on my chest after that one.' She pulled down the front of her t-shirt, closing one eye to focus. 'What you reckon?'

'I reckon you've had enough.'

'I'll drink to that.' She picked up her beer and clinked the glass against his. She took a long swig and burped loudly. 'Whoa! Apologies. That was a rogue one. I'm gassier than a fat kid with a coke addiction. And I'm not talking about the white stuff. Although I could do with a hit right now. You know where we can get some?'

'I'm not sure that's such a good idea.'

'Aye, you're probably right. Best stick to the booze.'

'So how come you're drinking alone? If you don't mind me asking.'

'Would you be asking if I was a guy?' She took another swig of beer and looked at him out of the corner of her eye.

'If you were a guy, I'd be encouraging you to drink more.' He grinned.

'Ha! Touché! You know what, I like you, Maxy. Is it short for Maximilian?'

'It is. My father was German.'

'What about your mam?'

'She's English. Well, she was born here, but her parents are Irish actually.'

'You don't say? I knew there was a reason why I liked you.' She downed the rest of her drink and stood up a little unsteadily. 'Right. I need to visit the little girl's room. Freddy! Get me a G&T. I can't face anymore beer.'

'I'll get it,' Max said. 'As long as you promise me it's your last one.'

'You drive a hard bargain. But it's a deal.' She gave him a lopsided grin and tottered off.

She came back a few minutes later and slumped back down on the stool.

'Feeling better?' Max asked.

'Aye, much better. I was pissing like Seabiscuit in there. Honestly, it was like Ride of the Valkyries. The poor lass in the stall next to me must have thought there was a tsunami coming.' Siobhan laughed out loud, slapping the counter.

'That's a very vivid picture you paint. Your drink's there, by the way.' He pointed to a freshly-made gin and tonic.

'Ah! That's deadly. Thank you kindly, fine sir.' She reached out carefully and gripped hold of it like a lifeboat in a storm.

'So, are you going to tell me what's wrong? There's clearly something bothering you, and it's a lot easier to talk to a stranger.'

'You don't let up do you, Maximilian?'

'I just want to make sure you're okay. Is that such a bad thing?'

Okay, fine, you asked for it, pal. But don't say I didn't warn you.' She took a sip of her drink and straightened her back. 'And for the record, I don't usually open up like this, but you seem all right. And I'm as pissed as a monkey.' She took a moment to compose herself and then continued: 'So... I've been having a relationship with this girl from work – she's actually the boss's daughter – so, as you can imagine, it's all been pretty hush-hush.'

'I had a feeling it was a girl.'

'Yeah, pretty obvious, right? I'm a drunken cliché, what can I say?' She let out a bitter laugh.

'So what happened? Did your boss find out?'

'Na, nothing like that. Nay-Nay's a bit of a closed book. She's been through a lot so I can't blame her. It's just tough, you know?'

'Nay-Nay?' He looked confused.

'Yeah, it's what I call her. Her real name's Anaïs.'

'Cute name. Is she French?'

'Her dad was, but her mother's very English. I swear if you took her knickers down, she'd have a red rose sticking out of her arse. Anyway, we had a big blow out this morning, and I told her I loved her, but then she ran off and I haven't heard from her since.'

'Maybe she just needs a little bit of time.'

'Aye, maybe...' Siobhan started to tear up again. 'Sorry, I get emotional when I'm pissed. Stupid mare.' She wiped her face with the back of her hand and looked away.

'It's okay. Don't worry about it. No judgement here.' He passed her a napkin.

'Thanks.' She forced a weak smile.

'Well, it doesn't seem that bad to me. I definitely think it's salvageable.'

'I haven't told you everything...' She gave him a sheepish look. 'There's someone else involved too – a guy called Liam.' She almost spat out his name. 'They've been spending more and more time together lately. She swears it's nothing, but I followed her tonight. That's why I'm here. They're having dinner down on the dock as we speak. When I left, they were holding hands at the table and staring into each other's eyes like a couple of lovebirds. God knows what they're doing by now. His tongue's probably down her throat – the smarmy prick!'

'I'm sorry.'

'You don't need to be sorry, Maxy, it's not your fault.' She finished the rest of her drink and stood up.

'Where are you going?'

'I'm going back to the restaurant to speak to her.' She took a step forward and the room began to spin. 'Whoa! Who turned on the carousel?'

'Come on, sit back down and have a glass of water.' He took her arm.

'I'm fine!' She shrugged him off. 'I just need to go and see Ani and make things alright.'

'If you go there now, you're just going to make things a hundred times worse.'

'But what if she goes back to his place and they sleep together? I don't think I could handle that. It kills me just thinking about it.'

'If she does that, then she's clearly not the one. If you really love her, you need to be patient. Trust me, I've been in your position before. It's tough. But if it's meant to be, she'll come to you. Maybe not tonight. But eventually.'

'I guess you're right.' She slumped back down, almost missing the stool.

'Whoa! Easy there.' He reached out and caught her just in time.

'Thanks,' she muttered.

'Where do you live?'

'Out east, near Clapton.'

'I'm heading that way too. I can drop you off on the way.'

'Are you sure? I don't want to put you out.'

'Yeah, it's fine, honestly. I'm in Walthamstow.'

'No shit? We're almost neighbours.'

'Here, put your jacket on and we'll get going.' He held it up and she struggled inside.

'Thank you, Maximilian, you're a gentleman and a scholar, so you are.' She leant on his shoulder for support and he guided her towards the door. 'Wait!' she said, suddenly becoming alert again. 'What about Freddy? You need to get his number.'

'I'll get it next time.'

'I need to give you mine too. Next time we're going to party like it's 1999.'

'Yes, we will.' He unlocked the car and bundled her inside.

'Hey! Be careful.' She fell face-first onto the backseat and struggled to sit up. But before she could say anything else, a huge fist crashed into her face and everything went black.

33

The waiter cleared the empty plates and Anaïs poured the last of the second wine bottle into Liam's glass.

'There. We don't need that anymore.' She put the bottle aside.

'I really need to pee.' Liam grinned like a naughty schoolboy and stood up, knocking the table with his thigh. 'Whoops! Sorry.' He stumbled off.

Once he'd gone inside, Anaïs poured the remainder of her wine into the water to join the other glasses she'd discreetly discarded of throughout the evening. Then she checked her phone and saw a message from Siobhan. She read through it, feeling a mixture of guilt and anger, and wondered what the other girl was getting up to. Probably getting pissed in Soho and trying to find a one-night-stand. She let out a sardonic huff. Surprised to find herself a little jealous at the thought.

'Everything okay?' Liam reappeared, taking her by surprise.

'Uh, yeah, everything's fine.' She put the phone away and forced a smile. 'Shall we get some churros to go? We could take them back to yours and watch a movie. If that's okay with you?'

'That's more than okay with me.'

'Great. Do you have any wine at yours?'

'I've only got beer. There's a little shop around the corner though. It's open all night so we could pop in on the way back.'

'Perfect,' she replied, catching the waiter's eye and calling him over.

They reached Liam's flat a little while later with a boxful of churros and a cheap bottle of red wine and he led her inside, turning on the light to reveal a sparsely-decorated hallway.

Anaïs glanced around at the off-white walls, which looked like they hadn't been painted in about twenty-years, and the tacky wood-effect laminate flooring, which was partially covered by a burgundy-coloured, Persian-style rug.

'I like the rug,' she said, taking off her heels and hanging up her jacket.

'Thanks. My mum gave it to me. She said the place needed a little colour.'

'She wasn't wrong,' Anaïs muttered.

'The bathroom's in there if you need it.' He pointed at the door directly in front of her.

'What's the one next to it?'

'Uh, that's my bedroom,' he replied, quickly leading her through another door into the main living area. 'So this is it. It's not much, but it's all mine.'

'It's, uh, very cosy. It's definitely a boy's place though.' She glanced at the framed movie posters on the walls, recognising the Pulp Fiction one hanging over the couch, and the Guardians of the Galaxy one above the TV, but she hadn't heard of any of the others. 'You've got an interesting taste in movies.'

'Yeah, there's a lot of obscure Eighties stuff that my older brothers got me into when I was a kid.

'Are they in London too?'

'No. Chris is a fireman in Manchester, and Paul's an engineer on the oil rigs so he's away a lot. His wife and little boy live in Sheffield though.'

'So you're an uncle?'

'I am.' He smiled. 'Do you have any brothers or sisters?'

'Nope. It's just me. Shall we open the wine and unpack those churros?' A wave of guilt rushed over her and she walked towards the small kitchenette on the other side of the room.

Liam followed her over and put the plastic bag on the counter.

'Everything okay?' He asked. 'You've gone very quiet all of a sudden.'

'Yeah, I'm fine.' She took the wine bottle out of the bag and forced a smile. 'Where are your glasses?' She slipped the little transparent pouch filled with the tranquilising powder subtly out of her bag and closed her palm around it.

'It's okay, I can sort everything out. I just need to wash some glasses and clean up quickly. I wasn't expecting guests. Go and choose a movie if you like. It'll only take a few minutes.'

'Are you sure?' she asked, not wanting to miss her chance.

'It's fine, honestly. It's not usually this messy, I promise. I've just been super busy since I started at *The Beacon*.' He gave an embarrassed smile.

'This is nothing. Try living with a bunch of girls, then you'll know what real mess is.'

She put down the bottle and wandered over to the nearby table, discreetly pushing the clutter aside and spotting the small notebook and a silver laptop hidden underneath. Bingo! She covered them back up and stepped over to a set of French doors.

'What's out there?' She peered into the darkness.

'Just a little garden and a whatchamacallit.' He glanced over his shoulder whilst he cleaned. 'You know? One of those little balconies.'

'A Juliet balcony?'

'Yeah. That's the one.'

'It must be nice in the summer.' She slipped the pouch back into her bag for the time being.

She was about to walk over to the couch when she caught a glimpse of her reflection in the glass. The image stopped her in her tracks and she gazed at the long wavy hair cascading over her bare shoulders, and the sleek black dress that clung enticingly to her delicate curves. She hadn't made this much effort in a long time and a small smile appeared on her lips. Then she saw Liam in the background and the image became distorted, her face twisting into a vile sneer, the smooth skin shrivelling up and turning grey, and she quickly looked away.

'Everything okay?' Liam appeared behind her, the bottle of wine in one hand and two glasses in the other. 'You look like you've seen a ghost.

'Uh, yeah, I'm fine,' she said, still a flustered.

'Okay, good. You can grab the churros then. I've already plated them up. And don't forget the chocolate dip.'

Once they were both sitting down, Liam poured the wine and turned on the TV.

'What do you want to watch?'

'How about we just listen to some music for a bit.' She hid her bag under the pillow beside her.

'Good idea.' He got back up and turned on a Bluetooth speaker on the windowsill. 'Any requests?'

'You choose.' She took a sip of wine. Her mind a swirl of conflicting thoughts.

'Okay. Wait a sec…' A moment later an up-tempo indie song began to play.

'Really?' Anaïs looked up at him.

'What's wrong with this?'

'We definitely need something more mellow. Here, let me…' She took the phone and scrolled through it. 'Here we go.' The intro to *At Last* began to play and Etta James' rich voice filled the room.

'I guess this works too.' Liam sat back down and put his feet up on the glass-topped coffee table.

Anaïs put hers up too and they sunk deeper into the small couch, their bodies sliding closer and closer until their legs touched.

She glanced out of the corner of her eye and caught him staring at her bare thighs but she pretended not to notice.

'This is nice,' she murmured, leaning her head against his shoulder and taking in the faint smell of his aftershave.

For a moment she forgot all about the powder, Siobhan, William, her mother, saving the agency – everything. And she closed her eyes, relaxing as Etta James faded away and Nina Simone's deep, dulcet tones took over. But her joy was short-lived when Liam's phone started to ring.

'Who the hell's calling at this time?' He muttered.

'Are you going to get that?' She saw William's name flash up on the screen.

'I'll call them back tomorrow. If it's important, they'll leave a message.'

'Are you sure? I don't mind,' she said, curious to know what the man wanted.

'Okay, just give me a sec.' He stood up and went out into the hallway, pulling the door behind him.

Anaïs waited for a moment. Then she got up and crept closer, peering through the small gap and listening to their conversation:

'I can't really talk right now… …' Liam paced up and down, speaking in hushed tones. 'I'm just at home, but I have company… … Mhm… … Yes, I'm with Laura… … We went out for food at a Spanish place in St Katherine's Dock… … I am still focused! … Look, let's just chat tomorrow. It's late… … I understand, but you have to see things from my point of view too…'

She crept back to the couch and took out the pouch, quickly pouring the contents into Liam's drink and stirring it with her finger. Once it had dissolved she picked up one of the churros and sat down.

Liam returned a moment later, his face red with anger.

'Everything okay?' She asked. 'You look tense.'

'Yeah, it's fine. Just work stuff.'

'You want to talk about it?'

'Not really. It can wait till tomorrow. I'd just like to chill with you, if that's okay?'

'I'd like that too.' She smiled. 'Maybe you should have some wine.' She eyed the glass, willing him to pick it up. Whatever the man had said it had clearly annoyed him, and she was eager to get this over and done with as quickly as possible.

34

Siobhan felt a flash of pain rip through her head and she let out a weary groan, an intense ringing encircling her like a swarm of angry bees. She tried to open her eyes. To say something. Do something. Anything! But her body wouldn't obey her commands.

'Wake up…' a faint voice echoed in the distance, drowned out by the incessant buzzing.

She felt someone or something shake her and she forced her eyes open, squinting up at a blurred figure.

'Who's there?' she murmured. 'What's going on?' She tried to focus but another flash of pain tore through her.

Suddenly the figure leaned closer, their face materialising through the fog.

'Max? Is that you?' It all started to come back to her.

'Nice of you to final join us.' He smiled.

She tried to sit up, but her wrists were tied behind her back. Her ankles bound together.

'What the fuck! Why are you doing this?' She wriggled and squirmed but the restraints wouldn't budge.

'Shh… just relax. I'm not going to hurt you. As long as you behave, that is.'

'I don't understand.' She looked at him in confusion. Then it hit her: the long dark hair, the thick unruly beard, the broad shoulders… 'William,' she murmured.

'Well done.' His smile grew wider. 'I was wondering when you were going to figure it out.'

'But how did you know who I was?'

'I know a lot more than you think. And now you're going to help me fill in the blanks.'

'Fuck you, you greasy-haired prick!' She spat in his face with a defiant glare.

'That's not very nice now, is it? I thought we'd made a connection back there at the bar.' He wiped his face calmly and stood up.

'Untie me and I'll show you what kind of connection we have.' She bared her teeth and leered at him, her body coiled like a snake, ready to attack.

'I don't think so,' he said, walking away.

'Where are you going?' she shouted, before instantly falling silent when she saw a woman sitting across from her in a green-sequined ballgown, the bloodstained material bunched up around her pale thighs.

She was about to say something when she realised the woman was dead, her stricken body propped awkwardly against the wall, a twisted grimace plastered on her ashen face, her lifeless eyes peeled back in perpetual terror.

'I see you've met Cecilia?' The man returned with a box of tissues. 'Although you two are old friends, aren't you?' He crouched down, blocking her view.

'I don't know what you're talking about.' Siobhan acted dumb. 'I've never seen her before.'

'Interesting… she seemed to know you: Siobhan Whelan, Operations Manager at the London and Districts' International Emergency Support-Centre for Women. That's quite the mouthful.'

'You've got the wrong gal,' she replied with as much bravado as possible. Although inside she was terrified. Whoever this William was, he knew even more than they thought, and he clearly didn't have a problem with killing people.

'Really?' He reached into her jacket and pulled out her purse. 'Then how do you explain this?' He took out her driver's license and held it up.

'Fine! It's me.' She let out a sigh. 'So I manage a women's charity. What's the big deal? Last time I checked that wasn't a crime.'

'It's a little late to be coy. Don't you think?' He took a tissue from the box and cleaned the rest of his face. Once he was done, he took out another one and dabbed it with his tongue.

'What are you doing?' She recoiled as he lifted it towards her.

'I'm just going to clean you up a bit. You're full of blood and snot. It's not a good look for a lady.'

'I ain't no fucking lady, pal! And if you come any closer, I'll bite your fucking fingers off.'

'Now, now, there's no need to be so aggressive. Like I said earlier, if you behave, I won't have to hurt you again.' He reached out and she jerked forward, snapping her teeth shut. But he moved away just in time, sending her toppling to the floor. 'You're not making it easy for yourself.' He flipped her onto her back like a stricken tortoise and pinned her down.

'Get your fucking hands off me, you prick! I swear I'm going to kill you when I get out of this!' She continued to struggle before finally gave up.

'Are you finished?' he asked, but she didn't reply. She just looked up at him, breathing heavily, her eyes full of anger and hatred. 'Good.' He wet the tissue again and gently dabbed at her nose and lip, every touch making her skin crawl. 'There!' he said, dabbing her one last time. 'That's much better. We can talk like respectable adults now.' He grabbed her by the shoulders and lifted her to a sitting position. 'I know your charity is a front for your real operation. And I know it's located underneath the restaurant. What I want you to do is tell me all about it: entrances, exits, security systems, floor plans, blind spots, who works there, what time they start, what time they finish, when they take their breaks. Everything. And if I find out you kept anything from me, I promise I'll come back and I'll kill you as slowly and as painfully as humanly possible. But that's nothing compared to what I'll do to your pretty little Anaïs. I spoke to Liam on the phone earlier, and she's at his flat as we speak. It won't be difficult to get my hands on her.'

The thought of Anaïs at Liam Patterson's flat sent a pang of jealousy through her, but she quickly cast it aside.

'You lay a finger on her and I swear it'll be the last thing you ever do. Believe me. Dead or alive, I'll hunt you down and make you pay, so help me God.'

'I'm not interested in hurting you or her. It's her mother I want, and the other two bitches she's working with. So tell me what I want to know and you'll be fine.'

'You're full of shit.' She laughed in his face. 'I'm not telling you nothing. You're not going to do anything while she's with that guy. And I doubt you'd have the balls to mess with Diane and the others either. If you were going to do something, you'd have already done it by now.'

'Is that so?' He smirked. 'The only reason I haven't done anything yet is because I want them altogether. That way they can see each other's faces when they die.' His face twisted into an evil sneer. 'And then once I've killed them all, I'm going to burn their little organisation to the ground. Now, are we going to do this the hard way or the easy way?'

'I guess it's going to be the hard way.' She looked him in the eye and gave him the smuggest smile she could muster. 'Do your worst, pal. You don't scare me.'

'Very well.' He walked out of the room and closed the door, leaving her alone with the corpse of Cecilia Davenport.

She sat there for a moment, her back against the wall, legs stretched out in front of her on the hard-wooden floor, and she looked down at the plastic cable-ties digging into her ankles. She guessed he'd used the same things on her wrists, and she looked for something she could use to cut them. But apart from the dead woman and the table, the room was empty.

'You know this is all your fault, right?' She looked at the woman who stared back with lifeless eyes. 'If you hadn't started blabbing to all and sundry, this sicko would never have found you, or us for that matter. And now look what's happened.' She glanced away for a second, then turned back. 'Jesus! Don't you know it's rude to stare? You look like shite, by the way.' She noticed the welts and bruises on the woman's arms and legs. 'You smell pretty funky too. Although I suppose I can't really talk.' She let out a snort which sent fresh blood trickling down her face. 'That is a nice dress though, I must admit. Green really brings out the colour in your – uh – cheeks.' She tried to raise her eyebrows, but her eyes were almost swollen shut from William's fist. 'Look. Don't try to guilt trip me. My conscious is clear. I was super nice to you when you came in. I showed you around. Explained everything. I even gave you a brandy when you were feeling nervous. And it wasn't the cheap stuff either. Then you suddenly get cold feet and demand your money back. Money that was meant for innocent women and girls who'd suffered abuse. Just like you now. Ironic, aye?' She let out a sardonic chuckle which sent another jolt of pain through her head. 'Fuck! I shouldn't have had all those bloody tequilas.' The memory of the alcohol made her stomach churn and she threw up on the floor beside her. 'Well, that's just great,' she muttered. 'So how do you suppose we get out of this, aye? You got any bright ideas over there?' She stared at the woman waiting for an answer. 'No? I didn't think so.'

A few seconds later, William walked back in carrying a small tool bag and knelt down beside her.

'What's happened here?' He glanced at the small puddle of vomit.

'I guess that's just the effect you have on people.'

'Is that so?' He opened the bag and took out a screwdriver, a Stanley knife and a pair of pliers.

'If that's meant to scare me, it ain't working. I like it rough.' She grinned.

'You really are a feisty one, aren't you?' He sliced through her t-shirt with the Stanley knife and yanked down her bra. 'Now, tell me what I want to know…' He picked up the pliers and opened the clamps, touching the cold metal against her skin and making her flinch.

'So you do feel fear, after all.' He smiled.

'Go fuck yourself.' She tried to sound strong, but her voice was barely above a whisper and she cowered away from him despite herself.

'Have it your way. This might sting a little.' He squeezed them shut and she let out a gut-wrenching scream. But despite the excruciating pain she still refused to speak.

'Your loyalty is very admirable. But you're just prolonging the inevitable.' He swapped the pliers for the screwdriver and plunged the blunt metal head into her ribcage. The fierce blow punctured her skin, sucking the wind out of her, and she gasped in agony.

For the next few minutes, he continued to jab at her body, systematically breaking her down, until she finally told him everything. Then he gathered everything up and left the room, turning off the light and leaving her curled up on the floor sobbing quietly in the darkness.

35

Anaïs and Liam continued to sit on the couch, listening to music and eating churros. He still hadn't touched the wine though, his mind seemingly elsewhere, and she began to grow more anxious.

'Everything okay?' she asked. 'You've barely said a word for the last fifteen minutes.'

'I can't do this any longer.' He sat up and faced her.

'Do what?' Her chest tightened, her eyes flitting between Liam and the untouched wine. This wasn't going the way she planned.

'Lie about my feelings. About the way I feel about you. Ever since you first walked into *The Beacon*, I haven't stopped thinking about you–'

'Liam, wait!' she tried to stop him, but he was determined to carry on.

'No. Hear me out. Please.' He stared at her with a wide-eyed innocence that broke her heart. 'I know you like me too. I can see it. You can't deny there's something special between us. I know we've only just met, and I'm a little drunk right now. But sometimes time is immaterial–'

'It's not that simple.' She looked down guiltily. Unsure of how to continue. She'd never expected things to become so intense. To have feelings. Yet he was right. She couldn't deny it.

'What is it?' he asked. 'Is there someone else?'

'No... Well, kind of... I don't know – like I said, it's not that simple.' She thought of Siobhan and suddenly felt even worse. She needed to pull herself together before this whole situation blew up in her face.

'Whatever it is, I don't care.' He took her hand and squeezed it gently. 'We can figure it out. Just give me a chance.'

The feel of his warm hands made her heart beat faster and her hairs stand on end.

'Liam, I…' She started to say something, then fell silent, her mind in turmoil, her eyes filling with tears.

'Look at me.' He lifted her chin and stared into her eyes.

She gazed back, her lips pursed, barely able to breathe. The tension between them almost unbearable.

'You're so beautiful,' he murmured, leaning forward.

This time she didn't resist. She closed her eyes and gave into her desires. But just as their lips met, the intercom rang and they leapt apart in shock, the spell broken.

'What now?' Liam glared at the door while Anaïs flopped down on the couch letting out a deep sigh.

What was she doing? She shook her head, annoyed by her weakness yet filled with a longing to taste his lips again, to sink deeper into the couch and disappear to a place where they could be together. Another world. Away from all this mess. Then Liam went out into the hallway and William's voice crackled through the intercom bringing her crashing back to reality:

'What the hell are you doing here?' Liam jabbed at the button.

'I just need to come up and speak to you for a minute. It won't take long, I promise.'

'I told you I've got company. Can't you come back tomorrow?'

'It concerns her too,' the man replied ominously.

Suddenly her stomach dropped and she reached into her bag, resting her hand on the taser.

'What the hell are you talking about?' Liam's voice rose and he glanced over at her.

'Let me up and I'll explain.'

'Fine! You got two minutes.' Liam buzzed him in and Anaïs perched on the edge of the couch, her back ramrod straight, a tight smile on her face as she glanced around, looking for potential escape routes. But it was no use. She was trapped.

Soon she heard footsteps on the landing, followed by a loud knock, and Liam opened the door.

'We can talk here?' he said, blocking the entrance. But the man stepped past him.

His large frame filled up the small hallway, and Anaïs' could see that he wore a flat cap and jacket, his bearded face indecipherable in the gloom.

She thought about calling her mother or Jackie, but before she could do anything, he entered the room and her fears multiplied.

'Hello, Anaïs.' He took off his cap and smoothed back his long hair.

'What are you talking about?' Liam appeared beside him. 'This is Laura. I already told you that.'

'Should you tell him or should I?' The man's eyes lit up.

'No. It can't be…' she murmured, her mouth falling open.

'Can someone please tell me what's going on?' Liam's eyes flitted between them, his face a mixture of anger and confusion.

'I'm afraid it is, my dear.' The American accent disappeared and he prolonged the last syllable, the words cutting through her like shards of ice. 'It's so nice to see you again.' He flashed the same wolf-like grin that had haunted her dreams for the past two years.

'Victor.' She forced out the word. Her voice barely above a whisper. She closed her eyes, hoping it wasn't real. But when she opened them again he was still there. 'It's not possible. I watched you die in the fire.'

'Haven't you ever heard of a Phoenix, my dear?' His grin grew impossibly wide, his mouth a dark chasm sucking her into a nightmarish abyss.

'Seriously, someone better tell me what the hell is going on, right now!' Liam stepped between them.

'Get out of here!' Anaïs cried. Terrified of what the man might do.

'Not until you give me an explanation.'

'I'll explain everything later, I promise. Just go. Leave us alone!' She spat out the last words, staring at him defiantly. Hoping he would listen. But before either of them could react, Victor took out a Stanley knife and swiped the blade across Liam's throat.

'No!' Anaïs reached out, but it was too late. Liam's face turned white and blood gushed from the wound.

He looked down at her in confusion, not seeming to understand what was happening.

'Laura, I–' He choked on the words. His hand rising as the realisation finally set in.

'Liam, I'm so sorry.' She looked into his eyes and her heart broke into a million pieces, knowing it was all her fault, wishing she could turn back time and do things differently.

He reached out, his hand shaking with the effort, and she touched his fingertips for a fleeting moment.

'You were right.' She smiled sadly, her lips quivering. 'Time doesn't matter.' She felt a spark of energy pass between them. Then he crumpled to the floor.

'Such a shame.' Victor glanced down at Liam's stricken body and tutted. 'He was starting to grow on me. Oh well…'

'Why would you do that? He was innocent!' Tears cascaded down her face and she glared at him with absolute hatred.

'Collateral damage, I'm afraid.'

'You're a monster!' She leaped up and lunged at him with the taser. But he was too fast, swotting her away with the back of his hand and sending her crashing through the coffee table in an explosion of glass.

She let out a groan, her body throbbing from the shards embedded in her skin, but before she could recover, Victor was on her in an instant, snatching the taser out of her hand and yanking her up by the hair.

'Not this time,' he said, flinging her onto the couch like a ragdoll. 'Now, you're going to do exactly as I say, or things will get a lot worse. Do you understand?'

'Go fuck yourself!'

'You've gotten quite tenacious since I saw you last. And even more beautiful, I might add. You're not a skinny little girl anymore. You're a woman now.' He looked her up and down, his eyes lingering on her exposed thighs.

'You're still a sick fuck!' she shot back, desperately trying to cover herself.

'That may be so, but am I really that different from your mother and her merry little band of men-killers?' He let out a little giggle.

'They're nothing like you. They only kill criminals. They don't rape and murder innocent women and girls.'

'Hmm, semantics.' He shrugged. 'Alas, we need to cut this conversation short. Time is of the essence. Come on. Get up. We're going for a little trip.'

'I'm not going anywhere.'

'Do you women always have to be so stubborn?' He sighed. 'It really is quite tiresome.' He looked at her impatiently, but she refused to move. 'Very well.' He reached into his pocket and took out a tuft of red hair. 'Do you recognise this?'

'What is it?' Anaïs asked, although something inside her already knew the answer.

'It belongs to your dear Siobhan. You two are very close, aren't you? One might even say *intimate*.' He grinned.

When he said Siobhan's name, her stomach lurched. She couldn't be dead too. She couldn't handle anymore loss. She glanced at Liam's lifeless body and quickly looked away, a wave of guilt and sadness washing over her.

'Don't worry, she's still alive. For now. But if you don't start behaving, I'll make sure she dies a slow and painful death.'

'What the fuck's wrong with you?' She suddenly exploded. 'Why are you doing this?'

'Why do we do anything? In the grand scheme of things, everything we do is inconsequential. We exist merely for a blink of the eye and then – poof – we're gone.'

'What kind of bullshit answer is that?'

'Do you really want to know why I do it?' He stepped closer, his eyes lighting up. 'I do it because I enjoy it. Because that look of fear in those pretty green eyes of yours makes me ache with desire. And when I get you and your mother, and all those other bitches who tried to kill me, together, I'm going to bask in your collective terror, revel in your helpless screams, and then bathe in your sweet, sticky blood.' He closed his eyes for a moment and took a deep breath, slowly exhaling. A look of serenity on his face. 'Now, up you get.'

Anaïs climbed to her feet a little shakily, wincing with pain as the broken shards of glass dug deeper into her torn skin.

'Now what?' she asked.

'Put your jacket on. It's cold outside.'

'What about Liam? You can't just leave him here like this.'

She glanced down, her eyes filling with fresh tears. She wanted to wrap her arms around him and tell him everything would be okay. To give him the kiss they never had. But it was too late. He was gone. Nothing left but an empty shell. The thought crushed her. But before she could say a last goodbye, Victor's hand appeared in front of her face, holding a white cloth, and she passed out.

36

Victor drove to South Bank and pulled in behind the National Theatre, parking as close as he could to the Hungerford Bridge.

He glanced around, making sure the coast was clear. Then he turned off the engine and checked on Anaïs. She lay unconscious on the backseat, barely visible under a grey blanket, and he stroked her hair softly.

'There, there, Sleeping Beauty. Soon this will all be over. But not before I've had my fun.'

He'd waited over two years for this opportunity, hiding in the shadows and patiently plotting his revenge. Tonight everything had fallen into place. Killing Liam had been unfortunate. But he always knew it would happen sooner or later. Everyone he got close to died eventually. That's just the way it was.

He climbed out of the car and threw Anaïs over his shoulder, covering her with the blanket and quickly making his way towards the bridge. When he got there, he swiped the card on the panel like Siobhan had told him and watched as the carriage travelled upwards and a duplicate emerged from below, taking its place.

'Well, isn't that clever,' he murmured, stepping inside.

A few seconds later, he emerged into a long cylindrical corridor and the lights came on automatically. He gazed around for a moment. Taking it all in. Impressed by the scope of their vision. Then he followed Siobhan's directions to the boardroom.

Thankfully, it didn't take long to get there, and he dropped Anaïs' limp body to the floor unceremoniously.

'You're heavier than you look,' he muttered, breathing heavily, before strolling over to the nearby table. 'Hmm, so how does this work?' He pressed on a discreet panel built into the glass and it lit up, revealing a digital menu. He glanced around and saw that there were identical panels located in front of the other chairs too, while a high-resolution holographic screen floated above him.

Intrigued, he scrolled through the options and clicked on the Metropolitan Police Database. He noticed straightaway that all the men wanted for violent and sexually-related crimes had been flagged, some of them already greyed out.

'Very efficient. Don't worry, my friends, I'll avenge you all soon enough. After tonight the London and Districts International Emergency Support-Centre for Women will be closed for business. Indefinitely.' He clicked onto another screen which brought up the CCTV feeds for the whole of Central and Greater London, while another showed the internal cameras set up within the underground complex as well as the Thai restaurant above. But before he could explore anymore, Anaïs began to stir.

Quickly he went over and grabbed her by the shoulders, dragging her to the table and lifting her onto one of the chairs. He strapped her wrists to the armrests with a pair of cable-ties, and then tied her ankles too.

'Don't worry, I won't be gone too long.' He left the room and made his way back up to the riverside.

A few minutes later, he reached the car and took a small handgun out of the glove compartment. He slipped it into his jacket, then took a pair of heavy-duty rucksacks out of the boot. The bags were filled with brick-sized blocks of plastic explosives which he'd been making in his basement for the past year, using illicit chemicals and specialised equipment he'd purchased on the dark web, and he carefully lifted them onto his shoulders.

Locking the car, he returned to the underground complex and headed straight to the utility room which, according to Siobhan, powered the whole place.

When he got there, he carefully emptied one of the bags, placing the blocks on top of the power units and activating the mini-detonators which were linked to a small remote-controlled digital timer that he'd set to five minutes.

Once he was done, he took the other bag and planted the rest of the blocks discreetly throughout the complex.

He noticed a plain black door on his way around and from Siobhan's description he guessed it was their so-called Treatment Room.

Curious, he opened the door and went inside.

'So this is where the magic happens,' he murmured, a small smile playing on his lips as he envisioned all the men who had met their demise there.

The room was empty apart from a metal gurney in the far corner, and he wandered over to a long rectangular mirror on the back wall, looking at his reflection.

'So this is where you like to hide and watch.' He blew on the glass and drew three female stick-figures on the cloudy surface. 'Not for much longer.' He swiped his hand through them and made his way back to the boardroom.

When he got there, Anaïs was fully awake and desperately trying to free herself.

'Someone's full of energy after their little nap.' He smiled, amused by her helpless struggles.

'How did you get in here?' She glared at him.

'I think you know how.'

'Siobhan would never help you.'

'Maybe not willingly. But I can be very persuasive.'

'I fucking hate you!' she screamed.

'Such anger.' A shiver of excitement passed through him. He ached to touch her. But he knew he needed to be patient. There was still a lot of work to be done before the real fun could begin.

'Whatever you're trying to do, you won't get away with it. We beat you once, and we'll do it again.'

'Maybe so. Although this time it'll be me who has the element of surprise. Now be a good girl and unlock this.' He held out her phone.

'I'm not going to do anything to help you.'

'Very well.' He reached out and grabbed her thumb, twisting it around.

'Stop! What are you doing?' she cried out in pain.

'This is what happens when you don't cooperate.' He held her thumb against the screen and it came to life. 'Now, where's your mother's number? Ah, here we go, "Maman", isn't that cute?'

He sent a short message, asking her to come to the underground complex along with Jackie and Andréa. Then he waited for a reply.

A few seconds later, the phone pinged and he read the message.

'Looks like they're on their way.' He went over to the table and opened the CCTV cameras on both entrances, the images magnified on the big screen.

'They're not going to fall for it.' Anaïs called out. 'You think you're so clever. But they'll see right through your plan. And this time we'll stop you for good.'

'Okay, that's enough from you for the time being.' He took a scarf from one of the rucksacks and tied it around her mouth. 'Don't worry, we'll talk again later, I promise.' He stroked her hair, enjoying the way she cowered beneath him.

A little while later, he spotted two figures approaching the bridge.

'Ah, our first guests have arrived.' His eyes lit up, recognising the faces of Diane Dubois and Chief Superintendent Jackie Njoku. 'I should go greet them.' He took out the gun and winked at Anaïs.

37

Anaïs watched with growing dread as Victor hid behind the door, waiting for her mother and Jackie to appear.

Soon Jackie's loud voice boomed down the corridor, and she tried desperately to warn them, but it was no use. They were walking into a trap and there was nothing she could do.

A few seconds later, the doors opened and Anaïs locked eyes with her mother for a brief moment, before Victor stepped forward and pointed the gun at their heads.

'Good evening, ladies.' He grinned from ear-to-ear. 'It's been far too long. Did you miss me?'

Instinctively, Jackie pushed Diane out of the way and lunged towards him. She managed to grab hold of his jacket and a tussle ensued.

Anaïs hopes rose as Jackie seemed to be getting the upper hand. But then a gunshot rang out, the sound reverberating around the room, and Jackie crumpled to the floor.

Anaïs let out a muffled cry, eyes peeled back in terror, as Diane rushed over and pressed her hands against the gaping wound on Jackie's shoulder.

'Leave her.' Victor pushed Diane away and pointed the gun at her head.

'But she's going to die if I don't stop the bleeding.'

'She should have thought about that before she tried to be a hero. And I hate to break it to you, but you're all going to die tonight. I didn't bring you here for a reunion party. Now go and sit next to your daughter.' He nudged her with his foot.

'Don't you dare touch me.' Diane glared up at him.

'I won't ask again.' Victor pressed the barrel of the gun to her forehead.

'Do as he says,' Jackie murmured. 'I'll be okay. It's just a scratch.' She forced a smile, but Anaïs could see from her mother's bloodstained hands that it was a lot more serious.

Diane hesitated for a moment, then gave in and walked over to Anaïs.

'Are you okay, ma puce?' she asked, leaning over and hugging her.

Anaïs nodded, tears filling her eyes. Desperately wishing she could hug her back.

'I said sit down,' Victor commanded. 'You need to get up too.' He kicked Jackie in the side and she let out a pained groan.

'Leave her alone,' Diane called out. 'Haven't you done enough damage already?'

'I haven't even started yet.' Victor glanced at her, a malicious glint in his eye, before turning his attention back to Jackie. 'Come on. Up you get.' He grabbed her by the hair and yanked her to her feet. She was too weak to fight him off and stood up shakily, shuffling towards the others. Blood dripped to the floor with every step and he put her in a chair next to Diane, gagging and restraining them both. 'Now, where's the other one?' He glanced up at the screen and searched through the cameras looking for Andréa. 'Ah, here she comes.'

Anaïs looked up and saw Andréa walking along the corridor, and her heart sank.

Victor approached the door and Anaïs glanced at her mother who stared back with an anguished look in her eyes. They both turned their attention to Jackie, her head lolling listlessly beside them, her blouse stained through with blood, and Anaïs knew that if they didn't do something soon, she'd bleed to death.

Desperately, she scanned the room, searching for something that could help them, and she spotted Jackie's gun lying just a few feet away. With Victor occupied, she scooched down as far as she could and tried to reach it with her feet, but it was tantalisingly out of reach. Gritting her teeth, she pulled against the restraints with all her might, the plastic digging into her skin, and she touched the handle with her outstretched toes. Come on. Come on... She fought through the pain and dragged it back towards her.

'What are you up to?' Victor glanced over his shoulder, eyeing her suspiciously.

Anaïs looked at him innocently, the gun hidden beneath her chair, and he turned back to the door.

A moment later Andréa entered, and he grabbed her around the neck, pushing the gun against her ribs.

'Nice of you to finally join us, Ms Jensen, I almost forgot about you. But then you've always been the quiet one, haven't you?'

'What's going on? What are you doing?' Andréa's eyes darted around as Victor pushed her onto an empty chair and strapped her down.

'Now that you're all here, we won't be needing these anymore.' He removed the gags from their mouths.'

'I'm so sorry, maman,' Anaïs blurted. 'This is all my fault–'

'Shh, don't blame yourself, ma puce. I should have seen it coming. He fooled us all.'

'But you don't understand. He killed Liam and he tortured Siobhan. For all I know, she's dead too.' Anaïs burst into tears, unable to control her emotions any longer.

'Oh, my beautiful girl, I'm so sorry. I promise I'll get you out of this. You just need to stay calm. Can you do that for me?'

'Well isn't this sweet?' Victor stood over them. 'Such a touching mother, daughter moment.'

'We need to get Jackie to a hospital,' Andréa called out. 'She's dying!'

'Do we have to go through all this again?' Victor rolled his eyes. 'If you'd turned up on time, you'd know that you're all going to die. But not until I've had my fun. You ladies put me through hell. Now it's payback time.'

'How are you still alive?' Diane asked. 'You should have burned to death in that warehouse.'

'Indeed, I should have. In fact, I almost did.' He pulled up his trousers and showed them his scarred legs.

'Who brought the *Peperamis*? I'm starving.' Jackie suddenly came back to life and let out a weak laugh before spluttering and coughing uncontrollably.

Victor glared at her for a moment, and then covered them up again.

'I'm glad you find it so amusing,' he said, the serene look returning to his face.

'So how did you get out of there?' Diane continued to question him.

'I know what you're trying to do, Ms Dubois, but I'll indulge you. After all, we're not going anywhere. And I'm in no rush. As I was saying before being rudely interrupted. I almost succumbed to the fire but as the flames engulfed me, the floor gave way and I plummeted to the basement below. Which, luckily for me, was flooded with ice-cold water from the river. The fall put out the fire and broke the chair. Although it also broke both my legs, which wasn't so lucky. Alas, it could have been a lot worse. After that I managed to drag myself to safety before the emergency services arrived.'

'So where have you been for the last two years?'

'I went back to Hungary. My family still owns a place in the countryside, just outside Budapest. I stayed there until I recovered, licking my wounds and plotting my revenge. And now here we are.' He held his arms aloft and looked around. 'I love what you've done with the place, by the way. It's almost a shame to destroy it all.'

'But how did you find us? And why now?' Diane persisted.

'So many questions.' He let out a little laugh. 'Is this really necessary? You're just delaying the inevitable.'

'Humour me.' She smiled.

'Very well.' He gave an impatient sigh. Although Anaïs could see that he was revelling in the spotlight. Enjoying every minute of this opportunity to show off his ingenuity. 'I've been following you for a while. But I knew it was pointless to try and pick you off one-by-one. As soon as I killed one of you, I'd never have got anywhere near the rest. You're a wily old bunch, I'll give you that much. No. I knew I had to be patient and find a way to bring you all together. My first bit of luck was seeing Cecilia Davenport leave the restaurant while I watched from the shadows. She was clearly in some distress, and when I followed her and dispatched of her driver, it didn't take much to find out what she knew – just some pliers and a few broken fingers.' He grinned. 'Then I set-up an email account using her details to reel in Liam Patterson. He was the perfect stooge: a hungry young journalist, desperate for a break–'

'You didn't need to use him!' Anaïs cried out. 'You could have just hired another lowlife thug like yourself.'

'True. But Liam was the perfect foil. So handsome and innocent. I guess you could say, I played you at your own game.'

'Cecilia Davenport never double-crossed us?' Diane looked shocked.

'On the contrary, she put up quite the fight. And then tonight, when I saw Liam and Anaïs canoodling at the restaurant and Siobhan spying jealously from afar, it just seemed too good an opportunity to miss. All the stars aligned, if you will.' He reached into his pocket and took out a small glass vial.

'What's that?' Andréa asked. 'What are you going to do?'

'All will be revealed soon enough.' He stepped over to the wall and turned off the lights, leaving just the holographic screen floating in the darkness, the flickering screensaver casting an eerie glow.

'Ah, much better. You can't have a party without a little ambience.' He walked back over and opened the vial.

'What's in there?' Andréa asked. But Anaïs already knew. Her mind going back to the forest...

'It's Lysergic acid diethylamide, or LSD for the layman, or layladies in this case.' He giggled. 'This is my very own recipe. Anaïs can attest to its potency. Can't you, my dear? As soon as it hits your bloodstream, it will take you to another dimension. Maybe you'll be safe there, but I doubt it.' He flashed a wicked grin.

'You can't give me that!' Andréa shook her head vehemently. 'I don't even take aspirin.'

'Well you're in for a treat tonight.' He lifted the dropper towards her mouth.

'No, please.' She tried to recoil but there was nowhere to go.

'Don't worry, you're going to like it, I promise.' He squeezed her cheeks, forcing her mouth open, and thrust it inside. 'There. That wasn't so bad, was it?'

He administered the drug to the rest of the women, and then disappeared from view.

A moment later the sound of heavy drums reverberated around the room, the deep bass bouncing off the walls.

'What's that? What's going on?' Andréa's eyes darted around.

'Just ignore it,' Anaïs replied. 'He's just trying to scare us.' But the drums were soon joined by a relentless electronic beat, the tempo steadily increasing and growing louder by the second.

'Make it stop!' Andréa cried out, yanking at her restraints.

'Don't try to fight it.' Anaïs called out above the rising din. 'You'll only make it worse.' But before she'd even finished the sentence, the walls began to subtly bulge and contract, faint shapes hovering in front of her, glowing translucently in the dim light.

She closed her eyes, telling herself it wasn't real, but when she opened them again, Victor loomed over her, dressed like the Grim Reaper, a dark hood concealing his face. She rolled her eyes at his theatrics, but soon the light intensified, morphing into a strobe-like effect, and his hulking shadow flipped back and forth on the wall behind, like a giant moth flapping its wings in the moonlight. She wanted to look away, but she was mesmerised as it moved faster and faster, matching the beat of the music.

Soon the whole room throbbed and pulsated like a living, breathing creature, the sound becoming a deafening roar, the lights blinding. Then, just as quickly, it fell silent and everything returned to normal.

For a moment Anaïs breathed a sigh of relief. She glanced at her mother and Andréa who both sat hypnotised, their eyes like saucers, while Jackie slumped between them, her chest barely moving.

She faced Victor again, glaring up at him. Determined not to show any weakness. But when he threw back the hood revealing the same mask he wore in Epping Forest, the red horns pointing towards her, a dagger in either hand, she let out a terrified scream.

38

Siobhan spat out dried blood and dust and lifted her head from the floorboards. She'd heard the man leave a while ago and tried to get herself up to a sitting position, but every movement sent a jolt of pain through her battered body, and she slumped back down.

'Come on, you can do this. Ani needs you.' She gritted her teeth and rolled onto her side. 'You're still here too, aye?' Cecilia Davenport came back into view, her green-sequined ballgown glowing softly in the gloom. 'This light is doing you plenty of favours, by the way. Maybe stay away from bright places from now on.' She started to laugh, but it turned into a spluttering cough. 'You wouldn't have some water over there by any chance, would you? Or maybe a bottle of champagne? You look like the kind of gal who carries one around in case of an emergency. No? I guess I'll just have to wait then.'

She rolled onto her back and tried to slide her wrists underneath her, contorting her body and grunting with the effort, but she couldn't manage to do it.

'I should have stuck to the bloody yoga classes.' She slumped back down, panting heavily. 'Right. Plan B.' She shuffled backwards and wriggled her body up the wall, like a fish flopping about at the bottom of a boat, until she finally managed to get herself into a sitting position.

'Now what? You got any bright ideas over there?' She looked at the dead woman. 'I didn't think so.' She pulled at the restraints again, but they didn't budge.

There had to be something she could do. She closed her eyes, wracking her brain, but all she could think about was how thirsty she was and how much her body hurt.

'Fuck!' she suddenly cried out in frustration, hitting the back of her head against the wall. 'Ah, Jesus!' She opened her eyes again and took a deep breath, holding it for a moment and then slowly exhaling. She took a few more breaths and her body started to relax, the tension seeping away.

'Okay, you can do this.' She scanned the room again and her eyes stopped on the woman's gaping mouth. 'You've got some pretty gnarly gnashers there, ain't ya?' She stared at her long sharp canine teeth. 'You're like a vampire... oh well, here goes nothing.' She let out an incredulous snort, shaking her head at the ridiculousness of the situation. Then she shuffled across the floor. Her progress was torturously slow, her body throbbing with every movement, but she refused to give up. Finally, after what seemed like a marathon, she reached Cecilia Davenport's corpse.

'Okay, focus, you can do this.' She looked up at the woman. 'I'm sorry, Cece, but things are about to get a whole lot weirder. Just putting it out there. Usually I'd buy a gal a drink before doing something like this, but we're going to have to skip the foreplay this time.'

She scooched around and shuffled backwards, wriggling onto the woman's lap. 'Jesus Christ! You're so fucking stiff!' She cringed, desperately fighting the urge to jump back off. 'Seriously, I'm having flashbacks here. It's like being back in Year Six and feeling Jacob O'Reilly's little boner rubbing up against me in gym class – that's when I knew for sure I was lesbian, by the way.' She glanced over her shoulder. 'Hey! Don't look at me like that. I don't see you coming up with any better ideas. I'm doing this for the both of us. If I don't get out of this, we're both gonna be stuck here, rotting away together, and that ain't gonna be pretty.'

She turned back and kept wriggling until her hands were level with the woman's face.

'Okay, here we go…' She took a deep breath and slid the plastic strap inside her mouth. 'This is so fucking grim,' she muttered, her wrists poised, hesitating for a moment, wishing there was another way of freeing herself. 'Come on, you can do this. Stop stalling and get on with it.' She was about to start sawing when she spotted something shiny nestled in the woman's hair.

'What's that?' She leaned closer, craning her neck to get a closer look, and saw that it was a silver comb. It had an intricate flower design decorated with a cluster of emerald and diamond petals, and she couldn't help noticing its sharp jagged edges. 'That could work. It would be a lot less messy too.' She glanced at the woman's face. 'I mean, it beats turning you into Cletus, the slack-jawed yokel, right? That's a *Simpsons* reference, by the way. You don't strike me as the cartoon type, or any kind of type right now, to be honest.'

She shimmied up as far as she could, balancing precariously on the woman's chest, and felt for the comb with her fingers.

'Come on, come on, I know it's there somewhere.'

She kept searching, her back squashed against the woman's face, the squelching sound making her grimace, and she fought the urge to throw up again.

'Fucking hell! I'm going to need therapy after this,' she groaned before finally touching the cold metal with her fingers. 'Aha, got you, you little bastard!' She grabbed hold of it the best she could and tried to prise it free, but it wouldn't budge. 'Come on! Give me a fucking break here.' She kept pulling, her face straining with the effort, and she felt it give a little. 'Yes! That's it. Come to mamma.' She readjusted her grip and yanked it with all her might, letting out a surprised yelp as it suddenly came loose, sending her tumbling to the floor with a heavy thud.

Quickly, she rolled onto her side and started rubbing the hard the edge of the comb against the plastic strap, but her hands were in an awkward position and she couldn't get any leverage.

Finally she stopped, her whole body throbbing with the effort, her tired fingers barely able to keep hold of the comb. She thought about giving up altogether, her energy completely zapped. Then Anaïs' face popped into her head. She couldn't let this man get his hands on her. She had to get out of these straps no matter what it took, otherwise they were all screwed.

'Come on. Think. There had to be another way.' Her eyes darted around and she noticed the narrow gaps running between the wooden floorboards. 'That's it!' She wedged the comb into one of them and pushed down against the hard metal, grinding her body against it.

For a moment nothing happened, but she kept going, her body screaming out with every movement until, suddenly, the plastic snapped.

She landed on top of the comb with a high-pitched cry. But the pain quickly turned to joy when she held up her unclasped hands.

With her hands free, she undid the straps around her ankles and clambered to her feet, gingerly hobbling over to Cecilia Davenport, the puncture wounds in her thighs throbbing with every step.

'Well, Cece, I guess this is it. I know I said some mean things, but I couldn't have done this without you.' She leaned over and hugged the woman, putting the comb back in her hair. 'And don't worry, I'll make sure someone comes back for you.'

She left the room and found herself on a narrow landing. She saw her jacket hanging over the wooden banister and snatched it up, quickly checking the pockets, but they were all empty.

Disappointed, she put it on, pulling the zip all the way up to hide her bare chest. Then she hobbled along the landing, using the wall for support.

She found a bathroom at the far end and quickly turned on the tap, shoving her head under the faucet and drinking greedily. When she'd finally had enough, she turned on the light and checked her reflection in the mirror.

'Fuck me! I look like an extra from the *Walking Dead*, and not one of the fresh ones either.' She tilted her face, taking in all the cuts and bruises. 'Thank God I've got a winning personality.' She cupped her hands under the tap and splashed water over her face, wincing when she accidently touched her nose.

Once she cleaned off most of the blood, she hobbled back outside and stopped at the top of a steep staircase. 'This is going to be interesting.' She peered into the murkiness below, then made her way down, clinging onto the banister for dear life.

She got to the bottom without incident and weaved her way through a minefield of cardboard boxes, which blocked up the narrow corridor, before opening the door at the end of the corridor and entering what looked like an old pharmacy, its windows all boarded up, the countertop and display units covered in a thick layer of dust.

Why the hell would he bring her here? Then it dawned on her: the strange man, the pharmacy, the vendetta against Anaïs and her mum. It had to be the guy who raped her. So it wasn't Max or William; it was Victor all along. This guy had more disguises than a *Scooby Doo* villain. The thought would have made her laugh if the situation wasn't so dire. She quickly searched the room for a telephone. She found one mounted on the wall behind the counter and picked it up, but there was no dial tone.

Frustrated, she hit it against the wall, and then hobbled towards the entrance, grabbing some Ibuprofen on the way.

To her relief the door opened when she turned the latch, and she made her way to the main road, flagging down a black cab.

'Evening, love. Everything okay?' The driver eyed her suspiciously. 'Looks like you've had a rough night.'

'I'm okay, pal, don't worry about me. Now, are you going to let me in or not? I'm in a bit of rush here.' She glared at him, holding onto the door handle impatiently.

'Get in.' He sighed, unlocking it. 'But if you get any stains on the seats, you're paying for it.'

'Yeah, yeah.' She climbed in gingerly and thought about asking if she could use his phone, but then she realised that she didn't know anybody's number anyway. 'Take me to South Bank – actually, scrap that.' She remembered that the man had taken her card. 'Go to The Sacred Lotus restaurant in Charing Cross,' she said, hoping Queeny was still there. 'And make it fast.'

'I'm sorry, love, but I can't go over the speed limit. It's not worth the hassle.'

'Look. I'll give you fifty quid, and I'll cover any fines you get. Just get a move on. And if you call me *love* one more time, I swear to God I'll shove my boot so far up your arse, you'll be tasting leather for a month. Capiche?'

'Uh, yes, ma'am.' He glanced in the rear-view mirror then sped up.

The taxi arrived outside the restaurant less than fifteen-minutes later, and the driver turned around to face her. 'That'll be fifty pounds, please, love–I mean, ma'am.' He quickly corrected himself.

'I just need to pop inside to get the money.'

'That wasn't the deal. How do I know you're not going to run off?'

'I ain't running anywhere, pal. Look at me, I can barely fucking stand up. Just give me two minutes, will you? Geez!'

'Okay, fine. Just be quick. I haven't got all night.'

He unlocked the door, and she struggled out, hobbling towards the entrance. She could see that the lights were off and her heart sank; then, to her relief, she spotted Queen Bea standing behind the counter, and she went inside.

'Jesus, darling, you scared me half to death.' Queen Bea looked up in shock. 'I was just about to lock up. What are you doing here? Is there something happening tonight?'

'No. But we have a bit of a problem–'

'Oh my God! What happened to your face?'

'It's nothing. You should see the other guy.' Siobhan tried to smile, but her whole face throbbed with pain and it quickly turned into a grimace.

'We should get you to the hospital.' Queen Bea stepped around the counter to inspect her wounds.

'Honestly, it's fine.' Siobhan waved her off. 'Right now, we have bigger things to worry about.'

'What's going on? Is it something to do with downstairs?'

'Yep. But before I tell you, can I borrow fifty-quid for the taxi?'

'Here.' Queen Bea opened the till and handed her the money.

'Thanks, Queeny, I appreciate it.' Siobhan hobbled back outside.

When she returned, Queen Bea was sitting at a table, pouring a dark spirit into two shot glasses.

'Sit down and drink this.'

'What is it?'

'It's Mekhong, darling. It'll take the hairs right off your chest, and everywhere else for that matter.'

Siobhan sniffed it hesitantly, and then took a sip. The harsh liquid burnt her throat and she winced. 'Oof! That's strong. I like it.'

'Good. Now tell me what's going on.'

Siobhan quickly told her everything and Queen Bea listened in stunned silence.

'Oh my God! That's awful,' she said when Siobhan finished. 'Do you think he's down there with them now?'

'I think so, yeah.'

'Should we call the police?'

'You know we can't do that.'

'No, of course not. You're right. But we need to do something.'

'That's why I'm here. Do you have your phone on you?'

Queen Bea took it out from her cleavage and handed it over.

Siobhan rolled her eyes, and then called Diane, but there was no answer. Undeterred, she tried Jackie and Andréa, but they didn't answer either. Finally she tried Anaïs, but it went straight to answerphone.

'None of them are picking up,' she said, handing it back.

'This is bad.' Queen Bea stood up and paced around nervously.

'Do you have a laptop or a tablet?'

'There's a laptop in my office, why?'

'Can you get it for me, please? I have an idea.'

Queen Bea disappeared and came back a few seconds later, handing Siobhan a black laptop.

'Thanks,' she said, turning it on and opening a web browser.

'What are you doing?' Queen Bea peered over her shoulder.

'Just give me a sec.' Siobhan typed her username and password into an online app and a copy of her desktop screen appeared. 'Right. Let's find out what's going on down there.' She opened the security cameras and her mouth fell open.

'Oh my God!' Queen Bea crossed herself and looked up to the ceiling.

'Praying isn't going to help us right now.' Siobhan watched as a masked figure swiped two daggers through the air, the women cowering beneath him.

'He looks like the Devil.' Queen Bea gripped Siobhan's shoulder. 'How are we meant to stop him? He's huge!'

'Aye, he is. But there's two of us.'

'You're not in any shape to fight anyone. And you don't expect me to go down there like this, do you? I'm wearing six-inch Manolos, and this dress is a Vera Wang.'

'And?' Siobhan looked at her. 'Is your fancy dress worth more than the lives of our friends. No. Our family? Because that's what those women are down there are, if you'd forgotten.'

'Of course not.' Queen Bea looked down.

'Good. Now go to the kitchen and get the two biggest sharpest knives you've got. We're going to sort this prick out once and for all.'

39

Anaïs watched with a mixture of awe and terror as Victor continued to swipe the daggers through the air, the pointed blades leaving shimmering trails like children's sparklers on Guy Fawkes night.

'Now, who am I going to slice open first?' His eyes shone through the dark slits in the mask, and Anaïs knew he was grinning underneath. 'I know. We'll do eeny, meeny, miny, moe...' He paced up and down, reciting the children's rhyme in a singsong voice, tapping each woman on the shoulder.

Finally he stopped in front of Diane and crouched down, ripping open her blouse and placing the tip of the dagger against her chest.

'Maybe we should start with the vivacious Ms Dubois.' He pushed the blade gently into the soft flesh above her heart, a trickle of blood running down and staining the white fabric of her bra, but she barely noticed.

'Stop it!' Anaïs shouted, pulling at the restraints as he pushed the blade deeper. But Diane still didn't react. Her mind elsewhere. Lost in her own little world.

'Hmm, well, that's no fun.' He wiped the blade on his robe and stepped away. 'How about you, Ms Jensen. Are you still with us?' He stroked Andréa's cheek with the blunt edge of the metal.

'No, please, leave me alone,' she whimpered, turning away.

'Why don't you start with me?' Anaïs called out, ignoring the colours and shapes dancing on the periphery of her vision. 'You look ridiculous in that outfit by the way. Like some kind of reject from a shitty nineties horror movie.'

'Is that so?' He walked over and ran his fingers through her hair. 'What happened to the sweet, innocent girl I remember? You've become so hard. So bitter. So discourteous. That Siobhan has been a bad influence on you, I fear.'

'She's a better person than you'll ever be. You're just a sad, pathetic loner. I bet you were the weird kid who got bullied at school too. You really are a walking, talking cliché.' She let out a contemptuous snort.

'Maybe I should start by cutting out your tongue.' He took off the mask and grabbed a handful of her hair, yanking it back. 'Now, what were you saying?' He lifted the dagger to her mouth and grinned.

'Go to hell.' She gritted her teeth, staring up at him defiantly.

*

Siobhan stepped out of the lift and led Queen Bea along the corridor. But she came to a stop when they approached her office.

'What's wrong?' Queen Bea asked.

'Shh.' Siobhan held up her finger. 'Can you hear that?'

A faint scratching noise came from inside, and she crept closer.

'Be careful,' Queen Bea whispered.

Siobhan grabbed the handle and the scratching stopped.

Bracing herself, she opened the door and yelped in surprise when Chewie leaped out and pinned her to the floor.

'Jesus, Chewie!' She tried to push him off as he lapped at her face with his rough, sloppy tongue. 'Not the face! I'm in pain here, you big dummy!'

He finally relented and she climbed gingerly back to her feet, stroking his head and tapping his side. 'It's good to see you too, boy.'

'What's he doing here?' Queen Bea frowned.

'Andréa must have left him here. Jackie doesn't like him being in the boardroom when we have meetings.'

'Shouldn't we put him back in there?'

'Wait a sec...' Siobhan said, an idea forming in her mind. 'Maybe we should take him with us.'

'But why?'

'We can use him as a diversion. Think about it. If Chewie goes in first, the guy won't have a clue what's going on. Then, when his attention's focused on the dog, you can slip inside and sneak up on him from behind.'

'Why me?' Queen Bea looked horrified.

'Because I can barely stand up right now. By the time I hobble in there, it'll be too late. Look. Don't worry. Once you're in position, I'll come in and confront him. All you've got to do is stick the knife in his back, and then I'll finish the job.'

'I don't know. It sounds so risky.'

'Do you have a better idea?'

'Can't we just set the dog on him? Isn't that why people get these big things?'

'Chewie's not a trained guard dog. He's a big softy, aren't you, boy?' She ruffled his head.

'Fine!' Queen Bea crouched down and undid the clasps on her shoes.

'What are you doing?'

'I'm leaving these here.' She slipped them off and put them by the door. 'If I've got to sneak up on this guy like some kind of ninja, I'd rather do it barefoot.'

'Good idea. Come on, let's go. We're wasting precious time.' Siobhan hobbled down the corridor and Chewie padded along beside her.

'Hey! Wait for me!' Queen Bea shimmied after them in her tight dress, yanking it up over her thighs.

When they approached the boardroom, Siobhan noticed that one of the doors was partially open.

'Great. We're in luck,' she whispered, coming to a stop. 'Now, listen to me, boy. You need to be quiet, okay?' She looked at Chewie and raised a finger to her mouth. 'You ready?' She glanced at Queen Bea.

'No. But what choice do I have?'

'None. Nice legs, by the way.' Siobhan grinned.

'Thank you, darling. I think that's the nicest thing you've ever said to me.'

'Let's hope it's not the last.' She crept up to the door and peered inside.

*

Victor grabbed Anaïs' hair even tighter and ran the dagger across her lips.

'So beautiful,' he murmured. 'Maybe I'll keep you till last, after all. It would be a shame to silence you so soon. You know how much I like it when you scream.'

She looked away and thought she was hallucinating again when she saw a blurry creature entering the room. But when it got closer, she realised it was Chewie.

'What are you looking at?' Victor followed her gaze and spun around. 'Whose dog is that?' he demanded.

'Chewie!' Andréa called out and he wandered over, putting his head in her lap.

'How did it get in here?' Victor glared at the dog, but Anaïs could see that he was apprehensive about getting too close.

'I don't know,' Andréa replied. 'I left him in Siobhan's office before I came in here.'

'Who else is down here? I thought it was empty.'

'It is,' Diane spoke up, suddenly lucid again. 'Chewie was probably bored of your constant drivel, just like the rest of us. Maybe he came in here to ask you to stop blowing hot air out of your behind and get on with whatever it is you're planning to do. I mean, honestly, you're the only person I've ever met who can make acid boring. I remember it being much more fun when I tried it back in the eighties.'

'Look who's decided to re-join us.' Victor grinned. 'Once I put a bullet in that thing, the fun can really begin.'

'No!' Andréa cried. 'You can't hurt him. Please!'

'Not so fast, pal,' An invisible voice called out. 'Lay one finger on the doggo and it'll be the last thing you ever do.'

Anaïs looked at the door and watched as Siobhan hobbled inside. 'Shiv! You're alive!' she called out excitedly.

'Aye. You didn't think I'd miss out on this, did you?' Siobhan gave her a quick smile, but Anaïs could see that she was badly injured.

'Look what the dog dragged in.' Victor raised his arms. 'You must have balls of steel to come back here after what I did to you. I'm surprised you can even walk.'

'I don't have any balls, pal. I've got a platinum-coated pussy and I'm here to fuck you up once and for all.'

'Very good.' Victor clapped the daggers together and let out a little laugh. 'You really are the Queen of the pithy one-liners, but that's not going to help you very much now, I'm afraid. How did you escape, may I ask?'

'Good old Cecilia helped me.'

'Cecilia Davenport's alive?' Diane called out.

'Not quite. It's a long story,' Siobhan replied. 'I'll tell you later. After I've dealt with this prick.'

While they continued talking, Anaïs caught a glimpse of Queen Bea sneaking up behind the man, a long kitchen-knife held out in front of her.

Their eyes met for a brief moment, but Anaïs quickly looked back at the others, not wanting to give her away.

'You're very confident for a woman who's already been beaten once this evening.' Victor grinned. 'Actually, multiple times if we're keeping count.'

'Let's see how tough you are when I'm not tied up.'

'Maybe you should come and sit down first. Have a little rest. You really do look terrible, my dear.'

'Come over here, and I'll show you how I'm feeling.' Siobhan raised her fists and held them up like a tired old boxer coming out for one last round.

'Very well, have it your way.' Victor raised the daggers and stalking towards her.

Anaïs glanced back at Queen Bea, but the woman was frozen to the spot, her eyes glazed over.

This wasn't good. But before she could do something to snap her out of it, Victor lunged forward and sliced open Siobhan's cheek with a glancing blow.

'No!' Anaïs watched in horror as Siobhan stumbled backwards and crashed to the floor.

Her voice triggered Chewie into action and he leaped up on Victor, clamping his jaws on the man's forearm.

'Ah! Get off me!' Victor tried to shake him off, but the dog held on tight, growling menacingly and clawing at him with his huge paws.

'Hurry up, Queeny! Do it now!' Anaïs called out, trying to rouse the woman into action, but she fell silent when Victor plunged one of the daggers into Chewie's side.

'Chewie!' Andréa cried, tears streaming down her face, as the dog let out a gut-wrenching yelp and wandered off into a dark corner.

'Now, where were we?' Victor smoothed down his cloak and stood over Siobhan who lay prone below him, blood seeping from the gash on her cheek. 'Ah, yes. It's time to put you out of your misery, once and for all.' He raised the dagger above his head, clasping it with both hands. But just as he was about to bring it down on her chest an ear-shattering gunshot rang out, and his eyes widened in surprise.

Anaïs stood behind him, the broken restraints discarded on the floor, the smoking gun held out in front of her, while Queen Bea held the knife beside her.

For a moment he didn't move, his arms hovering above him like a statue. Then he slowly lowered them, dropping the dagger to the floor with a metallic twang.

'Well that was unexpected.' He turned to face her, blood dripping from his mouth. 'Although I wouldn't celebrate quite yet if I were you.'

'It's over. You lost again. And this time I'm going to make sure you're dead.' Anaïs pointed the gun at his chest, desperately ignoring the shapes and colours that continued to plague her mind.

'Maybe so…' He smirked. 'But I'm going to make sure I take you all with me.' He opened his palm and Anaïs saw that he was holding a small black device.

'What's that?'

'It's a timer. I've planted explosives all through this place and the countdown has already begun.' His eyes lit up and she saw that the digital display was at four-minutes-and-fifty-five-seconds.

'You're bluffing.'

'I guess we'll find out soon enough.' His face broke into the familiar wolfish grin and she knew he was telling the truth.

'Queeny, cut the others loose,' she said, keeping her eyes on him. 'Now!' She raised her voice and the woman scurried off.

'You'll never get everyone out in time.' He continued to grin despite the hole in his chest.

'We'll see about that.' She pulled the trigger and another bullet crashed into him. 'That one's for Epping Forest.' He fell to his knees and she aimed the gun at his face. 'And this one's for Liam.' She fired again and he crumpled to the floor. 'And this is for everyone else who's ever had the misfortune of meeting you, you sad, pathetic, piece of shit!' She stood over his lifeless body and fired off the rest of the bullets, his body spasming with each thudding impact.

When the gun was finally empty, she dropped it in disgust and stared down at him, mesmerised by the growing pool of blood which glowed luminously in the gloom, glittering and pulsating, as if another version of him was about to rise from it, like an alien creature in a sci-fi movie.

'Come on, ma puce, it's over. He's dead.' Diane touched her arm, bringing her back to reality.

'We need to get that timer.' Anaïs crouched down and prised it out of his hand.

'How much time do we have?' Siobhan asked as they all gathered in the middle of the room.

'Just over four-minutes.' Anaïs glanced at the display.

'Maybe he really is just bluffing,' Andréa said hopefully.

'Do you want to wait to find out? Because I don't,' Anaïs replied.

'But what about Jackie and Chewie? We can't just leave them here.' At the sound of his name, the dog trotted over gingerly, the dagger still protruding from his side. 'Oh my God, Chewie, you're alive!' Andréa bent down and hugged him.

'Okay, well, that's one problem sorted,' Anaïs said. 'Now we just need to figure out what to do with Jackie.'

'We could use the gurney,' Diane suggested. 'It's in the Treatment Room.'

'I'll go and get it.' Anaïs ran out of the room and raced along the corridor, but when she opened the door to the Treatment Room, she suddenly stopped and held onto the doorframe for dear life as the black-and-white tiles disappeared, replaced by huge stone pillars rising from an endless black void.

She spotted the gurney on the other side, barely more than a silver speck on the dark horizon, and she closed her eyes. But when she opened them again nothing had changed.

'Fine! Have it your way.' She took a deep breath and leapt forward, landing on the pillar closest to her. The narrow surface rocked back and forth, and she swayed precariously before regaining her balance. She took a moment to compose herself and lined up the next one. But just as she was about to jump, the other pillars started to collapse around her, the abyss growing wider and wider.

'Come on, you can do this. Everyone's relying on you.' She leaped onto the one in front of her, but that started to give way too.

Panicking, she quickly jumped again, but without a solid base, she came up short, letting out a terrified scream as she clung onto the edge of the pillar by her fingernails.

'Help!' she cried out, her legs dangling in mid-air, her grip slipping with each passing second. Then, just when she was about to plummet into oblivion, a hand appeared above her.

'Come on, grab it.' Liam gazed down at her, his blonde hair and blue eyes shining like an angel.

'No. It's not possible. You're dead.' She looked up at him sadly, tears filling her eyes.

'Stop whining and hurry up.' He smiled, leaning closer.

Anaïs reached out, and he pulled her up effortlessly.

'Thank you.' She hugged him tightly, nuzzling her face against his neck. But when she looked again, he'd disappeared.

For a moment she was overcome with sadness. Then she saw the gurney in front of her, and she quickly cast it aside. Now wasn't the time to grieve. She could do that later, once she'd saved everyone else.

She grabbed hold of the handle and raced back to join the others.

'Jesus, Nay-Nay! Where the hell have you been?' Siobhan called out as she came screeching around the corner.

'Sorry. I had a bit of trouble finding it.'

'How much time do we have?' Queen Bea asked.

Anaïs looked at the timer and her stomach lurched. 'Less than two minutes.'

'Fuck!' Siobhan threw back her head.

'It's fine. Come on. We can still do it.' Anaïs crouched down and the three of them loaded Jackie onto the gurney, while Diane looked on in a daze and Andréa sat on the floor hugging Chewie.

'Okay, that should do it,' Anaïs said, breathing heavily. 'Queeny, you push her to the lift and I'll take care of the others.'

'What about me?' Siobhan asked.

'Here.' Anaïs gave her the timer and they locked eyes for a brief moment. 'Just make sure we get out of here in time. Okay?'

'Okay.' Siobhan nodded.

With the clock ticking, they raced along the corridor, Queen Bea leading the way, pushing Jackie along like a contestant in *Supermarket Sweep*, while Anaïs guided Andréa and her mother, and Chewie trotted along beside them.

'Less than a minute!' Siobhan called out from the back as the lift came into view.

Queen Bea reached it first and jabbed her finger at the button, pushing Jackie inside as soon as the doors opened.

A few seconds later, Anaïs herded Andréa and her mother inside. Then she turned and urged on Siobhan who had slipped further behind.

'Come on,' she shouted. 'We're running out of time–' But before she could say anything else, Siobhan stumbled and went sprawling to the floor, the timer slipping from her grasp and bouncing away.

'Push the button!' Diane called out, suddenly alert again.

'Wait!' Anaïs went to help Siobhan, but Diane grabbed her arm.

'It's too late, ma puce. We've got to get out of here now!'

'No! I'm not leaving without her.' Anaïs shrugged her off and ran to Siobhan's side, grabbing her by the arm and pulling her up. 'Come on. We need to get out of here.'

'You shouldn't have come back for me.' Siobhan looked up wearily.

'Just shut up and move your arse.' Anaïs forced a smile.

'I don't think I can, Nay-Nay. My legs are numb.'

'Yes, you can. Come on. We'll do it together.' Anaïs took her hand and they shuffled awkwardly along the corridor as the others shouted encouragement and waved them on.

Finally they reached the lift and Anaïs shoved Siobhan inside.

'Press the button!' She shouted, getting in behind her.

'It's not working!' Queen Bea called out. 'There's too many of us!'

'Try now.' Anaïs squeezed in further and the doors finally closed.

'How much time do we have?' Diane asked as the lift started moving.

'I don't know. I lost the–' But before Siobhan could finish the sentence there was a thunderous roar and the whole underground structure began to shake violently.

'We're all going to die!' Andréa cried, clinging onto Chewie for dear life as they all tumbled around like ragdolls.

'Everyone hold onto something,' Anaïs shouted, wincing as her head crashed against the wall with a heavy thud.

The next few seconds went by in a hazy blur as the lift reached the riverside and the doors slid open, spewing them out onto the promenade just as a huge fireball tore through the floor of the carriage.

The explosion shook the bridge to its foundations and Anaïs rolled over, watching as the sky lit up like a fireworks display.

'It's beautiful.' She smiled serenely, gazing up at the dazzling spectacle, momentarily forgetting about everything else. Then she passed out.

EPILOGUE

BERLIN

FOUR MONTHS LATER

Anaïs cycled across the Oberbaum Bridge, weaving in and out of the slow-moving traffic and embracing the cool morning air as she glanced up at the soaring, red-bricked turrets that stood in the middle of the gothic-inspired structure.

Soon she reached the other side and cruised through the East Side Gallery, the mile-long remnant of the Berlin Wall with its colourful graffiti and murals reminding her of those early-morning cycles through Brick Lane, back when her hair was green and life was simpler, and she smiled at the memory.

She stopped at a docking station up ahead, parking the hire bike and looking back down the road, but a man suddenly appeared, blocking the way.

'Hi,' he said, smiling. 'You look a little lost. Can I help?'

Anaïs gawped back. His blonde hair, blue eyes and boyishly-handsome face reminded her of Liam, and a pang of sadness and regret stabbed her in the chest.

'Is everything okay?' he asked.

'Yes, sorry, you just reminded me of someone for a second.' She glanced away in embarrassment.

'Someone good I hope.'

'He was.'

'I'm Sebastian by the way.'

'Nice to meet you. I'm Anaïs.'

'So where are you going this morning, Anaïs? Maybe I could buy you a coffee on the way.'

'That's nice of you to offer, but–'

'Hey! Nay-Nay! Where the hell did you go? You were meant to be waiting for me!' Siobhan came to a screeching halt and jammed her bike into a free slot. 'Who's this guy?' She stepped between them and looked the man up and down, making him shuffle uncomfortably.

'Sebastian was just asking if I needed some help,' Anaïs spoke up.

'Was he now? Thank you, Sebby, old sport, but we can take it from here.' Siobhan grabbed Anaïs' arm and dragged her away.

'Uh, okay, it was nice meeting you. Have a good day,' he called out.

'You too.' Anaïs glanced over her shoulder and smiled apologetically.

A few minutes later, they passed the German Federal Intelligence Service building with its brutalist architecture and endless windows and approached a quiet little café on the other side of the road. Her mother sat outside with Andréa and two almost identical-looking blonde women. The women wore matching black trouser-suits and dark sunglasses and remained seated while Diane and Andréa stood.

'Nice of you to finally join us.' Diane kissed Anaïs on either cheek, then hugged Siobhan half-heartedly.

'Morning, maman. Sorry we're late. We, uh–'

'Got a little lost,' Siobhan butted in. 'This city is like a maze.'

'Can we begin now?' one of the women asked in a strong German accent.

'Of course,' Diane replied. 'This is Lisa.' She introduced the woman who was the slightly shorter and curvier of the two. 'And this is Linda. They're agents from the Federal Intelligence Service.'

'Linda and Lisa, aye? That's cute. I'm Siobhan and this is Shanaïs.'

'This is the one you warned us about?' Lisa took off her glasses and looked at Diane.

'Uh, yes. I'd like to say she grows on you, but I'd be lying. And this is my daughter, *Anaïs*.'

'It's nice to meet you both.' Anaïs shook their hands.

'It's a shame Chief Superintendent Njoku couldn't be with us.' Linda spoke for the first time.

'Yes,' Andréa replied. 'She's getting stronger every day though. And she's got her hands full looking after Chewie and Artoo and Deetoo.'

'So who do I need to sleep with to get a coffee around here?' Siobhan looked around. 'I must have drunk a whole bottle of vodka last night, not to mention all the other stuff – I bet youse two know what I'm talking about, right? Don't tell me you don't go clubbing from time to time and get a little loosey-goosey – it's Berlin, Baby!'

'Yes, we are aware that this is Berlin,' Lisa replied, stony-faced. 'And you can get coffee when we're done. This won't take long.'

'Fine.' Siobhan sighed, slumping down into an empty seat. 'Let's get on with it then.'

'Very well...' Lisa glanced around, and then lowered her voice. 'As we discussed over the phone, there's an international sex-trafficking group operating in the city, which has been targeting local girls and tourists. We've been tracking them for a few months now through official and more discreet channels, but they've accelerated their operations lately and we need your help.'

'What makes you think we can help?' Siobhan asked. 'It sounds pretty hardcore to me.'

'We've been keeping an eye on you since Andréa's company started working with us, and we've been very impressed with your methods.'

'Okay, carry on...' Siobhan grinned. 'Flattery will get you everywhere.'

'This group is from Lithuania, close to the Russian border, and the Intelligence Service would like to extradite them back there to avoid a diplomatic showdown. But we would prefer to deal with them in a more appropriate manner.'

'You want to kill the Rusky bastards?' Siobhan said matter-of-factly.

'Yes. But we need you to infiltrate them first and find out who their leader is. Then we can bring them down. It won't be easy though. This group is highly-organised and very professional. They're also extremely violent. We've already lost two of our girls.'

'Girls?' Anaïs looked confused.

'Yes. You're not the only pretty face who is good undercover,' Lisa replied. 'We have our own private team here too.'

'There's something else,' Diane spoke up. 'While we've all been recovering, Alessandra came out to help. And now she's missing too.'

'Our sexy senorita, Alessandra?' Siobhan looked shocked.

'Yes.' Diane nodded.

'What the hell are we waiting for?' We need to find Ale and take these fuckers down. The only thing the Intelligence Service will be extraditing is their mutilated balls.'

'I agree,' Anaïs added. 'Just let us know what you need.'

'Very well.' Lisa smiled for the first time. 'Let's begin...'

Thank you for making it to the end of my new novel, *Ladies Who Lynch*. I really hope you enjoyed it.

If you'd like to learn a little more about me, and read more of my work, you can find me at **Jasonwride.com**.

You can also follow me on Instagram **@Jasonwr1de** to see more cheesy pictures and random stories about my day-to-day life.

Printed in Great Britain
by Amazon

86573624R00132